CRITICS LOVE ELI MARKS!

Praise for the Eli Marks Mystery Series

"An intriguing cross between noir and cozy, with fascinating details about magic tricks and plenty of quirky characters. An easy, enjoyable read for mystery buffs seeking a bit of an escape from the usual crime fiction fare."
  – *Library Journal*

"A finely-tuned, diabolical, sneaky, smart, stylish mix of magic and mayhem that plunges our hero Eli through a tangled web of danger and deceit that'll keep you guessing."
  – Steve Spill, Magician and Author of *I Lie For Money*

"With twists and turns, flurries of romance, and a cast of characters that seem to be the unholy spawn of *The Maltese Falcon* and *The Third Man*, *The Miser's Dream* keeps the pages turning and the reader delighted from start to finish."
  – Jeffrey Hatcher, Screenwriter, *Mr. Holmes*

"I loved this book. From beginning to end I was hooked. The story is fantastic and the cast leaves you wanting to know more. I can't wait to read the next book in the series."

– *Bookschellves*

"This is an instant classic, in a league with Raymond Chandler, Dashiell Hammett and Arthur Conan Doyle."
– *Rosebud Book Reviews*

"Has as many tricks up its sleeve as its likeable magician-hero. As the body count rises, so does the reading pleasure."
– Dennis Palumbo, Author of the *Daniel Rinaldi Mystery Series*

"A wonderfully engaging, delightfully tricky bit of mystery. Fans of magic will delight in John Gaspard's artful use of the world of magicians, onstage and offstage. It's a great story and great fun!"
– Jim Steinmeyer, Author of *Hiding the Elephant: How Magicians Invented the Impossible and Learned to Disappear*

"A real winner of magical proportions. Filled with snappy, delightful dialogue and plenty of sleight-of-hand humor, Gaspard's latest mystery in the Eli Marks series does not disappoint."
– Jessie Chandler, Author of the Shay O'Hanlon Series

"The author does a fantastic job juggling the separate plots and keeping readers' minds thoroughly engaged…and the pure entertainment of the industry will leave all readers hoping that there will be a 'number three' very soon."
– *Suspense Magazine*

"*The Ambitious Card* is intelligently written and…entirely engrossing."
– *Ellery Queen's Mystery Magazine*

"The deftly-plotted mystery is enriched by Eli's relationships with his ex-wife, her new husband, his old-school stage magician Uncle Harry, and an interesting collection of people and places in and

around St. Paul...This stylish novel is filled with interesting details, snappy dialogue, and appealing characters."
— *More Than a Review*

"This story is very well-written and fun to read. I would definitely read another Eli Marks Mystery."
— *A Simple Taste for Reading*

THE LINKING RINGS

AN ELI MARKS MYSTERY

JOHN GASPARD

THE ELI MARKS MYSTERY SERIES

THE LINKING RINGS

An Eli Marks Mystery

First Edition | December 2017

www.elimarksmysteries.com

ISBN-13: 9781078283090

ASIN: B07V4T1XTG

Printed in the United States of America

ACKNOWLEDGMENTS

Thanks to Teller, Tina Lenert, Dustin Stinnett, Jim Cunningham, Bill Arnold, Amy Shomshak, Steven Paul Carlson, Scott Wells, Suzanne, Joe Gaspard, George Campbell and Amy Oriani

For John Fenn -- thank you, Maestro!
We'll be in constant touch.

"Sometimes magic is just someone spending more time on something than anyone else might reasonably expect."
Teller

CHAPTER 1

There were many attractions I had hoped to see on my first visit to London. The inner workings of the city's jail system had not been one of them.

Especially on day one.

When planning the trip, I had assumed my biggest concern would be jet lag. I was wrong. While it proved to be a real issue, it came in at a distant second to raising bail.

At the moment, though, jet lag was all I had on my mind as I suppressed yet another yawn. Coming to The Magic Circle directly from the airport had been Harry's idea, because his plan was to spend as little time in London as possible. Consequently, all I had seen of the city so far had been the interior of Heathrow airport, some blurry views of a rainy metropolis from within a careening cab, and now the second floor meeting room of the venerable magician's club, The Magic Circle, located somewhere in the mysterious heart of London.

"Every time you yawn, you make me yawn," Harry growled in a poor imitation of a stage whisper.

"I've noticed that," I said, doing a considerably better job of keeping my voice down. "It's kind of cool."

"Easy for you to say," he said. "You don't have to go on stage in forty-five minutes."

That was true. My role for the evening's gala event was strictly that of an observer. Harry's responsibilities were far more substantial, and he leaned forward to listen closely to the instructions that were being given to him and the evening's other performer by the club's Executive Director.

The room was beginning to fill with magicians, and Harry and his soon-to-be stage partner were at the top of that particular food chain. The reactions they were getting exemplified an odd phenomenon I've experienced through a life spent observing my magician uncle: while in the presence of normal people—that is to say, non-magicians—Harry was looked upon as your run-of-the-mill cranky and charming old man.

But let him walk into a room full of magicians, and it's as if the Dali Lama has just arrived. He was, as he liked to put it, an *occasional* rock star.

Although at this moment, he was one of about a half-dozen Dali Lamas in the room. It was a virtual *Who's Who* of magicians of a certain age. But right now my focus was on the two who were about to go on stage.

I turned and looked at the other magician, a man I had never met. Of course, I had certainly heard of Oskar Korhonen. He was a highly skilled magician from Finland who was world-renowned for his dexterity with a deck of cards. Such dexterity was all the more astonishing because Oskar was missing his left arm. A childhood accident had appeared to doom his dream of making a living as a magician, but his perseverance had clearly paid off. His one-handed shuffle was a thing of beauty, made all the more poignant in terms of card shuffling because it was really his only option.

He stood next to Harry on slightly wobbly legs, wearing his customary red checkered plaid tuxedo, a fashion statement that made him instantly recognizable within the magician world and certainly a curiosity outside of it.

"*Mitä?*" he asked, leaning forward to hear better, as the multiple conversations in the room were starting to build to something just this side of a din.

"Why don't we move this conversation into the theater?" the

Executive Director suggested loudly, recognizing the room was only going to get noisier. He gestured toward the door, and the two older magicians made their way through the room, the growing crowd parting respectfully to let them pass. When they reached the doorway, Harry stopped, bowed slightly, and motioned to his fellow magician.

"After you, doctor," Harry said with a wide smile.

"No, no, doctor, after you," Oskar replied in his charming Finnish accent. Harry finally acquiesced and went first, followed by Oskar, who gave him a warm pat on the back.

I was puzzled by the exchange, as I knew for a fact Harry wasn't a doctor in any sense of the term, and I had never heard of Oskar Korhonen being referred to in this manner. I made a mental note to ask Harry about it later. Since I was now alone in a crowded room of strangers, I turned to my traditional method for dealing with new people: I ignored them all.

Instead, I began to investigate the display cases lining a far wall. As it turned out, it was to be the first—and least deadly—of a number of investigations I'd be taking part in that week.

* * *

The beauty of The Magic Circle, I quickly discovered, was there was no need to pretend to look at the displays to avoid talking to strangers. The exhibits were genuinely fascinating, each one offering at least one treasure. At the first display case, I was stunned to discover the crisp white glove magician and ventriloquist Jay Marshall had fashioned into his long-time stage partner, Lefty. I snapped a photo of the famous glove and texted it to my friend Nathan back at home, recognizing this act alone qualified me as a certified magic geek. He replied seconds later and I could read between the lines of his two-word text message (Wow. Cool.) that he was just as excited by the find as I was.

I became increasingly enthralled with each display as I examined them. Moving in closer, I read a program from a stage show by Chung Ling Soo (a.k.a. William Robinson), purportedly from the performance in which he died from a mishandled Bullet Catch routine. I then was captivated by posters and handbills from celebrated comedian and magician Tommy Cooper, who had also died on stage in the middle of a performance.

"That particular display is a bit on the morbid side, I'm afraid," said a soft and refined voice behind me. "But be sure to get a good look at the Cups and Balls set in the next case. A rare item, not to be missed."

I turned and was stunned to see I was being addressed by none other than Laurence Baxter, a legend in the magic community. He was shorter than I had anticipated but just as dapper and natty as he appeared on TV. And make no mistake, Baxter had appeared on British TV more than any other magician in the last forty years. The closest magic equivalent in the US might be David Copperfield, but a better analog would probably be Johnny Carson in terms of name recognition and national adoration. Although, as Uncle Harry had often commented, Baxter's fame did not extend much past Dover; however, throughout Great Britain he was a certified superstar. And despite his advancing years, he still looked trim and full of energy.

"Cups and Balls," I repeated, trying not to sound like a starstruck geek. "In the next case."

Baxter was clearly accustomed to this reaction from the public (laymen and magicians alike), so he gently turned me toward the next case and indicated a worn and tarnished set of brass cups, each one displayed with a rather faded red ball atop it.

""Doesn't look like much, does it?" he said as I leaned forward to get a closer look at the set.

Not sure if this was a trick question or not, I mumbled an indecipherable response. He continued on as if what I said had made sense.

"That, my young friend, is the very set of Cups and Balls the Duke of Cornwall used when he applied for admission to The Magic Circle."

I nodded in sympathetic agreement for a few moments, then realized I could cover my gross ignorance no longer.

"Forgive me," I said. "Should I know who that is?"

He smiled a devilish grin. "'Round these parts," he replied, sporting a comical American accent, "He is more commonly known as His Royal Majesty, Charles, Prince of Wales."

"Oh. My," I said.

"Indeed."

I looked at the worn props. "How did he do on the test?" I asked.

Baxter considered his words carefully before speaking. "Well, he was granted admission, let's just leave it at that."

I turned to him. "Are you being diplomatic?"

"Always." He gave me a practiced smile and put out his hand. "I'm Larry, by the way. Larry Baxter."

"I know," I said, glancing down at his hand while he shook mine. "Everyone knows."

He shrugged modestly. "I've learned to never make assumptions. And you are?"

I had been distracted looking at his hand and stammered a response.

"Oh, sorry, Eli Marks," I said. "You have the same ring as my uncle," I added, gesturing at his right hand.

"Well, if your uncle is Harry Marks, that would make perfect sense," he said, holding up his hand and admiring the ring. "We both got our rings at the same time. All of us did."

"All of us?"

"The Magnificent Magi," he said, moving to a display case in the corner and gesturing for me to follow. "There we are, in all our glory. Such as it was."

He indicated a slightly faded black-and-white eight-by-ten photo on the display's second shelf. I leaned in for a closer look and immediately recognized a much, much younger version of Uncle Harry's beaming face. He was surrounded by several other young men, each smiling up at the camera during what appeared to be a dinner or a party of some sort. Upon further inspection, I also recognized younger versions of Laurence Baxter and Oskar

Korhonen, each holding up a right hand to display their matching rings.

"We were going to go with the other hand for the rings, but we opted for the right in deference to Oskar. Didn't want the old boy to feel left out."

"What's the occasion?" I asked as I scanned the other smiling faces.

"We were all admitted to The Magic Circle at the same time, quite a group of us, so we decided to call ourselves The Magnificent Magi and celebrated the occasion with matching rings. Silly, perhaps, but I still wear the ring for sentimental reasons. I think all the boys do," he added, glancing at the photo. "Except poor old Archie, of course."

He gestured toward one fellow in the photo: a long-faced young man who was either feeling badly at that evening's photo opportunity or who always sported a sad and sour expression.

"What happened to Archie?"

He clucked his tongue. "Tragic, really. He died," he said, then moved in closer and lowered his voice. "Suicide. Terrible business."

He turned toward the room and shifted his mood, once again becoming the upbeat and buoyant character everyone knew. "But that's in the past, and tonight is all about the future and celebrating two performers who have not graced this stage in too long a time."

I nodded in agreement. "Harry was really thrilled to get the invitation," I said as we looked out at all the magicians, young and old, who were filling up the room. Waiters had started to move through the space with glasses of champagne, and Laurence snagged two as the tray sailed past us.

"It will be delightful," he said, thrusting one of the glasses into my hand. "And, as I said, long overdue."

A thought occurred to me, and I realized Laurence might have the answer I was looking for.

"Can I ask you a question?"

"Always."

"I noticed Harry and Oskar addressed each other as 'Doctor,'" I said. "Is that also a shared trait among the Magnificent Magi?"

I could be wrong, but I think Baxter came *this* close to doing a classic spit take, then gave me a pained smile and shook his head.

"Are they still doing that? Some jokes will never die, I suppose." He took a more complete sip of his champagne. "It is a practice common to all the Magi with the exception of myself," he said. "You see, I read Medicine at University and was headed toward a career as a doctor before the magic bug took complete hold of me. Early on, I made the mistake of calling myself Dr. Baxter—I do have the degree, after all—and the lads have never let me forget it.

"Consequently, all the Magi refer to each other as 'Doctor.' Except me. None of them call me 'Doctor.' They never have, silly buggers." He smiled, downed his drink, and placed it on another passing tray. "Lovely to have met you, Eli," he said, once again putting out his hand.

"The pleasure is all mine, Mr. Baxter," I said in return. "Or should I say Dr. Baxter?"

He shook his head good-naturedly. "Why start now? Call me Larry."

"That may take awhile," I admitted.

"As you wish, Dr. Marks," he said, giving my hand a quick squeeze before moving back into the crowd.

* * *

There's a funny thing about magicians: get just about any number of them into a room together and the place suddenly turns into an impromptu performance venue. This was no exception, and mini-shows popped up all over the room. I had finished looking at the displays and was still feeling the adrenaline rush of meeting Laurence Baxter. So I turned my attention to the room, which in the past few minutes had transformed into a sea of magicians demonstrating their skills to other magicians, who were patiently (or not) awaiting their turns to demonstrate right back.

Closest to me was a young man with slicked-back jet-black hair wearing a tattered tux and bright yellow sneakers. He was demonstrating his virtuosity with a deck of cards, but I would be hard-pressed to call what he was doing a traditional magic trick. Instead, he was manipulating the cards, practically juggling them, his hands orchestrating the cards into a shower of tumbling, well-controlled movements. The small crowd around him, consisting of young men about his age, was cooing in appreciation at his skill and dexterity. I found it impressive as well, although I could hear my Uncle Harry's voice in the back of my head, growling, "Yes, that's all well and good, but when is he going to actually *do* something?"

He didn't get the chance, as one of his audience members squinted across the room and declared, "Angelika is here!"

"And she's performing? Brilliant!" said another teen boy in the group.

That was all it took for the crowd to rapidly disperse and just as quickly reform across the room. The young man in the tux and yellow sneakers scowled at the interruption and didn't bother to follow his audience.

"Ah, she's nothing to run home for."

I didn't want to disagree with him, but from this distance she certainly appeared to be worth a quick trot. She was dressed in a bright Victorian-style outfit, consisting, primarily, of a tight red corset along with a very short red skirt and black lace stockings. Her blonde hair was tied up in a messy ponytail on the top of her head, while on her feet she wore high black shoes with what looked like painfully sharp pointed heels.

"Not a fan?" I suggested as the young man squared his deck of cards and began to put them back into the case.

"Of her? Not bloody likely," he grumbled. "She's all knickers and knockers, that one." He pocketed the deck of cards and smiled up at me. "You're not from around here, are you?"

I shook my head as I put out my hand. "No, from the States. Eli, nice to meet you."

He took my hand and then his face brightened. "Not Eli Marks by any chance?" he said.

"That would be me," I said, anticipating his next statement would be some glowing comment about my Uncle Harry.

"Fantastic," he said, now pumping my hand enthusiastically. "I'm a huge fan of your Card-Presto, use it all the time. Saved me a small fortune on cards over the years."

"Well, thanks, glad it's of use," I said, taken aback the conversation was actually about me and not my nearest relation. The Card-Presto, a device designed to help flatten decks of cards, and thus increase their longevity, was one of the few magic items I had ever produced. It was a small but consistent seller. "And you are?"

"Liam. Liam Sutherland. This is fantastic. Eli Marks. My, my."

I shrugged modestly.

An awkward moment of silence, which Liam broke. "Well, mate, I'm helping out backstage so I have to be off. But if you're around after, I'd love to buy you a pint."

He barely looked old enough to be buying alcohol at all, a pint or otherwise, but I'd always been lousy at guessing a person's age. "I'm not going anywhere," I said. "That would be great."

"Brilliant," he replied happily, turning to go, repeating my name as he headed toward the door. "Eli Bloody Marks, what do you know."

I basked in the momentary glow of celebrity for a few seconds, than made my way across the room to watch Angelika to see if there was, in fact, anything more to her than, as Liam so expressively put it, knickers and knockers.

* * *

While her appearance and costume may have helped draw a crowd, I could immediately recognize it was her skill with a deck of cards that kept the growing audience in rapt attention. By the time I joined the group, she was in the midst of what looked like an Ambitious Card routine, joking playfully with a teenager she had pulled from the swarm buzzing around her. He was a gawky and gangly kid, his looks and manner absolutely screaming "nerdy magician." She had

9

grabbed him by the shoulders and was manhandling him, getting him into a position of her liking. With the stage arrangement set, she nodded at him dramatically. He placed his chosen card back in the deck and Angelika began a complicated series of cuts and shuffles.

"Oh, you lads are burning me," she complained with a smile.

The crowd laughed in agreement. There is no audience harder to fool than a group of magicians. Oddly enough, no group is easier to fool as well, because with knowledge often comes complacency.

"Now, you lads think you know every move I'm making here, don't you?" she teased with a wicked smile. "Every false cut and shuffle, every break, am I right?"

The group produced sounds of assent, and she increased the speed of her shuffles and cuts.

"Perhaps. Perhaps. Yet I possess a secret weapon which you young gents sadly lack," she said, scanning the group and forcing them to look her in the eye. "It's true and it's effective and it will help me fool you boys. Every. Single. Time. Never underestimate the mis-directional value of some well-placed...cleavage."

With that, she glanced down at her chest, which was attractively shaped and featured by her bustier. Every eye followed her gaze. I don't know if she actually made a move with the cards right then, but at that moment she could have snuck an elephant into the room and no one would have noticed.

"Back up here, boys," she said a moment later, laughing and pointing to her eyes. "Back up here, please." Nervous laughter all around as they realized how she had maneuvered their gaze at what was likely a critical moment. She turned to the young man who was helping her with the trick and he locked eyes with her, terrified to look anywhere else.

"See anything down there you like, Brian?" she asked. He sputtered a noncommittal response. "Is it warm in here? You look a bit...sweaty," she added seductively, gesturing to his forehead. "Have you maybe got a handkerchief on you?"

He nodded and quickly reached into his back pocket. As he did, his expression changed from one of embarrassment to amazement. Instead of the handkerchief he had gone after, he pulled a playing card out of the pocket. He glanced at it, and then held it up for the small crowd: a Queen of Hearts, with his name scrawled across the face.

"That's how it's done, boys," she said with a laugh.

The crowd burst into applause, including several loud whistles of appreciation. She took a deep curtsey, modestly placing one hand over her cleavage as she did so. It may have been my imagination, but I thought she winked at me before turning away from the group.

"She's really good, isn't she?" a familiar voice said behind me. I turned and was surprised to see Megan standing next to me. As soon as I saw her, I started to feel a bit guilty, like the wink was something I had requested. For her part, Megan seemed nonplussed by the exchange and actually excited by the magic.

"I mean, I only saw the end of it, but she really had them engaged," Megan continued. "You know, the way you and Harry talk about engaging an audience."

I was a little thrown by the arrival of my girlfriend and this sudden topic of conversation.

"Did you already make it to the hotel?" I sputtered, pulling out my phone to check the time. "Was there any problem?"

She shook her head, smiling broadly. She clearly wasn't suffering the same degree of jet lag I was feeling.

"We're all checked in," she said. "It's adorable. I don't know where the desk clerk is from, 'cause we had a lot of trouble communicating with each other, but we eventually got it all sorted out. It was great! I think you're going to love it."

Because Harry had wanted to spend so little time in London, we had timed our arrival a bit on the tight side. Our plan, which apparently had worked, was once we landed, Megan would take the bags and get us checked into the hotel, and then come meet us at The Magic Circle for the evening's special show. Which, if my phone had properly updated, was going to start in about ten minutes.

"We should probably head into the auditorium," I said, looking

11

around and noticing the steady stream of people leaving the room. I patted my pockets for the two tickets Harry had given me, and we joined the line of people waiting to ascend the spiral staircase up to the theater.

Once we got onto the narrow staircase, I made the mistake of glancing down. The surface on the first floor had been painted to make it appear like the spiral staircase continued on into infinity. Looking up offered a similarly disquieting effect, so I instead concentrated on looking at the back of Megan's head as we made our way up and up, finally arriving at the small auditorium.

* * *

"Ladies and gentlemen, mesdames and messieurs, domain and herrian, you are in for a rare treat this fine evening."

Laurence Baxter had been on the stage for all of ten seconds, and he already held the audience in the palm of his hand. The sightlines in the theater were terrific. Even from my tenth-row seat, I felt like he was talking directly to me. The audience was clearly thrilled to be there watching Baxter do his thing, and Megan and I were immediately caught up in the excitement.

"Can everyone see me all right?" he asked as he pulled out a deck of cards. "And can you see these? In case you are unfamiliar, these are playing cards."

The laughter from the audience had a sense of anticipation to it, like they knew where this was headed. To be honest, from where I sat, the cards were not all that visible. Certainly a traditional card trick in front of this size audience would require some real finesse.

"Perhaps you can see them better if I do this," Baxter said, and with a practiced flick of his wrist he sent one, then two, then three cards sailing through the air and up into the balcony. I turned and looked over my shoulder at their trajectory, which was so precise that people in the front row of the balcony were able to grab the cards out of the air as they sailed over their heads.

"As I always say, if you can't bring the people to the cards, then bring the cards to the people," he said with a laugh as a round of applause died down. "And, just to prove these are, in fact, ordinary cards, can I have the quick assistance of a volunteer?"

Moments later a middle-aged man stood rather sheepishly next to Baxter, who quickly demonstrated for him the necessary wrist moves required to flick cards with such speed and precision. As expected, Baxter continually bested the volunteer, whose plucky efforts landed a series of wingless cards about eight feet away, in and around the front row seats.

Upping the ante, Baxter then called for some help from backstage. Moments later, Liam, the young card juggler I had spoken to earlier, pushed a wheeled table on stage. Sitting atop the table was a large watermelon. This new addition was on the opposite side of the stage from Baxter and his volunteer, and once it appeared, it provoked a quick wave of applause from many in the audience. Once the large melon was properly positioned, Liam disappeared backstage.

"Perhaps it was the sheer distance which was tripping you up," Baxter suggested, handing more cards to the volunteer and gesturing toward the watermelon across the stage. The man was a good sport and gave it his all, but not one of the cards landed anywhere near the table, instead drifting sadly and aimlessly before fluttering to the stage.

"You have to account for the air currents in the room," Baxter said patiently, taking the deck of cards from the hapless volunteer. He quickly wet his index finger, held it up in the air to test the currents, and then begin to flick cards—one after another—at the watermelon.

His aim was perfect, and each card not only hit the watermelon, but pierced the rind, holding fast. Within moments, half a dozen playing cards were protruding from the watermelon. The audience applauded wildly as Baxter escorted his volunteer back to his seat and then returned to the stage. He had done a magnificent job of warming up the crowd.

"Thank you, thank you, for recognizing and rewarding me for what is, admittedly, a unique and wildly unnecessary talent," he said. "And, speaking of talent, tonight—or rather, the next fortnight—is a celebration of talent. A rare opportunity for audiences to experience performers who are, with the exception of one another, the definition of peerless." He lowered the handheld microphone as the audience applauded; this crowd was evidently aware of the line-up that had been brought in for this special series of performances.

"It is, as they say, a once in a lifetime occasion." He put one hand into his pocket and began to casually walk the stage. "I'm particularly pleased to be able to introduce tonight's two perform-ers, for we go way, way back." He exaggerated the final "way," and winked at the audience. "Of course, I was just a mere lad when I met them, and they were already well into their dotage."

This produced the laugh he intended, which he waved away with his free hand. "No, no, I admit, tonight's performers are my contemporaries. I will own up to that. I'm a big enough man to admit that. In fact, I've even invited several of them—a few of whom are a step above street buskers and pickpockets—*into my own home* while they are here in London," he continued, making it sound like the grandest of gestures.

"Mind you, I've put away the good silver," he added quickly. "I'm not a bloody idiot."

More laughter and applause from the crowd, and I remem-bered "I'm not a bloody idiot" was a well-known catch phrase of Laurence Baxter's when he'd been appearing on television regu-larly in his own long-running prime-time show.

"Tonight's two special performers are each receiving a recogni-tion which is long overdue: by order of the Society's President, each is being bestowed The Devant Award, named in honor of the first president of the Magic Circle."

This produced a thunderous ovation, the volume of which was surprising because the auditorium probably only held a hundred and fifty seats or so, including the small balcony above us. Laurence Baxter smiled at the enthusiastic response and even placed the microphone under his arm so he could join in the applause.

Once it had subsided, he took the microphone in both hands.

14

"Ladies and gentlemen, please join me in welcoming two unparalleled performers as well as dear, dear friends. Oskar Korhonen...and Harry Marks!"

Another deafening ovation as he stepped toward the wings. The curtain parted, revealing the two older performers.

It was clear the two magicians had been positioned in a tableau, but it was also immediately apparent something had gone askew. Oskar was seated in a majestic, high-backed wooden chair with Harry standing right next to him in what I'm guessing had been intended as a regal pose for the pair.

The applause rapidly slipped away, and a few people laughed and then just as quickly stopped, realizing this was not intended to be a comic entrance. Somewhere in the auditorium, someone shrieked.

Oskar was slumped over in the chair.

Harry stood over him. He didn't look out at the audience. He wasn't dazed, but instead looked deeply puzzled.

He was looking down at Oskar Korhonen, who had a large knife sticking out of his back.

CHAPTER 2

H arry was arrested.

Not immediately, of course. First, there was a shocked reaction from the crowd. Legendary British reserve was in short supply as it quickly dawned on the audience this was, in fact, not part of the show. Screams were followed by calls for "Is there a doctor in the house?"

Laurence Baxter was the first to the tableau, looking a bit mystified at what was expected of him, his medical education being long past. He looked at Harry, he looked at Oskar, he looked at the bloody wound in the one-armed man's back, and—from where I was now standing—he looked a bit pale and wobbly. Perhaps it had been for the best that he had abandoned medicine in favor of magic.

The cries from the crowd had summoned a stern old woman to the stage, clutching a First Aid kit in her bony hands. I recognized her as the lady who had been running the coat check. My first impression of her—that she was a dead ringer for Mrs. Danvers from the first film version of *Rebecca*—was reinforced as she slowly moved across the stage. Despite her slow pace and obvious frail condition, she took immediate and complete charge of the situation.

"Oh, Miss Hess, thank god. There's been an accident," Laurence Baxter said as he turned to her with evident relief.

"So I've heard," she said calmly, in what I recognized as probably a German accent. "Move. Let me see what this fuss is."

He stepped aside, and she moved in, glancing first at Harry and then down at the body.

"Yes, well, we will not need this," she said, thrusting the First Aid kit into Baxter's trembling hands. "This man is beyond bandages and antiseptic spray. If the police have not been called yet, they must be."

"But, what...why?" Baxter nearly whimpered.

"Because this man is dead," she explained with flat simplicity, and then she hobbled off the stage as slowly as she had arrived.

* * *

The police reached the same conclusion Miss Hess had come to, albeit without her Germanic directness.

In a matter of moments, the auditorium was overcome with a rush of activity. EMTs sprinted in, followed immediately by the police. The order was given for the auditorium to be cleared, and the crowd moved down to the second floor Devant Room and the first floor Clubroom, where the police would likely question potential witnesses.

I had other plans. I grabbed Megan's hand.

"Eli, we're going the wrong direction," Megan said as I maneuvered us toward the stage.

"I have to get to Harry," I said loudly over the hubbub of the retreating crowd. Megan must have agreed with me, for she tightened her grip on my hand as we made slow but steady progress.

We pushed upstream, against the moving crowd, until we reached a door to the left of the stage. I gave it a firm push and was relieved to feel it open. A moment later we were backstage, which was just as chaotic but not nearly as crowded as the auditorium.

The first person I encountered was Liam, the young magician

who had so admired my Card-Presto product. He was pale and shaken, wiping at his nose with his sleeve. He saw me and shook his head.

"I moved the chair where they said to," he said, his voice choking. "That's all I did was move the chair."

"Yes, boy, and you keep moving," Miss Hess said, coming up from behind him. "This is no place for you now, move along. *Geh weg! Schnell, schnell.*"

"Oh, give it a rest," another voice cut in. I turned to see Angelika, the female magician I'd seen earlier. She was moving through the backstage area, headed toward the door we had just come through. "Give the poor lad a moment to breathe, for bloody's sake. You heartless old crone."

She draped an arm over the teenager's shoulder while the old German woman mumbled something unintelligible before turning and heading away, making her way slowly through a small crowd of police.

"Come on, they need us out of here, love," Angelika said to the teen. "Let's head downstairs and see what's what."

We stepped aside, she guided the boy through the door, and the two of them disappeared back into the auditorium.

* * *

We finally spotted Harry, deep in conversation with a man and a woman I guessed were the British version of plainclothes detectives. They were just outside of an area which had been quickly cordoned off by the crime scene team. Their version of a CSI tech was snapping photos of Oskar, who was still slumped over in his large wooden throne. Harry glanced my way and nodded, which I took to mean that, under the circumstances, he was doing okay. It made me feel a little better, but not by much. I wanted to walk over and confirm this with him. However, given the demeanor of the police who were questioning him, I suspected Harry was out of bounds, at least for the next few minutes.

"Eli!"

18

I turned toward the sound of my name and saw Laurence Baxter waving me over to a small group huddled on the far side of the stage. Steering clear of the crime scene, Megan and I snaked our way across the backstage area and joined the small assembly. I recognized the hefty British comic magician Angus Bishop and a renowned mentalist who went by the single name Borys. Like Baxter, both were in their seventies, and although they were not as decrepit as Miss Hess, neither had the same youthful energy Baxter projected.

Joining the group as we arrived was another older gentleman with the whitest hair I had ever seen. While his deep tan appeared genuine, there was something about his hair that didn't. Although probably just as old as his contemporaries in this small group, his frosty hair gave him an ageless and timeless look. He leaned into the group and whispered conspiratorially but not quietly.

"Harry didn't do it, I'm sure of it," he said in a clipped American accent. "I couldn't get very close, but from what I could see, it appeared the knife actually came out of the base of the chair, attached to an armature of some kind. It traveled up on an arc, sweeping up behind the chair directly into the occupant's back. Then, via some mechanism I couldn't discern, the arm swung back underneath the chair."

"But the knife did not," Laurence Baxter added dryly.

"Sadly, no," the white-haired man agreed. He glanced over at me and Megan, then back to Laurence Baxter, who immediately picked up the social cue.

"Ah, yes, this is Harry Marks's nephew, Eli," he said, reaching out and patting my shoulder. "And..." he continued, tossing the next introduction to me.

"And this is Megan," I said, unnecessarily putting my arm around her shoulder. I wasn't sure what other words were needed to describe our relationship. Calling her my girlfriend made me feel like we were still in junior high, while referring to her as my partner sounded like we worked together in a law firm. It was my strategy to lock down a more permanent relationship status while on this trip, but for the time being, I just let her name hang in the air.

Baxter continued the introductions. "Brilliant. Of course, this is Angus Bishop," he continued, gesturing toward the broadly built gentleman to his left. "And Borys," he added, indicating the thin, wiry man who was dwarfed next to Angus. "And, of course, Davis De Vries," he added, referring to the man with the amazingly white hair.

"I certainly know you all by reputation," I said, quickly shaking hands with each of the older gentlemen. Angus, not surprisingly, had a strong grip in proportion to his bulk. I've never actually met a longshoreman, but I suspect some of them would be intimidated by Angus's size and girth, despite his advancing years.

Borys was slighter of build, short and rail thin with wide eyes, which had both a feral and fearful quality. His grip was nonexistent, like shaking hands with a wisp of air, while Davis De Vries shook my hand enthusiastically for several seconds longer than necessary.

They all then turned to Megan, clearly far more interested in shaking hands with her. Having spent more than her fair share of time in the company of old magicians who fawned over younger women, she complied graciously.

"I'm not a magician," she explained to the group, "but Eli prepped me on all the performers who were going to be part of the celebration. Except," she added, turning to Davis De Vries, "for you."

"Just so," he said, breaking into a wide smile. "I'm the performer behind the performers. The man behind the curtain, as it were."

"De Vries builds many of the best illusions we all use," Baxter said, then noticed Borys was shrugging at this description. "That is to say, all of us who do big-box illusions."

"Mr. De Vries created the The Baker's Dozen," I explained to Megan. "We saw it last year at the *Magic Live!* convention in Las Vegas. You know, the illusion where it appears the magician cuts the assistant into thirteen even slices?"

Megan reflexively shuddered at the memory, producing a slight chuckle from De Vries.

"Not to worry, I'm currently working on a gluten-free version," he said, offering a practiced one-liner. Polite chuckles were had all around.

"He'll also be unveiling his latest creation this week, although he's too modest to tout it," Laurence Baxter added. "The Catherine Wheel. Should be a corker."

There were excited rumbles of agreement on this point, and then, collectively, the group suddenly seemed to realize that a somber attitude would be more appropriate given the situation. For example, the fact Oskar Korhonen was still slumped over in his chair on the other side of the stage.

"Well, yes, anyway," Baxter continued, "we must do whatever the police require of us to sort this mess out as quickly as possible. A terrible thing."

There were nods of assent all around, but no actual plan was suggested. I was about to point out this missing element when I noticed Harry and the two plainclothes police officers moving toward us. I thought they were coming to talk to us, but their pace didn't slacken as they veered around the group, heading for the stage door in the back.

Harry's wrists were handcuffed, but he was able to turn toward me and speak before they pulled him through the door and into the stairwell.

"These are not the linking rings I was planning on employing this evening," he said with a weak smile, gesturing to the cuffs while clearly working hard to keep any fear out of his voice. "Don't worry, Eli. We'll get this sorted out."

The small group watched as the stage door closed ominously behind him. The group of old men then turned to me.

I'm sure their expressions mirrored mine and we were all thinking a similar thought: getting this all sorted out might not be quite as easy as Harry was suggesting.

* * *

One of the uniformed constables told us which police station Harry had been taken to, so I excused Megan and myself from the group, with the promise to keep them all apprised of what we learned. Laurence Baxter pressed a business card in my hand, and then Megan and I headed downstairs to call a cab.

Megan reminded me we needed to retrieve our coats, which meant standing in a short but slow-moving line in front of the coat check window.

As we inched forward, I could see the attendant, Miss Hess, inspect each claim stub closely, as if there had been a recent rash of counterfeit claims and subsequent missing coats. After each examination, she would disappear into the bowels of the cloak room for what seemed like a long time for such a simple and direct mission. Then she would return and hand over the coat, still bristling with suspicion as she shooed the person away and indicated the next in line should get a move on. Very few actual words were exchanged throughout; instead, this was all communicated with a harsh series of grimaces, scowls, and Teutonic-sounding grunts.

Since we had arrived separately, we each presented her with our own claim tickets. She looked closely at both tickets and then just as intently at the two of us.

"You arrive unaccompanied and yet depart jointly," she said, more statement than question, lacing the comment with what sounded like a heaping dollop of judgment for good measure. "That is curious."

"Life is curious," I countered, deciding this scary old lady had not cornered the market on enigmatic phraseology.

"In more ways than you'll ever know," she replied quietly as she turned to retrieve our items. Each of our coats, neither of which struck me as being particularly heavy, were of sufficient bulk that the old woman felt the need to bring them to us separately.

She struggled with each coat as if its pockets were loaded down with heavy stones. Finally, she finished with us, handing Megan her coat without a word, then signaled to the patron behind us that their time had in fact come.

* * *

"A flight risk? That's absurd," I huffed indignantly. Sadly, my voice cracked on the last word, thereby sucking any authority out of my intended outrage.

The police detective, a tired woman in her early forties who identified herself as Detective Inspector Matthews, sighed and continued her explanation of their reasons for holding Harry in a jail cell overnight and why my request to see him had been denied. Her accent was a delightful mix of British and Indian, but currently that was the only thing about her that might be considered delightful. To be fair, I imagined she wasn't finding me to be particularly enchanting, either.

"As I explained, Mr. Marks, this is a capital crime. Your uncle's behavior is, at the very least, questionable."

"Really? How do you figure?"

DI Matthews sighed deeply and looked down at her notes. "He arrived at two thirty this afternoon from the US for—he claims—the sole purpose of being on stage with the victim this evening. He booked a hotel for one night only. He came to the scene of the crime directly from the airport, and although he claimed to be staying in town for just one night, he had checked two large bags for the flight. He and the victim were alone backstage for several minutes. He was standing next to Mr...." She glanced down at her notes. "Next to Mr. Korhonen when he was killed. And he is holding a return airline ticket that will take him out of the country tomorrow at noon, a mere twelve hours from now."

She set her notes down and looked across the table at me. "All in all, singly and in its totality, this is behavior we on the force would judge to be, at the very least, questionable."

"He didn't kill him—" I began, but she held up a hand.

"This is not for you or me to determine, sir," Matthews said firmly. "If the decision is made to charge your uncle, which I believe to be highly likely, our legal system will do an excellent job of determining his guilt or innocence. But for the time being, specifically this evening, he is considered a flight risk and will remain under our supervision until tomorrow at the earliest, at which time our prosecutors will determine and present their next steps."

Although the accent and some of the terminology was different, this all had a very familiar ring to me.

My ex-wife was an Assistant District Attorney back in Minneapolis, and her new husband was a hulking Golem who made his living as a Homicide Detective. I had been on the receiving end of his sleep-inducing officiousness on more than one occasion. If experience has taught me anything, it was that it was fruitless to argue with City Hall. Particularly if City Hall had taken the human form of an underpaid and overworked Homicide Detective.

"Now it is my recommendation that you return to your hotel and come back in the morning, and at that time we will have more information to share on your uncle and his situation, vis-à-vis this ongoing murder investigation."

I'm sure there are some fundamental differences between the US and British criminal justice systems, but the way all their people straighten up papers and close folders to signal the end of a conversation is eerily identical.

* * *

It was a return trip to the hotel for Megan but the first for me. The streets were dark, and my sense of direction was a shambles. So, instead of being adventurous and exploring the subway system, we hopped into a nearby cab. Megan had the hotel's name and address at her fingertips, and a few minutes later we pulled up to what was going to be our home away from home for the next week on our first vacation as a couple.

The exterior looked a little worn and rundown, but I chalked it

24

up to poor street lighting and a moonless night. The interior, however, had no such excuses to fall back on.

"Isn't it adorable?" Megan whispered as we made our way down the front hallway toward the small lobby. "It's like stepping back in time."

"You mean before the invention of the vacuum cleaner?" I suggested. I looked down, convinced small puffs of dust were emanating from each step we made on the worn carpet.

The fuzzy first impression the foyer made was reinforced tenfold the moment we entered the small lobby. Mismatched Christmas lights had been strung haphazardly over the front desk, although most of the bulbs weren't lit. A worn lopsided couch sat by the window, next to a rack filled with faded tourist brochures. Beside the rack was a wobbly-looking card table with what could only be called a vintage PC atop it. The computer's screen glowed a sickly green.

Someone with either no sense of irony or the finest wit since Oscar Wilde had printed up a small dot-matrix placard touting the table as the "Busness Center." Yes, "business" was in fact misspelled.

"What was the Yelp rating on this place?" I asked Megan quietly as we waited for the harried desk clerk to finish what sounded like an angry phone call. His tone was indignant, which was evident regardless of the language. It sounded like Russian, but my knowledge of that language was confined to villains trying in vain to kill James Bond.

"Oh, the reviews were terrible, but I read through them and the criticisms were just dumb Americans complaining about moronic things," she explained happily. "I love it here."

Before I could inquire as to which things the dumb Americans had railed against, the desk clerk finished his call by slamming the receiver down hard on the cradle and saying something that sounded like a curse, regardless of the language. He then looked up and gave us—well, Megan at least—a toothy smile.

"You are back," he said as he turned to the crooked set of

wooden cubbies hanging precariously on the wall behind him. "Your night, it was good?"

"It was interesting," Megan said as he handed her the key. It was attached by what appeared to be baling wire to a plastic tag bearing our room number.

"Interesting is good?" he asked, still smiling his toothy grin. His short-cropped hair stood straight up on top of his head, while his bright blue eyes bulged just the tiniest bit.

"Interesting is good, yes," Megan agreed. "Good night."

"Good night to you and to you too, sir," he said, waving at us happily as we moved out of the lobby and back to the hallway. I followed Megan, who took a confident left, leading us to the elevator door. She pushed the up button.

"Russian?" I asked.

She shrugged. "I have no idea. But he's clearly not from around here."

"Well, neither are we," I said, and then looked over at the elevator doors as they wobbled open. A dim light illuminated the elevator car, but that term was giving it way too much credit. It was like a phone booth, but smaller.

"This may be the smallest elevator I've ever seen," I said. "I've seen dumbwaiters more spacious."

"I know, isn't it great?" she beamed as she stepped in. I turned sideways and wedged myself into the small box. Megan pressed the button for the fourth floor. The doors quavered shut and, with a small lurch, the elevator began to climb.

"You know, I once made a refrigerator box fort that was bigger than this elevator," I observed, marveling at the tiny space. "How did you ever get upstairs with all of our luggage?"

"Oh, that was easy," she said, turning so my elbow wasn't digging into her shoulder. "I just piled all the bags in here, hit the button for our floor, then ran up the stairs."

"Let me guess: you beat the elevator by a considerable margin," I suggested as the car whined and stuttered its way up.

"They call it a lift. And, yes, I had plenty of time to catch my breath, if that's what you mean."

I was going to continue the conversational topic, but I began to fear we'd run out of oxygen in the small space, so I just nodded and waited for the ride to be over.

* * *

Sleep came quickly and my only dreams consisted of continually awaking, thinking I was trapped inside a coffin. You might think I was flashing back to our ride up in the lift, but when it came to small spaces, our room gave the elevator a run for its money. I had already assembled a growing mental list I was sure would match up, point by point, with the complaints generated by the "dumb Americans" on Yelp.

For her part, Megan loved the place, so I wisely kept my mouth shut. The fact was, the inconveniences were minor, and we had come to London to see the sights, not to become roving hotel critics. Seeing her happy and having fun erased any other issues I might be having with our accommodations.

Once we were showered and dressed, we made our way to the communal breakfast room and showed our room key, which entitled each of us to what was advertised as a traditional English breakfast. Moments after we had settled in, before they had even offered coffee or tea, a waitperson delivered two overflowing plates to our table and then disappeared as quickly as she had come.

I looked down at the plate that had been put in front of me, then looked to see if a similar disaster had befallen Megan.

"What is this?" I asked, my voice a little hoarse, either from lack of use or flat out fear.

"It's a traditional English breakfast," Megan said brightly.

"No, seriously, what is this?"

She picked up her fork and pointed tentatively at each of the alleged food items on the plate as she introduced them.

"I think this is back bacon, those are fried eggs, this looks like a grilled tomato, that's gotta be a mushroom of some kind, those are sausages, and this pile here is baked beans." She sat back, clearly proud of her achievement. She had tried to sound authoritative, but I could tell she was flat out guessing at a couple of items.

I looked at the plate again, then at the wait staff as they bustled around the room. "Did we do something wrong? Are they mad at us?"

A buzz alerted me to a text from Laurence Baxter, informing me that he'd secured a lawyer (a "solicitor" in his terminology) who would be meeting with Harry as soon as they would allow him this morning. Baxter suggested meeting at the police station at ten thirty. I texted back we would see him there.

"You can always spot the Americans," Megan whispered, nodding at a couple as they entered and were seated by the hostess. "Even before they say a word."

I was about to question the validity of this statement, when the female half of the duo said in a too-loud and grating American accent, "Oh, do we have to sit by a *radiator*?" She spat out the word like someone who had been relocated against their will to a site less desirable than Chernobyl or Love Canal.

Megan was ahead, one love, and I made the mental note that, if asked, I would say we hailed from Canada.

The game then became guessing the nationality of the people who weren't obviously Americans. Megan had a better facility with languages than I did, so she was able to offer linguistic predictions with far greater speed and accuracy than I could. For example, her prediction the little boy with the Harry Potter glasses was French proved dead on when he continually ignored his mother's request to stop swinging his legs while he sat, repeating the word "*non*" over and over again.

Two love.

We did agree the family across from us—grandmother, mother, and a younger boy—were likely Russian, or perhaps Ukrainian. They ate silently, but I heard the grandmother whisper "*Etta dyedooshkye*" to her tablemates. My wish to be able to translate it was granted a few moments later when the woman I was assuming was her daughter whispered to the younger boy, "For PopPop."

With these instructions in place, the two each handed the grandmother an item from their plate—a roll from one and an apple from the other—which she stealthily slipped into her purse.

My study of this interesting family dynamic was interrupted by the appearance of two very large and very loud Americans, who squeezed into the table directly next to ours and began a long series of complaints concerning just about everything in sight. Before they could add us to their list, we finished our coffee and quickly exited.

* * *

The police station was no less cheery in the light of day.

Laurence Baxter met us at the front door and filled us in as we made our way down to the gray airless visitor waiting area. There was a surprising amount of activity for a Sunday morning, probably all stemming from Saturday night incidents, hopefully all less deadly than the one at The Magic Circle.

"My solicitor is in with Harry now," he said quietly. "He said, given this is a capital crime, they are well within their rights to hold Harry for seventy-two hours before charging him."

"So he thinks they're going to charge him?" I said, speaking much louder than intended.

Baxter shook his head. "He's not sure. My understanding is the prosecutor will bring the facts of the case before a magistrate tomorrow morning. The magistrate will determine if there is enough evidence to warrant pressing charges." He gestured toward three empty chairs in the crowded waiting room. "So, at the very least, Harry isn't getting out today."

I exchanged a look with Megan as we sat. It was clear we were both thinking the same question, but I said it out loud first. "Which one of us is going to call Franny?"

Megan shrugged, and I shrugged in return.

We had agreed to hold off calling Harry's soon-to-be new bride until we had more information. Currently, I wasn't quite sure if what Laurence Baxter had related counted as enough intelligence to bring Franny up to speed without simultaneously throwing her into a panic.

"She told him not to take this trip," Megan reminded me softly.

"I know, but it seems unlikely Franny would take this down the 'I told you so' road. At least, not right away. Plus, she was planning on picking him up at the airport." I looked at my watch, which I had yet to re-set. "It's not even six a.m. in Minneapolis. We might as well wait until she's up. No need to get her out of bed at this point."

Megan nodded in agreement, and I turned to Laurence, but he held up a hand.

"Here's Wexler-Smith," he said, looking toward the heavy steel door that stood between visitors and the poor souls they had come to visit. Just coming through the entry was a middle-aged man in a perfectly tailored pinstripe suit, making him the odds-on favorite as the best-dressed person in the room. His bushy white mustache and eyebrows gave him a sad hangdog appearance, which was reinforced by his slumped posture and slow, ponderous step.

"Nothing too positive to report, Baxter, sorry to say," he said in a low, Nigel Bruce like growl. "Too much red tape, high visibility of the crime, flight risk, foreigner, it all adds up. Bad business, if you ask me. Strictly by the book on this one, that's my guess."

Laurence Baxter nodded at the recitation, then introduced us to Simon Wexler-Smith, his long-time solicitor. The sad-faced man mumbled some words of condolence as he shook hands with me, then Megan.

"What are our next steps?" Baxter asked once the social niceties had been acknowledged.

"Wait for the magistrate's decision," Wexler-Smith replied confidently. "Not much we can do until then, I'm afraid. Hands tied and all that."

"Any chance I can see Harry?" I cut in, looking from the lawyer to Baxter. "Like, this morning? Now?"

Figuring Wexler-Smith was the one with the power, I concentrated my attention on him, but he turned impotently to Baxter. The solicitor may have been an expert on the law, but Laurence

30

Baxter was a bona fide star in this country, and that would likely count for more.

"Let me see what I can do," Baxter said quietly, unnecessarily straightening his suit jacket as he headed toward the main desk.

Five minutes later, I was being ushered through the imposing metal door, which closed with a sickening thud behind me.

* * *

Getting through that entry was just the first step in a journey, which included emptying all my pockets, going through two different scanners, and then a full body pat down by a clammy-handed middle-aged constable who, I sensed, had already reached his maximum level of tedium by this early hour. Regardless of how my day was going to go, I thought as they led me down the third blank hallway, his was likely to consist of performing this same series of actions on a never-ending stream of strangers. It made me feel a little better, but not much.

My Uncle Harry was not a large man—he resisted the word 'elfin,' but it wasn't far off the mark. However, when I first spotted him on the other side of the glass in the cramped booth where they'd placed him, he seemed even smaller than usual. I sat down on the hard plastic chair on my side of the glass. We reached for our respective phone receivers at the same time and then paused before saying anything into them. My receiver was warm and a bit sticky.

"I know what you're thinking," he finally said, his voice sounding tired, distant, and tinny through the receiver. "And I agree. Orange is not my color."

He glanced down at the jail-issued jumpsuit and gave an exaggerated shudder. "And I don't even dare consider how they may have hung up my tux," he added. "If they've hung it up at all."

For Harry, and many magicians of his era, the proper care and storage of one's tux was an issue of paramount importance, right up there with cleaning your coins and ironing your silks. In fact, once he was dressed in his tux before a show, Harry absolutely refused to sit down, as he felt bending his knees would negatively impact the line of his trousers. It was possible that attitude may have helped to save his life the night before, as it was Oskar who— apparently harboring no such qualms about the line of his tux— had opted to take a seat in the deadly chair.

"Are you doing okay?" I asked, figuring we must be on a set time limit and wanting to make the most of what might be a short conversation.

He shrugged. "Not bad. The people have been nice. The cell, however, is tiny. Miniscule."

I thought of mentioning the size of our hotel room but quickly decided this was not the right time for a quick game of travel adversity one-upmanship.

"Have you talked to Franny?" he continued, his brow furrowing in worry.

I shook my head. "Megan and I decided to wait until I'd seen you," I said. "So we could give her a more complete report."

He nodded at the decision, but I could tell he was concerned about her reaction to the news.

"She told me not to come," he said. "She said there were bad vibrations."

"You met her more than halfway," I countered. "Only staying one night, getting in and getting out quickly. It was a good compromise."

"Yes, with apparently sparkling results."

I didn't have a helpful response, so I changed the subject.

"What have they told you about what happened to Oskar?"

"Nothing directly, but I've heard enough to piece most of it together," he said, leaning forward as he shifted into magic instructor mode, a persona I had experienced my whole life. "Apparently, there was a device in the chair. As soon as one sat on the cushion, the pressure triggered the release of an arm on a powerful spring under the seat. It shot up out of the back of the chair, on a semicircle, and plunged the knife into the poor fellow's back. Then the arm retracted. Very clever, actually," he added, acknowledging his grudging admiration at the design of the deadly device.

"That's basically what Davis De Vries thought happened," I said, quickly recounting my short conversation with the small group of old magicians backstage.

"Yes, of course De Vries would figure it out quickly," Harry said. "Those sorts of mechanics are right up his alley."

I don't think he recognized the implications of this statement, but he was already onto another topic before I could press him on it. I made a mental note to come back to that thought at some point.

"The thing is, Buster, it was only a couple moments before the curtain even opened that the two of us decided who would be sitting and who would be standing," Harry said, turning as the door to his cubicle opened behind him. A guard stood there, silently indicating the time was up. "We'd gone back and forth on that decision for nearly thirty minutes, and we finally just decided it with a coin flip."

He turned to the guard and acknowledged his presence, indicating we were wrapping things up.

"Harry, I want to do something to move this thing along, but I have no idea what I should be doing."

He turned back to me, standing, but still holding onto the receiver. "I thought of it the moment I woke up and then kicked myself for not thinking of it last night. We've got to get in touch with McHugh."

As soon as he mentioned the name, I wanted to kick myself as well. McHugh was the one person who should have been my first phone call the previous night.

"Yes, of course," I said, also standing, although I wasn't entirely certain why. "How do I find him?"

"What day is it?" Harry asked, moving as slowly as he could to hang the receiver back up on its hook.

"Sunday," I said quickly.

"Perfect," Harry said as he backed away from the chair, still holding the phone. "Tower Hill tube stop. Seven thirty tonight! Sharp."

The guard took the receiver from Harry's hand and hung it up. I nodded furiously that I understood. As he was being ushered out of the cubicle, he turned and added one final thought. I could hear his voice, distantly, through the not-so-soundproof glass.

"And Eli," he said.

"Yes?" I shouted.

He was able to get his last words in before the door slammed shut.

"Wear comfortable shoes!"

CHAPTER 3

Although Henry McHugh was not visible when we stepped out of the Tower Hill tube station, the size of the crowd milling about assured me immediately that my limited understanding of the London underground system had brought us to the correct location.

"Are all these people here for a Jack the Ripper walk?" Megan said, scanning the swarm of tourists of all shapes and sizes.

"No, they're here for the *best* Jack the Ripper walk," I corrected. "Henry McHugh is considered to be one of the top living experts on the killings. Ripper walks are available every night of the week from lots of companies, but McHugh only does his on Sunday nights. When he's in town. And feels like doing it."

"What makes him the expert?" Megan asked as we snaked our way through the throng to pay. "I mean, was he on the case during the murders?"

I stopped and gave her a long look, checking to see if she was just pulling my leg.

"Megan, the Jack the Ripper murders took place in 1888," I said. "Do you know how old that would make him?"

"I get fuzzy on dates," she said with a shrug and we continued toward the front of the crowd as I pulled my wallet out of the relative safety of my front pocket and sorted through the unfamiliar bills.

Twenty pounds and ten minutes later we were on the move with the mob, straining to hear McHugh's voice above the general din produced by a large multilingual crowd moving through the cobblestoned streets of London's East End. Twice I had nearly gotten close enough to wave and get his attention, but with no success either time. The people treated him like a superstar, with fans quickly moving in for one-on-one questions each time he finished his short Ripper recitation and began the brief stroll to the next location. The crowd's reaction to him was, I realized, the same way magicians would approach my Uncle Harry. Perhaps this bizarre form of celebrity was what had bound the two men together as close friends.

I had met Henry McHugh a handful of times during my life. The most recent encounter had been at my Aunt Alice's funeral, which he had traveled from London to attend. I knew long trips like that were becoming fewer and fewer for him, but I also got the sense this singular event was one he simply felt he could not miss. I still remembered my uncle's look of surprise and relief when McHugh walked into the memorial service. Harry had not cried until that point, but seeing his old friend seemed to offer the permission he had been waiting for. To be honest, I still teared up when I thought about it.

While I pondered his relationship with Harry during the walking segments, McHugh had my complete attention each time he stopped and addressed the crowd on the topic of Jack the Ripper. Virtually all the original murder sites have changed radically over the years, so it required his oratory skills to bring each location to life once again. He was certainly up for the challenge, weaving a story about life in London's East End, which covered more than just the lurid details of the murders—although there was no shortage of gore in the retelling. But he also tied in the socioeconomic issues of the time, along with the racial and ethnic stereotypes that permeated the investigation of the crimes.

From time to time he would mention this suspect or that,

outlining quick details on what actions of theirs had added them to the list of potential suspects as one of the world's most infamous serial killers. And then, just as quickly, he would demolish the argument with some well-researched facts. After having done this with several of the best-known subjects, a frustrated listener finally yelled from the crowd: "Well, if it wasn't him, who do *you* think did it, for Pete's sake?"

McHugh smiled at the question, which I was sure he'd been asked about as many times as I'd asked someone to take a card. He waited until the crowd had stopped laughing and then gave his well-practiced response. He didn't say it loudly, but he knew at that moment everyone could hear him.

"I believe he was a local man," McHugh said, with just the trace of a smile. "And he didn't like prostitutes."

* * *

"Just how many suspects are there in this Jack the Ripper thing?" Megan whispered after McHugh had introduced—and shot down —another two possibilities.

"I'm not even sure McHugh could give you a number," I said, taking her arm so we weren't inadvertently separated by the moving crowd. "Everyone has their favorite. In fact, the only time I can remember my Aunt Alice and Uncle Harry having an actual fight was on this very topic."

"I never met your Aunt Alice, but the way Harry talks about her, I can't imagine the two of them ever fighting."

"And they hardly ever did. But one of Alice's favorite mystery writers wrote a book—a non-fiction thing about the murders— suggesting a new and unlikely suspect. And Alice made the mistake of telling Harry she thought the author got it right on the nose. And that's how she put it," I added, smiling at the memory. "'She got it right on the nose.'"

"And Harry didn't share this view?"

"Well," I said. "A lot of people didn't share that view. But Harry was the only one of them who was living with Alice. The two of them eventually agreed not to talk about it, but I know it irked both of them to the end."

We increased our pace to catch up with the crowd. "What will be the one thing that bugs the two of us until the end of time?" she asked, looking up and smiling at me. I stopped and kissed her on the forehead.

"I don't know, but I can't wait to find out," I said as we rounded a corner and rejoined the group.

* * *

"In the early morning hours of Sunday, September 30," McHugh was saying to the rapt crowd, "mere minutes after the interrupted murder of Elizabeth Stride, our killer struck again. Here, in Mitre Square. Claiming the life of Catherine Eddowes. Right here, on these very cobblestones upon which we stand."

The old guy really had a way of spinning a story, and the added detail about standing on the same cobblestones from 1888 sent a chill up my spine. The way Megan squeezed my hand suggested this reaction was not unique to me.

"At approximately one forty-five a.m., when PC Edward Watkins discovered the body, he literally stumbled upon a bloody mess. The killer had cut the poor unfortunate woman from her breast bone all the way down to her—oh my stars and garters, is that Eli Marks?"

I was surprised, as one would be, to hear my name in this context, and realized McHugh must have finally spotted me in the crowd.

"My goodness, it is Eli. Hello old boy, good to see you, we will talk anon, won't we?" With that, he gave me a cheerful wave, and then returned to his description of the crime scene—including what sounded like a very complete listing of the internal organs that had been appropriated and spirited away as part of the bloody act.

Once the conclusion of the walk had been reached, McHugh was surrounded by those attendees who wanted to ask just one more question, offer one more possible suspect theory, or pose for a selfie with him. He was kind and patient with one and all, so Megan and I stood quietly off to the side, awaiting our opportunity. Seeing there appeared to be no end in sight, he waved me over.

"This won't take as long as it looks," he said, stepping toward me and lowering his voice. "Why don't you go grab a table at that pub, and I will join you presently."

I glanced across the street at the pub, called The Ten Bells, and then turned back to him. "Sure thing," I said. "We'll wait for you there."

"Brilliant. I can't wait to find out what our friend Harry has been up to."

* * *

Megan and I had no trouble snagging a table in the rustic old pub, but I soon realized an actual conversation with McHugh was still at least a few minutes away. A mini-mob of acolytes followed him into the bar in order to buy a copy of his book and get it autographed. This must have been a regular occurrence, for as soon as he entered, one of the large barmen pulled a cardboard box out from under the counter and set it by McHugh's feet at the table we had secured.

"Back in the day," he said as he settled in and starting pulling fresh copies of *The Jack the Ripper Omnibus* out of the box, "I would carry a supply of the books with me. But with later editions getting bulkier and me getting—well, bulkier as well—it seemed a prudent solution to strike a bargain with the pub owner. He stocks the books, and we split the take. A fair arrangement all around, don't you think?"

As I was coming to learn, about sixty percent of British questions are rhetorical. Figuring this one fell into that majority, I took drink orders and headed to the bar while McHugh signed books and fielded compliments on his oratory and writing skills. By the time I returned with three ales, the crowd had dwindled to

McHugh, Megan, and one last devotee who was fanning the dying flames of his argument. McHugh smiled patiently at the young man.

"To me," the fellow concluded breathlessly, "the evidence is irrefutable."

"Well, sorry to be the one to refute it then, old boy, but prison records clearly place our friend behind bars well before and well after the deaths of the canonical five," McHugh said with more patience than I might have mustered. "To the best of my knowledge, prisons didn't even offer conjugal visits at the time, let alone day passes to commit the odd serial killing."

"Well, then, I guess we'll have to agree to disagree," the fellow said.

"The story of my life," McHugh replied with a smile, finishing up his autographing duties as he handed the signed book to the young man, who nodded, tipped his cap, and scurried out of the bar.

"Do you ever get tired of having the same arguments over and over?" I asked as I set the ale in front of him.

"Hardly. After all, I was married for over forty years," he said, bringing the glass to his lips and taking a long sip. He sat back and let out a deep satisfied sigh. "To the perfect drink at the perfect time in the perfect place with the perfect companions," he toasted, before taking another long sip. Once sated, he leaned forward.

"So, tell me of magical Minneapolis and the musings of our mutual mystical friend, Harry Marks."

The whole story took longer to recount than I had expected, and throughout the telling McHugh's countenance shifted continually, reacting to each twist and turn of Harry's first two days in London. He offered no interruptions or asides, just a steady stream of "my mys" and "good heavens" as I unfolded the tale. I finished by recounting my conversation with Harry in the jail's visiting booth and his admonition to pull McHugh into the narrative.

"Just so," McHugh said once I had finished. "Although, due to my retired status, I'm not entirely certain what help I can provide, but my years in the service might, at the very least, help grease some wheels. If that is in fact the expression."

I nodded and was about to continue, but Megan jumped in before I could form my first question.

"How long have you been retired?" she asked. McHugh considered the inquiry.

"Officially, I handed in my badge over fifteen years ago," he said. "Due to injuries sustained while off duty. But I have been asked to consult on a number of cases in the intervening years," he added, taking another sip of his ale.

It was then I remembered the story, as recounted to me by Uncle Harry: McHugh and his wife had been mugged late one evening on the way home from the theatre. Outnumbered and wishing to keep his wife out of harm's way, McHugh wisely handed over all their valuables when requested to do so. But it was to no avail, as the muggers took shots at the couple as they departed. McHugh survived, a nearly imperceptible limp the only reminder of the crime. His wife hadn't been so lucky.

With little to occupy his time, he took any and all requests to speak on the Jack the Ripper case, bringing him to the States more than ever before. And, with most of those trips came a swing through Minneapolis to see his old pal, Harry Marks.

"So they're going before the magistrate in the morning, you say?" he mused, stroking his chin. "I suspect I can make a phone call or two, which might minimize Harry's future incarceration. And, if we're lucky, forestall any long-term confinement on his part."

Before offering any details on this plan, McHugh held up an empty mug, which was my cue it was time to make another trip to the bar.

* * *

Less then twelve hours later, Megan and I found ourselves seated in another pub, this one around the corner from the police station Uncle Harry had been calling home since Saturday night. After meeting us out on the street, McHugh had settled us into the warm establishment and gone off to, in his casual phraseology, "have a quick chat with a few lads." A text moments later from Laurence Baxter informed me that he, too, was at the station, pulling whatever strings he could.

I passed this information along to Megan, and we agreed it was looking like Harry had a formidable team on his side.

The pub served breakfast, but we had already grabbed a bite at our hotel, which we had both taken to referring to as *Fawlty Towers*. Although, in retrospect, I think Megan thought the title was more of a joke than I did.

I had steered clear of the traditional English breakfast that time around, in favor of cold toast and coffee, while Megan availed herself to the porridge, which she proclaimed far superior to the oatmeal at home. I suggested the bar wasn't set particularly high for that contest, but she insisted I sample a bite, and I was forced to agree with her assessment. They may have conceded the Revolutionary War, but when it came to hot oats for breakfast, the British were the clear winners.

Many of the same characters we had seen the day before put in another appearance. The Harry Potter kid was bratty as ever, and the Russian grandmother repeated her admonition of "*Etta dyedooshkye*" to her tablemates as they squirreled away bits of food for "PopPop." And then a couple of Americans came in complaining about the low thread count in the sheets and its impact on their delicate flesh, which we took as our cue it was time to head out and meet McHugh.

* * *

"Enter a free man!"

We turned to see Laurence Baxter, looking insanely dapper for such an early hour, holding the pub's door open wide. He gestured expansively as Harry entered, squinting at the sudden change in illumination. He appeared bleary and out of place in his rumpled tux, his hair nearly as disheveled as the rest of him. Baxter patted him warmly on the back and directed him toward our table, nearly slamming the door shut on McHugh, who had followed the two magicians in.

Megan quickly jumped up and met Harry at the halfway point, pulling him in for a long, warm hug.

"Oh, Harry, we were so worried for you."

"You and me both, my dear," Harry said, his voice raspy and strained. "You and me both. Have you talked to Franny?"

"We called her last night after we met up with McHugh," I said as I pulled out a chair for him. "Megan brought her up to date."

"She said she was going to hop on a plane," Megan added. Harry immediately shook his head, holding up a hand.

"No, no, Franny hates to fly. She just hates it," he said.

"Not to worry," I said, patting his arm. "We talked her out of it. She's going to sit tight until we hear more."

"Oh, thank goodness," he said, visibly relieved. "She didn't want me to take this trip. I should have listened to her."

"I think we've turned a corner," Laurence Baxter said as he joined us. In his scant moments in the bar, he had managed to flag down one of the wait staff and place an order. Now he silently directed the waitress as she carefully placed a cup of tea in front of Harry. Baxter nodded his approval as she smiled shyly at him and scurried away. Such is the power of celebrity, I thought.

"Perhaps," McHugh said as he joined us. He pulled out a chair and lowered himself down heavily. "But I don't think we're entirely out of the woods just yet." He glanced over at the tea Harry had begun to sip, then looked up at Baxter. "Brilliant. Any chance you could grab a cup for me as well?"

The expression on Baxter's face suggested it had been quite a while, if ever, since someone had asked him to serve them tea. He looked around, but no help was in sight. He pursed his lips for a moment, nodded, and then turned and headed back to the bar.

"What do you mean?" I asked. "About not being out of the woods?"

"Well, there's no question the case against Harry is circumstantial, but the problem is that the circumstances themselves are extraordinary," McHugh began. "He had means, he had opportunity. Only the motive is missing, but to be candid, I've seen cases where the best of three was all that was required to tip the balance. And not, I'm sad to say, in the direction we would prefer."

"The thing is," Harry said quietly, "if they look back far enough, they could find a motive." He could see the shocked reactions on our faces. "Not a strong motive, mind you, but it's there. If they were to dig."

"What possible reason could you have to kill Oskar Korhonen?" I said.

"As you might imagine, I've had a lot of time to think since Saturday night," he said slowly. "And something did occur to me. It's been years. A lot of years. It had to do with the Marks Pass."

"Oh, the Marks Pass," Laurence Baxter said as he returned, placing a cup of tea in front of McHugh. He did it so carelessly I was surprised he didn't miss the table and have it land in McHugh's lap. "I had forgotten about that. Quite the brouhaha at the time, wasn't it?"

McHugh righted the tea in its saucer. "What is the Marks Pass?" he asked, turning to Harry. "It sounds like something your pioneers went through on their way to the California Gold Rush."

"It's a card move I did some work on. A means of getting a card from any location in the deck to the top," Harry said quietly. "It's really just a refinement, based on the Hermann Pass."

"Don't downplay it," Baxter said, leaning in. "It was and is quite elegant. And less knacky than Hermann."

"It is pretty slick," I agreed. "Plus you could do it one-handed."

"And what does this Marks Pass have to do with Oskar Korhonen?" McHugh said, trying to get the conversation back on track. "Other than the fact he possessed, as I gather, only one hand."

"Back in the seventies," Harry said, "Oskar produced a training video for magicians."

"Interesting." McHugh had taken a small pad from his pocket and he began to take notes. "Are there a significant number of one-armed magicians in need of training?"

Harry shook his head. "It was really about looking at old tricks in new ways, which, as you can imagine, one is forced to do if you have half as many hands as the average magician. There was some really fine thinking in the video. Out-of-the-box stuff, as they say."

"First rate," Baxter agreed.

I don't think I had ever actually watched the tape, but as the third magician at the table, I felt obliged to nod along in order to complete the trifecta. So I did, adding an ineffectual "Good stuff" to the conversation to confirm my contribution.

"Anyway," Harry continued, "in the tape he demonstrated the Marks Pass. Without *any* accreditation."

"Not a word," Baxter said bitterly. "Not a word in the demonstration itself, nothing in the credits, it wasn't mentioned on the box. Just shameful, really."

McHugh looked at the two old magicians, a puzzled expression on his face. "So you're saying he stole a move of yours and profited from it? That's your motive for killing him?"

"Oh, no, he didn't steal it, didn't claim it as his own," Harry said quickly. "And he certainly didn't profit from it, I mean, not in any significant way."

"Oh no, a video like that, I can't imagine it selling particularly well, can you?" Baxter said to Harry, and they both agreed it probably hadn't.

McHugh looked like he was getting a tad frustrated. "Then what's the difficulty?"

Baxter and Harry regarded him and then each other. Baxter turned back to McHugh.

"He didn't credit the move," he said slowly, as if to a child.

"That's one of the worst things you can do in the magic community," Harry explained. "We're very big on giving credit where it's due. It's all about crediting your sources."

"Indeed," Baxter added quickly. "In our world, if you credit properly, you can get away with murder."

He instantly realized the implications of this unfortunate turn of phrase. "That's not to say anyone ever does, of course. Murder someone, I mean."

"No, of course not," McHugh said, closing his notebook. He

took a sip of tea and settled back into his chair. "Thank you for the information. Regardless of its implications at the time, though, I doubt that particular incident will loom large in the prosecutor's case."

"So what happens next?" I asked, hoping to steer the conversation away from Harry's possible motives for killing Oskar.

"We'll follow two tracks, really," he said, folding his hands across his chest. "Right now, this murder investigation is shining a very bright light in a very dark room. Currently that light is focused solely on Harry. I'd like to see the lads on the police force widen the beam a bit, as it were."

"To consider other suspects?" I suggested, thinking of one or two names I could add to their list. Davis De Vries had inside knowledge of how the murderous chair had worked, for instance.

McHugh snorted. "They are going to have to *look* for other suspects before they can consider others, and I see precious little evidence they're even doing that. Right now Harry is the shiny object that has their full attention. My next step will be to have a conversation with the Chief Inspector and remind him or her of all the points that don't count against our Harry as their prime suspect."

"And those points are?" Baxter said as he waved at a passing waitress and indicated Harry's tea needed a refill. McHugh held his cup up as well, but the action was either ignored or unseen by Baxter.

"Well, in addition to the dearth of motive on Harry's part, there is also the question of timing. He had hardly been in the country three hours when the murder occurred. And, of course, there is the issue of the chair. A unique item, that one, and certainly not something Harry had packed in his carry-on bag."

"No, that chair has been in use for years at The Magic Circle," Baxter said. "It's never given us any trouble in the past."

McHugh arched an eyebrow at this. "No, I suppose it hasn't."

He consulted his notes, flipping back a couple of pages. "They tell me the mechanism appears to have been inside it for years, but that it was possibly recently oiled and adapted to hold the knife.

Apparently, it was triggered when the subject sat in the chair. Any idea what its previous purpose might have been?"

Harry and Baxter exchanged a look.

"Probably a clever way to deliver a load of some kind to the magician," Harry said.

"Or produce an object quickly, out of thin air as it were," Baxter added.

"Davis De Vries might have some thoughts on that," I suggested.

McHugh clucked his tongue thoughtfully at this and made a quick note, then flipped to the next page in his small notebook. "Well, we got Harry out on bail. That's a good first step. My guess is they will hold his passport until they are sufficiently persuaded he had no involvement in the case."

"How long will that be?" Harry asked. I could tell he was worrying about the impact his absence would have on Franny back home. Although not yet newlyweds, the pair acted like a long-married couple and had become virtually inseparable over the last year or so.

"Probably be a few days," McHugh said. "At most, a fortnight."

"Oh, my, where will I stay for that long?" Harry said, setting down his teacup and patting his pockets. "I had a reservation for Saturday night at the Wesley Hotel by The Magic Circle, but I have clearly lost it by now, being Monday and all."

"You can always stay at our hotel," Megan offered brightly.

Before I could verbalize a response to the contrary, Laurence Baxter slapped the table with his hand.

"Nonsense," he said. "You must stay at my house. I have a little place out on the Heath. In fact, you all must come." He scanned the group and then added, "I mean, the visitors. The Americans."

McHugh smiled wryly and nodded. "Yes, of course, obviously."

Baxter's tone left little doubt there was to be no argument on the subject. I could tell Megan was disappointed at the prospect of leaving our own version of *Fawlty Towers*. She glanced at me, and I did my best to look sad. I'm pretty sure she saw right through my performance, and I was reminded of an expression Harry used to say to me when I was a teenager.

"You look like an undertaker trying to look sad at a thirty thousand-dollar funeral," he would say. I glanced back at Megan and doubled my efforts, trying to look twice as disappointed.

Deep down, of course, I knew neither one of us was buying it.

CHAPTER 4

The "Heath" Laurence Baxter spoke of turned out to be Hampstead Heath, a posh suburb of London. Its exclusivity was evidenced by the numerous large houses and small mansions I noticed as we approached Baxter's home. He had insisted on driving us, so after a quick stop at our hotel to check out and pick up our bags, Harry, Megan, and I found ourselves cruising through the tree-lined lanes while Baxter provided a running commentary on the surrounding geography.

"Hampstead Heath is one of the highest points in London, and you'll see the proof of that to your right, just around this curve."

Ever the obedient tourists, we all turned to the right as the trees parted, revealing a large green park that rolled on and on. In the distance was an amazing view of the heart of London.

"This must be one of the best views of the city," Megan said as she leaned around me to get a better look out the car window.

"Yes," Baxter agreed. "Of course, the London Eye provides the best view of London, primarily because it's one of the few views that doesn't include the London Eye."

He laughed at his own joke. I had seen photos of the London Eye, a very tall Ferris Wheel-type structure. No fan of heights, I wasn't planning on getting close to—let alone inside—the London Eye any time soon.

"Didn't someone once say the same thing about the Eiffel Tower?" Harry asked from his position in the front seat. He had been strangely silent throughout the entire trip.

"Perhaps," Baxter admitted, "but it applies in this instance tenfold. Ah, here we are."

He turned left, and we got our first view of Laurence's Baxter "house." A three-story mansion, complete with a turret on one high corner and what looked like a small glass greenhouse on the roof. The massive gray stone and red brick structure was situated directly across the lane from The Heath, giving the impression it was all part of the same sprawling property.

"Laurence, are you sure you've got enough room for us?" Harry teased as he gazed up at the imposing structure.

"Make your jokes, Marks, but this is one of those rare occasions when we are actually quite near capacity," Baxter replied. "Several of the Magi performing this week are staying with us. Borys, Angus, Davis De Vries, Hector Hechizo. Oh, and Roy and Roxanne Templeton. Let me see, is that all of them?" He pulled the car to a stop in the portico outside the front door, scratching his chin thoughtfully.

"Yes, I believe that's all of us," he finally said. "Now, let's get you three settled and then have some lunch."

* * *

The contrast between where we had stayed the night before and where we were staying now could not have been more, I don't know, contrasty. It was no exaggeration to say you could have fit four or five of our hotel rooms into the one bedroom Baxter brought us to (plus still have space for a handful of the hotel's elevators as well). The room, and the house itself, was an artful mixture of old-world elegance and modern convenience.

"When I bought it," Baxter explained as he gave us a quick tour of our new surroundings, "I have to admit it was a bit of a fixer-upper, if that's the right expression."

I assured him it was. I couldn't speak for all the American

tourists on Yelp, but I felt it was possible the type of high-ranking reviews this locale might generate would have caused the app to explode.

"I've put Harry across the hall from you," Baxter said, taking several long strides from the center of the bedroom to the doorway. He gestured down the long tastefully decorated corridor. "All the other magicians are on this floor. I was tempted to put Borys up on three," he said with a devilish grin. "You know, keep the mentalists at a bit of a distance, a little outside of the club and all that. But my better angels prevailed.

"And, speaking of the third floor," he continued, turning me toward the staircase at the end of the hall, "we've got a pretty decent workout room upstairs. You know the drill, some ellipticals, bicycles, free weights, that sort of thing. And, if you like flowers, my dear," Baxter said, turning to Megan, "you should take a look at the greenhouse on the roof. Not dazzling this time of year, I'm afraid, but there are some lovely specimens."

"A greenhouse," Megan said happily. "I love greenhouses."

And that was all it took to inspire a continuation of the guided tour, this time to visit the greenhouse, which was up a flight to the third floor, and then up a spiral staircase and out an aged wooden door that deposited us on the roof.

Once we were out in the air, Megan headed to the small greenhouse and immediately started *oohing* and *ahhing* over either the flora or the fauna, whichever one applied in this situation. Baxter marched forward to the edge of the roof and gestured to the majestic view of the Heath in the near distance and an equally impressive view of London on the far horizon.

"This is why I bought this place," he said with pride, then turned to me and motioned I should join him near the edge. "Come enjoy this magnificent view."

"It looks great from back here," I said, sticking close to the door and the stairway. I had found one of the best ways to confront my fear of heights was to stay away from them. While many other treatments had been employed, both traditional and arcane, no other method had proved to be as effective as simple avoidance.

51

"No fan of heights, I see," Baxter said.

"Guilty as charged," I agreed. "But it is an amazing view."

"You should see it during the New Year's Eve fireworks display. Dazzling from this vantage point. Looks like The Blitz all over again!"

I nodded in agreement, although I wasn't entirely clear why any Londoner would want to recreate the Blitz. I looked down, surprised to see I was standing on a grass lawn, which covered most of the roof. Baxter noticed and walked over to me.

"It's not really grass," he said quietly, sounding a little disappointed at the admission. "I tried, lord knows I tried, but the drainage issues up here were, to put it lightly, insurmountable."

I looked down at my feet. "I don't know," I said. "It looks pretty real to me."

"Thank you, but it would never pass close inspection," he said rather sadly.

I tried to imagine a reason why such an inspection would be required, but couldn't think of one. "Anyway, it looks nice," I finally said.

"Yes, I do like it. They lay it just like sod, in long strips. Remarkable, really," he said. "All right, enough of the tour," he said suddenly, clapping his hands together. "Let's eat!"

* * *

Lunch was nearly as impressive as the house itself.

A typical lunch for me at home usually consisted of simply standing in front of the open refrigerator, grazing on whichever foodstuffs seemed like they hadn't gone bad yet. That was a far cry from the spread Laurence Baxter set out for his guests, and it included the ritzy novelty of servants bringing in food and carrying away plates.

Once Harry, Megan, and I were seated, we were reintroduced to Angus Bishop and Borys, two magicians we had met briefly backstage at The Magic Circle. Although Baxter had rattled off a long list of names when we arrived, only one other magician joined us for lunch. He introduced himself as Hector, a large and jovial man from Spain, whose English was far superior to my Spanish. He seemed to find everything I said both fascinating and hilarious. I liked him immediately.

As we all got down to the serious business of eating an amazing lunch, Harry inquired as to the whereabouts of the other houseguests.

"Dr. and Dr. Templeton went into the city for even more shopping, God luv 'em," Angus said between large bites from a sandwich that would have made Dagwood Bumstead proud. "And I'm not sure what happened to Dr. De Vries," he added, wiping at a glob of mayonnaise that had missed his mouth and landed on his cheek. He licked the finger clean and continued to work on the sandwich.

"Dr. De Vries went back down to The Magic Circle," Borys said in his deep somber voice. Both magicians had been adding the moniker "doctor" to the names, in keeping with the way all the Magi addressed each other—with the exception of the one actual doctor in the group, Laurence Baxter.

Borys was an amazingly still and focused man who looked far younger than his years, given he was a contemporary of the other Magi. Like many mentalists, he cultivated a spooky quality, which he maintained in full force even while offstage. His accent was hard to pin down, but I suspected it was some form of Slavic.

"His shipping cases with The Catherine Wheel arrived," Borys added.

"Ah, yes, the legendary Catherine Wheel," Uncle Harry said as he took another bite of the egg-white omelet the kitchen staff had prepared for him. "Let me ask you this: since he's arrived, how many times has he casually mentioned the whole enterprise packs into two cases and can be assembled by one man using no tools whatsoever?"

Angus and Borys exchanged a quick look.

"Three times just this morning," Borys said. Angus was still chewing, but he shook his head. "Four?" Borys ventured.

Angus nodded.

"He's proud of that fact, is he?" I asked.

"Eminently," Laurence Baxter said before Harry could respond. "He hardly ever talks about the illusion's effect, just goes on and on about how easy it is to transport. As if conveyance were the primary concern behind a magic trick."

Angus shrugged. "You forget, mate, that's important to a lot of us poor working stiffs. Not every magician has a fleet of semi trucks carting our shows about, with peons and minions to set up and tear down for us." He gave a sidelong glance at Baxter to make sure his jab had landed. Baxter pursed his lips at him, confirming it had.

"Once, the airline lost all my luggage," Borys said in his deep voice, which seemed much too large for his small frame, "and I was able to procure everything I needed to perform a dazzling show from a stationery shop for under ten American dollars. You magicians, you're all about the silly big boxes."

Hector laughed and held up a deck of cards. "Not me, my friend, not me. All I need is this. And these." He wiggled his fingers at the rest of us in a manner that was somehow both charming and just a little bit obscene. "I can take one deck of cards and make it play for ninety minutes."

I glanced over at Megan and noticed she wasn't eating, just looking at the group and smiling.

"Is everything okay?" I asked.

"This reminds me of home," she said. "Sitting around with you and Harry and the Mystics at the bar. The accents are different, but the sentiments feel about the same." She patted Harry's hand and he smiled warmly for the first time all day. "It's a good feeling."

"Yes, it is," I agreed and turned to ask Hector a question about the make and model of the cards he was holding. And then I froze.

Standing by the door to the kitchen, icy and still, was the creepy old woman from The Magic Circle. She had entered quietly and stood staring at us with a look on her face that might have been utter contempt or complete indifference. Either way, it was unnerving.

Baxter noticed the expression on my face and must have recognized its cause. "Yes, Miss Hess?" he said without turning to acknowledge her.

"Do we know how many to expect for dinner?" she said in her clipped German accent. "Preparations must begin."

Baxter looked around the table. "What do you say, gents? You made it through lunch, want to give dinner a go?"

General assent all around, then Megan touched my elbow. "We have those theatre tickets tonight, Eli. Do you think we should eat in town before the show?"

I had completely forgotten about the tickets. "Yes, that's a good idea," I agreed and then turned to Harry. "Harry, do you want to join us? It's the show I told you about, the one with my friend from high school, Jake North."

I don't have much experience dropping names, but I must have just dropped a big one, if the reaction from around the table was any indication.

"Jake North, you say?" Baxter said, in a tone that was hard to read. The looks on Angus's and Borys's faces also suggested surprise at the mention of the name.

"You guys know Jake and his sitcom?" I asked.

"That bloody sitcom," Angus mumbled. "You know, when I talk to Americans, they are always so impressed by the Brit shows of ours they've seen. They think all we produce are shows like *Downton Abbey*, *Sherlock*, *Dr. Who*, and *The Office*, because we're polite enough not to send you our rubbish. The least you colonies could do is return the favor."

"And make no mistake, *Blindman's Bluff* is rubbish," Borys said.

"I've only seen it dubbed into Spanish, but, *si*, I would have to concur," Hector nodded. "*Es basura.*"

"It's bad enough we're subjected to that tripe, but now the bloke keeps popping up on every chat show on every channel," Angus said between bites of a rich-looking apple cobbler. "Gotten to the point you can't turn on the telly without seeing that silly git doing his lame tricks. Celebrity prats doing magic, God help us."

"Celebrities doing magic," Borys said, spitting out the words. "The worst. Just the worst."

"*Lo peor*," Hector agreed. "*Justo lo peor.*"

I didn't need more than my high-school understanding of Spanish to determine celebrities doing magic on talk shows was a sore subject among this group.

"Well, regardless, the whole thing strikes me as a bit deceptive," Baxter said, "given I am led to understand the play he's in doesn't even feature any magic."

"I guess not, I understand it's a comedy-mystery," I said. "Jake got into magic when he did the movie about the life and death of Terry Alexander."

The mention of that film steered the table away from the discussion of celebrities doing magic into an intense discussion of the Bullet Catch and the impossibility of effectively presenting magic in movies. Since I had helped with the presentation in that particular movie, I decided not to join in on the conversation. Thankfully, Harry pulled us back on track.

"It's a comedy, you say? Jake's play?" Harry said, steering the discussion back to our plans for the evening. "That might be just the thing. If the invitation still stands, I would love to join you."

"This will be fun," Megan said, and Harry beamed at her.

"Terrific," I said. "Anyone else up for it?"

Polite refusals all around. No one even bothered to come up with an excuse, which I took as a continued indictment of Jake and his magic-heavy TV appearances.

"Now, if you'll pardon me," Harry said, "I think I'll go lie down for a bit, in my ongoing attempt to reset my internal and infernal clock." With that, he pushed himself back from the table, nodded to Laurence Baxter, and headed toward the large dining room's entryway.

"Remember which room is yours?" Baxter called to him.

"Not a problem, I left breadcrumbs," came Harry's reply from the hall. That produced smiles all around.

Baxter turned to me. "He's holding up nicely, don't you think?" he asked quietly. "I mean, given the events of the last few days."

I was about to agree he was, when Angus chimed in.

"If I was him," Angus said, matching Baxter's low volume, "the thing that would bother me the most is remembering he and Oskar flipped a coin to decide who would sit in that bloody chair."

"So he must be thinking it could have been him?" Borys said.

Angus shook his head. "That would be my first thought, doctor," he said, glancing over his shoulder. "My second thought would be, if the knife was meant for me, and they missed me the first time..."

He let the words hang in the air, and then breathlessly finished the thought. "When might they try again?"

CHAPTER 5

The crowds of people pushing through Leicester Square were a stark contrast to the peace and quiet I'd experienced at the Baxter estate out on The Heath. Laurence Baxter had attempted to send us to the theater district with his car and driver, but we opted to hop on the Underground and experience the adventure of taking the tube. Harry led the way, his knowledge of the subway system seemingly undiminished in the several years he'd spent away from London.

"Best transit system in the world," he said as he marched confidently through the stations, down corridors and up seemingly endless escalators and stairs before we emerged into the brightly lit streets around the Leicester station. The sudden crush of people was simultaneously exhilarating and a little frightening.

Confident we'd successfully made it to the right neighborhood, we searched out a restaurant for a quick dinner. Harry's knowledge of the territory was invaluable, as he steered us past a number of chain restaurants and "tourist traps" until we found ourselves on a narrow street sprinkled with tiny, ethnic restaurants. We left the selection to Harry, who picked a small Greek bistro, and soon we were noshing away on hummus and stuffed grape leaves. It was only a matter of minutes before we found ourselves equally stuffed.

Despite the possible murder conviction, which hovered over his head, Harry focused the conversation on local sites of interest and Megan cross-checked our planned itinerary against Harry's past experiences. He pooh-poohed her interest in the National Portrait Gallery ("eminently boring," he proclaimed), and instead insisted she add Highgate Cemetery to our list of must-sees. He also suggested two short day trips we hadn't thought of and then agreed with my veto of The London Eye.

"If it's a view you want, grab lunch in the restaurant on the top floor of the Tate Gallery," he suggested. "That's a view worth paying for."

Before we knew it, dinner was over. It was time to go to the theater, and I realized that not a moment had been spent talking about Harry's current legal issues. As it turned out, I think this was his favorite part of the evening.

What came next certainly wasn't.

We had no trouble finding our playhouse among the several dotting the area, as Jake's name shimmered in enormous letters on the marquee. In fact, the play's title, *A Pretty Taste for Paradox*, appeared to be an afterthought, taking second billing to the American television star's name.

Given the size of the crowd milling around in front of the theater, I was concerned we wouldn't be able to snag the necessary third ticket for Harry. Once we had made our way to the front of the box office line, a clerk behind the thick glass typed and pecked at a keyboard, searching for an elusive single seat. There was nothing available in our row, but she did eventually find a seat in The Queen's Box, just to the left of the stage. Harry would be joining a party of three, while we would be situated in less posh seats in the stalls. Once we learned there was no intermission, we settled on a place to meet after the show and then took our seats. I looked up at the box and saw Harry as he entered and took his seat just as the house lights dimmed.

And then *A Pretty Taste for Paradox* began.

The mild applause that occurred when the curtain came up was nothing compared to the thunderous ovation Jake received when he made his first entrance. The action of the play came to a halt while the audience went nuts. Jake, for his part, just stood there smirking, that same smirk I remembered from high school plays, in which he would ad lib, break up the rest of the cast, and then just stand there like the outburst was entirely outside of his control.

Jake's movie-star good looks and natural charm and ease onstage were as evident now as they had been back in high school. I recognized that immediately. He was simply performing to a larger audience, and one with the type of disposable income that doesn't think twice about high-priced theatre tickets.

He was playing "The American" in an extremely broad take-off of Agatha Christie-style mysteries. The story—what there was of it —concerned a series of mysterious deaths at an old English manor home and the many curious and stereotypical characters staying there. I wasn't familiar with the play, but I got the sense it must have been slightly retooled to include in-jokes about Jake and his popular, albeit trashy, TV series.

As the main character on *Blindman's Bluff*, Jake played a lothario who pretends to be blind in order to impress and subsequently seduce women. It was a far cry from *Masterpiece Theatre* and was insanely popular with American audiences but reviled by critics.

As an apparent nod to that show, Jake blurted out his show's most famous catchphrase—"What are you, blind?"—at odd moments in the story. This was much to the delight of the audience, although it didn't add much to the plot or the pacing of the show.

I wasn't sure if it was the play or my current situation, but my mind kept turning back to the charges that hung over Harry's head. Certainly the police must understand, I thought, that it had been the simple toss of a coin that had placed Oskar and not Harry in the fatal seat. If the toss had gone differently, I would likely be sitting at a wake this evening instead of a slightly uncomfortable theater seat.

There was also the question of motive, of which there was precious little on Harry's part. I didn't know much about Oskar's relationship with the other Magi, but I couldn't imagine that anyone, including the London police, would take the position that a pilfered card move from thirty years before was considered a strong enough motive for a minor assault, let alone a cold-blooded murder.

As the show dragged on, I kept drifting back to these thoughts, thinking I must be the only one in the theater not enjoying the play. However, a quick glance at Megan and the expression on her face told me I wasn't alone. I looked up at Harry and could see his attention had wandered from the stage. He was looking around the old theater, which clearly offered more of interest than the play.

The conclusion of the show when it (blessedly) arrived was delayed, if only briefly, by a quick polling of the audience. At the moment of climax, the action on stage froze, and one of the actors stepped out of the story and up to the footlights.

"And now, ladies and gentlemen," he said in what was probably a fair Cockney accent (but what do I know, I was raised on Dick Van Dyke in *Mary Poppins*), "it's time to reveal the identity of the killer. But that is not for us to decide. *You* have seen all the evidence, *you* have listened to each of the suspects being interrogated, and now *you* are going to decide who is tonight's killer!"

The hubbub this created suggested the majority of the audience was aware of this feature of the show, while the minority—such as Megan and myself—needed to get ourselves up to speed on this new twist.

The voting process involved a small, remote-control-style device, which was attached to the armrest of each seat. I hadn't noticed it before, but I pulled it from its slot and examined the face of the device. There were five buttons, labeled one through five and then a green button at the bottom labeled "ENTER."

The actor at the footlights then introduced the five suspects, who each stepped forward in a fun or menacing manner as they held up a large cardboard number. Then voting commenced. The theatre became more energized than at any point in the evening as the actor counted down from ten, and the patrons conferred with their seatmates before pressing one of the numbers and casting their votes.

I was torn on who to vote for, so I sneaked a peek at Megan's choice—the charming malaproping old British Colonel who had some of the best lines in the show—and simply followed her lead, then looked up to see the results.

A video tally screen consisting of five columns had been lowered, and the screen was awash with a flurry of numbers as the end of the countdown approached and voting finished.

"And our murderer is...Number Three, The American! There's a surprise," the actor said dryly from the footlights. There was wild applause and cheering, and then as Jake stepped forward we also heard some good-natured booing.

The key moments of the play were then recreated, with Jake narrating the action, showing how he got away with each of the murders. Given that the story was structured so any one of five characters could, conceivably, be the murderer, the solutions he presented strained credibility, to say the least. But the audience didn't seem to care, and at the end they gave the cast a rousing round of applause. Jake was even called back out to take a final bow of his own.

As the curtain descended and the applause died down, I turned to Megan.

"Are we going to the stage door to say hello?" she asked. Her tone suggested "no" would be her preferred answer.

"I thought we might," I said.

"What can we possibly say?" Megan said. "I mean, without telling the truth?"

I shrugged. "I don't know. Maybe Harry will have an idea."

I looked up at the Queen's Box. Harry was waiting patiently for the others to exit before he could leave. I caught his eye. He shook his head and gave me not one but two thumbs down. I got the distinct impression, for this moment at least, he would have preferred to possess at least a couple more thumbs.

"Then again, maybe he won't," I told her as we stood up and headed up the aisle.

* * *

"Looks like we could have dodged a bullet on this one," Harry said quietly, "had we only taken a slightly closer look at the critical blurbs heralded on these posters."

We were standing at the fringe of a large crowd of people who had gathered around the theatre's stage door, ostensibly to catch of glimpse of the departing cast. However, given the chatter going on around us, it was clear the primary target of this potential love fest was none other than my old high school chum, Jake North.

I looked over at the posters on the theatre's outer walls—bright, colorful sales tools with more than their share of exclamation points. Large, capitalized words like "Hysterical," "Stunning," and "A Bright Light" touted *A Pretty Taste for Paradox* as the one show to see this season in London's West End.

"Turns out," Harry continued as he stepped up to the poster for a closer inspection, "'Hysterical' refers to the costumes, which were, at best, amusing. 'Stunning' is in reference to the set, which ironically was the least wooden thing on the stage. And without the benefit of my glasses, I can't quite read what 'A Bright Light' refers to. However, if my personal experience is any indication, it may have been the errant lighting instrument, which was shining in my eyes for the majority of the ordeal."

My intended witty riposte was cut short by a sudden cheer from the crowd as the stage door swung open and Jake North stepped out of the theatre. He feigned a look of surprise at the gathered crowd, putting a hand first to his mouth and then to his heart to demonstrate his intense humility toward their completely understandable affection for him.

In what sounded like a practiced speech, an unctuous under-ling who clung to his side announced, "Mr. North would love to sign autographs, but he must rush off to a previously scheduled television appearance. Watch for him later tonight on BBC Four!"

The underling repeated this announcement as he, with the help of three beefed-up bodyguards, forged a path for Jake through the crowd, snaking him toward a waiting car at the curb. Fans pushed and waved programs and called his name lovingly, but all they got in return was a smirk and a wave from Jake, who seemed to be relishing his role as the lead salmon heading upstream through a river of fans.

It was looking like we were going to be spared the embarrassment of telling him what we thought of the show, when he happened to turn my way just before getting into the stretch limo. Our eyes locked for a second, and I could see the wheels spinning as he tried to place me in this out-of-context environment. And then all the cherries lined up, and it clicked for him.

"Eli," he said, stammering a bit. "You're. Here. In. London."

"Just for a few days," I yelled back.

"Cool," he said, looking around for a moment like he had forgotten why he was standing there. The underling pointed toward the open car door. Jake turned back to me.

"We should talk. Or something. Great to see you!" he added, then slipped into the car. It was already moving before he had shut the door.

"Well, thank goodness," Megan sighed as the crowd began to disperse. "I couldn't think of one positive thing to say to him about the show."

"My go-to has always been, 'Boy, it sure looked like you were having fun up there,'" I suggested. I turned to Harry, but he was staring after the car, scratching his beard thoughtfully.

"It's probably apocryphal," he said. "But they say Noah Webster was once discovered by his wife while in the midst of canoodling with the chambermaid. 'Noah, I am surprised by you,' she bellowed at him. And he looked over and said, 'No, my dear. *I* am surprised. *You* are shocked.'"

Harry continued to the watch the car until it turned a corner and disappeared from sight. I knew enough not to ask, that the explanation would come at Harry's pace, not mine. A few moments after the car was gone, he turned back to the two of us.

"Your friend Jake," he finally said. "He was either surprised or shocked to see you. The trouble is, I can't quite figure which it was."

CHAPTER 6

The subway ride back to Hampstead Heath was a quiet one for the three of us. It might have been a product of our shared jet lag or a physical reaction to slogging through *A Pretty Taste for Paradox*. I was leaning toward the latter, and Harry must have agreed, for out of the blue he said, "It just didn't work."

"What didn't work?" I asked.

"The play we just saw," he said, still clearly annoyed by the experience. "A mystery should have a solution, a single solution that is clean and clear and elegant. Not five muddled solutions. Nonsense, it was just nonsense."

"And not even clever nonsense," I added.

"Not in the least," he agreed.

We sat for several moments in silence, rocking with the movement of the subway car. And then a thought occurred to me. "Of course, you've always been a fan of Anthony Berkley's novel, *The Poisoned Chocolates Case*, and that mystery had how many solutions? Five?"

"Six," he said. "But that book was really more of a parody of the genre, don't you think?"

"So was Jake's play."

"Not in the same class," he countered. "It did not satisfy. Solving mysteries is in our DNA, I think. It's one of the few skills humans can hold over the other species. Our eyes are poor, we're not that strong, we can't run fast..."

"Speak for yourself," I interjected, but he rolled right over me.

"But we can string together ideas—pieces of evidence—to tell a story. To solve a mystery," he said. "It's something McHugh and I have discussed at length, from his perspective of a police investigation and my perspective of a magician creating a story for an audience. Our audience wants—needs—a satisfying solution to a story. Without it, they feel cheated."

He looked up at me. "Don't you feel a little cheated? I know I do."

"Sure," I said, smiling at him. "But keep in mind I paid for all three tickets. So, if nothing else, I get to hold the title of most cheated."

"Let it so be bestowed," he said.

I'm not sure why that made me feel better, but it did. If only a little.

As we rode along, I began to think about the mystery we were in the midst of. Harry was a murder suspect. Someone wanted him or Oskar dead and—perhaps—didn't care which one it was. Both men were magicians and Magi. And both appeared on that stage together the other night for the first time in what? Forty years?

Why them? Why now?

I mulled over these questions and others, reaching nothing resembling a conclusion by the time we had reached Hampstead Heath.

* * *

"Is that Dr. Harry Marks I spy, slouching toward Baxter's Folly?"

The voice was vaguely familiar, but the laugh that followed made it immediately clear that it belonged to Roy Templeton.

The three of us turned in unison to see Templeton and his wife and stage partner, Roxanne, on the same path a few yards behind us. We were, as he had correctly observed, heading up the lane toward Laurence Baxter's mansion. There was a smattering of stars in the sky and a half moon, but most of the ambient light seemed to emanate from the skyline of London, visible across the heath.

"Dr. Templeton," Harry said, clearly thrilled. "I heard rumors of your presence in this vicinity but no proof as of yet."

"Here is my proof, and I think it's safe to say it's at least eighty proof or better!"

"I would expect nothing less," Harry said as the couple approached. Hugs were had all around while Megan stood off to the side, trying not to look as awkward as she probably felt. Recognizing the imbalance, Harry and I quickly made introductions, and before long all five of us were fast friends, slowly making our way up the charming lane toward the looming mansion.

I had known the Templetons since childhood (mine, not theirs). As I was growing up, our infrequent trips to their show in Las Vegas were always utterly memorable and instructive. As I furthered my studies of magic, I recognized how enlightening it was to see essentially the same show over the course of a number of years. The show didn't change much, but I did, and I watched it through different eyes every time.

Their act was a cunning blend of comedy, magic, pantomime, and even elements of commedia dell'arte. Of course, I didn't recognize any of that until I was an adult. As a kid, I just found it a hilarious story about a married couple on stage who really seemed to despise each other...until the end, when their onstage antics merged together to artfully demonstrate the enduring power of love. All this, plus pratfalls, fart jokes, and balloon animals—a perfect storm of elements—designed to appeal equally to kids and adults.

Both Roy and Roxanne had always seemed ageless and timeless to me. Even at his now-advanced age, Roy had lost none of his rubber-faced wackiness nor his dancer's grace. Roxanne was also winning in the battle against aging, although I suspected her jet-black hair required some chemical assistance and her unlined face may have come courtesy of the occasional expensive nipping or tucking. Or both.

While Roy was exactly the same on stage or off—loud, boisterous and always moving at one hundred miles per hour—Roxanne's off-stage persona was sharply contrasted to how she came across in their stage show.

She never spoke during their act, but instead offered slow-burn reactions to Roy's antics. The faster he moved, the slower she responded. So advanced was her comic timing, I had seen instances where she brought the house down with the merest shifting of her gaze from one point onstage to another. Nothing moved but her eyes, and it sent the crowd into hysterics.

Little of that subtlety was evident in her off-stage persona, which rivaled her husband's in energy and volume, with the bawdy and welcome addition of a sharp, ribald take on life, which Roy lacked. As my late Aunt Alice used to say of her, "Roxanne has no inside voice. She's all outside voice."

They were, in short, a fun couple, undiminished by their advancing years, and their sudden appearance immediately increased the vitality of our late-night stroll.

"Holy crap, did Baxter give you a tour of the compound?" Roxanne asked immediately. "My first question after he showed us our bedroom was, 'Thanks, Larry, but where's the gift shop?'"

"If Roxanne doesn't find a gift shop, she'll make one," Roy added, setting off a laughing jag between the two.

"I brought in two suitcases," she continued, "and the gal helping me pointed out one of the bags was empty. 'Don't worry, honey,' I said. 'It won't be when I leave!'"

"And have you met Baxter's version of Brünnhilde?" Roy asked, lowering his volume dramatically and glancing nervously at the house. "She's like Mrs. Danvers without the warmth."

"Exactly, right?" I excitedly agreed.

"There's a whole lotta scary packed in that little Teutonic frame," Roy continued.

"We ran into her first at The Magic Circle," Roxanne continued, "and she read us the riot act about where we had stashed our cases. Then to arrive out here and find out she's Baxter's Frau Blücher? Well, I nearly wet myself."

"No 'nearly' for me. I did!" Roy responded, sending them both back into a laughing fit.

Roxanne rubbed her eyes and then suddenly threw a chummy arm around Megan while we walked. "You poor thing," she cooed. "Trapped in Kane's Xanadu with a cluster of carny folk."

"Actually, I'm pretty used to it. I get it a lot at home, with Harry and the Minneapolis Mystics," Megan said.

Before our trip I had told her about the Templetons, and I think they were living up to my description. Megan moved closer to Roxanne. "When they start talking about the efficiency of one invisible dove harness over another," she said in a stage whisper, "I tune them out immediately."

"Wise girl," Roxanne said and then turned to me. "Don't let this one slip away, Eli."

"I'm doing my best," I agreed.

Roxanne then turned back to Megan. "I think my mother put it best when I told her I was marrying Roy. She said, 'A magician? Really, dear? Is that the best you can do? I was so hoping you would hold out for a mime.'"

She followed this with a dramatic pause and then another paroxysm of laughter, which carried our small group up the long driveway toward the front door.

* * *

We lowered our voices as we entered the large house, afraid our rollicksome party would wake the household. We needn't have bothered, as it appeared everyone was still wide awake and looked like they planned to stay that way for the foreseeable future.

"My excellent good friends," Laurence Baxter said, coming out of his study when he heard the front door open, "you have returned intact, I see, from your sojourns into the slums of the West End and the shopping mecca known as Covent Garden."

His tone and manner suggested that drinks all around had been offered and accepted several times in the last hour or so. Through the doorway into the large study I could see the other

70

magicians—Angus, Borys, Hector, and De Vries—chatting while a butler offered cigars from an expensive-looking wooden box.

Baxter looked over at Roy, who bowed dramatically. "My lord."

"What news?" Baxter said regally.

"None, my lord," Roy responded, taking on a Shakespearean attitude, "but that the world's grown honest."

"Then is doomsday near?" Baxter answered in what sounded like a practiced routine, but Roy suddenly cut him off.

"What the hell? You've started drinking before me?" Roy cried with mock outrage as he glanced into the study.

"Yes, but not to worry, it took five of us to match your intake. Fear not, I have ordered reinforcements," Baxter replied, gesturing toward a young maid who was heading toward us from the kitchen, carrying a tray with two more liqueur decanters and a tea service.

Pacing her was Miss Hess, who seemed to be directing the girl's every move. If she was going to be so picky about how things were done, I thought, why didn't she just do it herself? And then I realized the frail old woman was probably unable to carry the heavy tray. Instead, she clicked her tongue at the girl as she set the tray in the study and stopped to rearrange the placement of the decanters before they both exited silently.

"Cigars and port, gentlemen?" Baxter said, looking first at Harry and then at me.

"What about the ladies?" Roxanne said.

"You'll have to get your own ladies," Roy said. Roxanne provided a quick rimshot sound effect, and the two laughed like the old comedy team they were.

Roxanne turned to Megan "Come on, honey. If we spend any time in there, we'll come out smelling like a wet dog on a humid day. Why don't we go upstairs and braid each other's hair?"

"Um," Megan said, reflexively touching her hair. "I'm not sure—"

"That's code for there's a liquor cabinet in my room," Roxanne added as she headed toward the stairs.

Megan nodded, finally understanding. "Got it," she said as she followed Roxanne. She turned back to me as she started up the stairs. "Don't wait up," she said, deftly stealing my next line before I could utter it.

"But, but," I stammered, as Harry patted me on the back and pushed me toward the study.

"She's in good hands, Buster," he said. "And I for one could use a drink."

* * *

As it turned out, Harry was not the only one in need of a drink, although it was his first of the evening. Some of the others might have lost count.

Ever the good host, Laurence Baxter filled glasses for the newest arrivals and refilled the glasses of those who were already warmly ensconced. The only detractor was Borys, who held up his hand at the offered glass and instead headed directly to the tea service.

"Tea, anyone?" he suggested, looking around the group as he pulled a small leather pouch from within his suit coat.

"Not if it's the awful swill you lug about," Angus shouted from his corner.

"We have other options, if it's tea you're after," Baxter suggested, but Angus shook his head and sipped his drink.

Borys caught my eye as he opened the pouch and pulled out a teabag. "Eli, a bit of tea?" he said quietly. "It will, I think, aid sleep better than the other options here."

Baxter had just pushed a full glass of port—whatever that was —into my hand. "No thanks," I said, not sure either choice was the right one for me. "I'm good."

"As you wish," Borys said, as he placed the teabag in an empty cup and poured in hot water from the tea set's china pot. The water turned instantly black.

"You still keeping that foul stuff under lock and key?" Angus asked as Borys slowly stirred the dark liquid. He added two lumps of sugar and continued stirring, then looked from Angus to me, probably seeing the confused look on my face.

"Angus mocks me because I take precautions with my tea, always keeping it upon my person," Borys said. He turned to Angus as he continued. "As Angus is well aware, I often find myself sharing dressing rooms with unscrupulous sorts, otherwise known as magicians. They not only delight in stealing my tea, but in some cases go so far as to replace it with an odious substitute called...Lipton's."

He said the last word like he had a bad taste in his mouth, and given the look of the tea he was sipping, it may well have been the case. Angus burst out laughing.

"Oh, when I did that, it was classic," he said. "Just classic."

"Be that as it may, I learned a good lesson there, and now I'm wise enough to keep my valuables close to my heart," Borys said, patting his coat at the approximate spot where the pouch was located in an inside pocket. "And I have Angus to thank for that," he added, holding up his teacup in a mock toast. Angus mirrored the action across the room with his glass of port.

"Speaking of toasts," Baxter said somberly, "I think it might be appropriate to raise a glass to our fallen friend, Oskar."

The room turned quiet with soft murmurs of agreement from all quarters. There was a moment of hesitation, as no one was quite sure who was actually making the toast. Since he had come up with the suggestion, Laurence Baxter followed through and stepped to the center of the room.

"For Oskar. A fine man. A fine friend. And a world-class magician." He held his glass up and looked around the small assembly. "To Oskar!"

We all held our glasses aloft and repeated, "To Oskar!"

"To Oskar," Davis De Vries added a second too late.

We all drank our port, except Borys, who sipped his tea. I sipped gingerly at my port as well, not wanting to be the drinking lightweight who ruined an emotional toast with an explosive coughing fit.

As we drank in silence, I looked around the room, wondering

—not for the first time—if any of the other Magi might qualify as suspects for Oskar's murder.

Lawrence Baxter had been there the night of Oskar's untimely death, as had De Vries, Borys, and Angus. They were all long-time members of The Magic Circle, and none of them would have been out of place wandering around backstage before a show. Hector and the Templetons might have been there as well—the crowd was large and I was jet-lagged, so I felt I shouldn't rule them out, either.

But rule them out for...what? Murder? Really?

The group had known each other for years—since long before I was even born—and there seemed to be such love and affection among them. However, as rivals in the same industry, I'm sure it couldn't have been all sweetness and roses all those years.

"Would it be too soon," Roy Templeton said, snapping me out of my musings, "to perform a broken wand ceremony for Oskar at one of the performances this week?"

"Oh, I think that's a lovely idea, Roy," Baxter said, and there were sounds of agreement all around. "Yes, we must schedule that. We also need to reschedule Harry's show," he added, glancing over at my uncle. "Only, of course, if you are still inclined."

Harry shrugged. "From what they tell me, Larry, I'm not going anywhere for a while. I might as well put on a show while I'm here."

"Harry could be the lucky magician to inaugurate De Vries' Catherine Wheel," Roy Templeton suggested with a smirk, which produced laughter throughout the room.

"*Si, si,*" Hector agreed. "Harry can be the guinea pig."

"I would pay top dollar to see that," Baxter said.

"That's because you can afford top dollar," Angus said with a laugh. "But I'd dearly love to see old Harry on that spinning devil!"

"There's no way he's strapping me to that contraption," Harry said over the laughter. "No damned way!"

I had to agree with him and hoped no one would realize that, as the youngest magician in the room by multiple decades, I was actually the logical choice. Although I hadn't seen the illusion in action, Harry had told me all about it on the flight to London because Davis De Vries had tapped him for some advice on the design. From what I'd heard, it was not a trick I would enjoy performing.

As Harry had explained it, the Catherine Wheel was a large wheel, about ten feet in diameter, which stood upright on a support. During the performance, a magician was strapped to the wheel, looking a whole lot like Da Vinci's Vitruvian Man. In fact, Vitruvian Man was De Vries' original name for the device until Harry convinced him no one would get the reference. His second choice, Ixion, was also rejected, as Harry felt the average person had never heard of the Greek mythological figure who was secured to a spinning, burning wheel by Zeus. So the name the Catherine Wheel—the popular spinning firework, not the less-popular medieval torture instrument—won by default.

Once the magician was strapped in, a motor behind the device would start to spin the wheel, slowly at first and gaining speed. As it turned, sparks and small flames would fly out of the end of the wheels' "spokes," like the traditional spinning Catherine Wheel used in fireworks displays. While the magician was being spun around and around, two assistants would stand in front of the wheel, grasping a large silk. At the same instant, they'd hold up the cloth to hide the magician from view, but only for a second. The assistants would then drop the silk, revealing that the wheel—still spinning and shooting out sparks and flames—was now empty.

According to Harry, after the magician vanished from the Catherine Wheel, there were then a couple of options to make him reappear. Depending on the layout of the theater, he could emerge standing in the back of the auditorium. Or one of the assistants could wrap the other assistant in the silk very quickly, and then just as quickly unwrap her, revealing she has transformed into the magician.

Given what I knew about the device, if I were to perform the trick, I'd most likely be revealed backstage, on my hands and knees, saying goodbye to my dinner.

As it turned out, I was saved from being volunteered for such debasement when De Vries began to vigorously shake his head and wave his hands from his corner of the room.

"No, not Harry, not Hector, and, god help me, not Laurence," he said, still laughing from the suggestion. "I am very pleased to say I have stumbled onto a bit of a coup, as it were, in regards to the premiere of the Catherine Wheel. A big name has offered to help me with the unveiling."

This produced a barrage of guesses, as all the pros in the room tossed out their best guess as to who this mystery magician might be. De Vries smiled slyly while he shook his head at every idea. He waited until the last suggestion had been uttered.

"No to all and sundry," he said in his clipped American accent. "Excellent guesses, but all one hundred percent wrong. And the irony of it is, the fellow is among us at this very moment."

He gestured grandly at Roy Templeton, who was leaning on a chair across the room. Roy looked around, as surprised as any of us, and then began to take a deep bow.

"I'd like to thank the members of the Academy," he began.

"Not you, you clown," De Vries snapped, continuing to wave his hand in a gesture we now understood as the international sign for "idiot, get out of the way."

Roy stepped aside, revealing a television, which was playing silently in the background. And there on the TV, performing some card magic, was none other than Jake North.

"Oh, heaven help us, not that silly prat," Angus said, practically spitting out the words.

"I thought you said he was a big name," Roy said. "More like a big ass."

Hector mumbled something in Spanish. I didn't understand the words, but the sentiment was unmistakable.

"Criticize to your heart's content, my boys," De Vries said smugly, "but right now he is the biggest thing in the West End, with a hit television series to boot. And people love him." He noticed the TV remote on the table next to his chair and picked it up. He studied the controls for a moment before selecting one button. Suddenly, the room was filled with the sound of Jake doing a card trick for a smiling television host. Something funny must have just been uttered, because all we heard when the sound clicked on was the recognizable sound of an audience laughing heartily.

"Here's another thing about cards that's similar to dogs," Jake was saying. "Sometimes they only know the one trick. And that's okay, a one-trick dog is no shame and neither is a one-trick card. I mean, changing color is a pretty good trick all on its own."

The host nodded in agreement as I got up and started to cross the room toward the television.

"Of course," Jake continued, "on the other hand, maybe your card is the *leader* of the pack. In that case, it's easier to simply make the entire pack change color."

With that, he picked up the tabled deck, flipped it over, and spread the cards, revealing the deck now had the same color backs as the host's card. The audience did more than "ooh" at this revelation—they practically screamed before breaking into thunderous applause.

I was standing in front of the TV now, staring at Jake as he smiled his million-dollar smile at the camera, and then he turned and smirked at the audience as they applauded. I pivoted slowly and looked at all the magicians in the room. They were staring at me, clearly wondering what was wrong.

"That's my routine," I finally said when I found my voice. "He stole my routine."

CHAPTER 7

I f you ever want to grab the attention of a room full of
magicians, the only four words you need to utter are "He stole
my routine."

I turned back to the TV screen and watched as Jake completed
the final phases of my trick, feeling a little woozy as I came to the
realization that one of my signature bits was being broadcast
throughout Great Britain. And I was not the magician performing
it.

"That's *your* routine?" Roy Templeton asked as Jake wrapped
up the trick, revealing that—like a well-trained dog—the chosen
card had learned to roll over in the middle of the deck.

"Well, it is, admittedly, a pretty standard Ambitious Card
routine. And I'm sure others have done the 'a pack of cards is like a
pack of dogs' analogy," I said. "But those are my variations, and
that's my patter, almost word for word. The thing is, I never
published it or recorded it, so I'm not sure how he..."

I let the words trail off as a fuzzy recollection began to form in
my brain. While I struggled to retrieve it from the depths of my
memory, the other magicians in the room began discussing the
implications of my accusation.

"Oh, that's low, very low," Roy Templeton said, patting my back
paternally.

"All it takes is one bad apple," Laurence Baxter agreed.

"Completely extraneous," Angus said in a low growl and then noticed everyone was now staring at him. He thought back on what he had said and then quickly amended it. "Egregious," he said with a nod of comprehension. "I mean it's completely egregious."

"Oh, such a bad, bad thing to do," Hector Hechizo added, shaking his head ruefully.

Davis De Vries, who had apparently booked Jake to perform at the unveiling of his Catherine Wheel illusion, was gnawing on a fingernail and looking nearly as white as his hair.

While the others continued to commiserate on my behalf, I had a sudden realization.

"It was at the reunion," I said, turning to Harry. "Remember when Jake was in town for our high school reunion?" Harry nodded in agreement, and I turned to the rest of the group. "I did that trick at our reunion, in front of him. In fact, as I remember it, he was dying after botching Vernon's Triumph, and I stepped in and saved his ass with my Ambitious Dog routine. And now he goes and steals it..."

I looked back at the TV, which was now onto another show. But that didn't mitigate the anger I felt.

"You'll have to take him to task on this, Buster," Harry said. "Take him to task, and I mean pronto. We all know what happens if you let this sort of thing drag on, right?"

He turned to his peers, and they all nodded in agreement.

"Or it will be Archie Banks all over again," Borys suggested. His comment was greeted with more vigorous nods and grunts of approval.

"Who's Archie Banks?" I asked, although there was something vaguely familiar about the name.

"He was one of the Magi with all of us, early on," Harry explained. "A talented man, but sadly he possessed a tendency toward performance larceny. On a grand scale."

"He was a tosser," Angus added. "Stole with both hands, didn't care from who. A real pyromaniac."

"Kleptomaniac," Harry corrected.

"Whatever." Angus took another long sip, clearly disgusted we'd raised the memory of Archie Banks.

"He stole my book test, word for word, and that was the jewel of my act," Borys said, starting to fume at the memory.

"He copied three of my best big-box illusions, really smart stuff," De Vries added, a little relieved, I think, the subject had veered away from Jake North. "Not only copied them for his act, but then he had the temerity to sell knockoff copies as well. And then, to add insult to injury, he accused me of stealing the ideas from him!"

"The SOB even snuck in and nicked my best ad libs, choice stuff," Roy said as Baxter refilled his glass.

"Well, with any luck, Eli's current situation can be resolved with less acrimony," Baxter said as he continued around the room, refilling glasses. "And certainly less bloodshed."

That got my attention. "Bloodshed?" I said, looking from Baxter to Harry for some clarification. The two men exchanged looks and reached a soundless decision as to who would provide the explanation.

"Sadly," Harry said, "Archie Banks died. A failed failed suicide attempt."

That phrasing struck me as odd. "A failed failed suicide attempt," I repeated slowly. "But wouldn't that mean he survived?"

"Only if his goal was to kill himself," Harry said.

"Are there other goals in a suicide of which I'm unaware?" I asked, feeling like we were headed into some sort of morbid *Who's On First* routine.

"The feeling at the time was Archie was only *attempting* suicide, with the goal of being prevented before the act was completed," Baxter explained.

"God knows he had tried it before, always pulling out at the last second," Harry mused.

"I remember he called me once, middle of the bleeding night, said he had taken a handful of pills," Angus said, shaking his head at the memory.

"He was going to jump off a bridge. He was going to shoot himself. He was thinking of hanging himself," Roy continued, ticking off each method with his fingers. "Got so annoying, I was ready to do the deed myself."

This brought the group up short. Realizing the implications of what he had just said, Roy laughed it off. "But you know me, my follow through is rubbish."

"Unfortunately, in this one instance, Archie was not stopped and was, therefore, successful in his suicide," Harry added. "But unsuccessful in his suicide attempt."

"A failed failed suicide attempt," I repeated quietly, right on the edge of understanding. "How did he do it? What method...?"

"Gas," Harry said. "He had expected his girlfriend to come home and discover him in time. And, as luck—or fate—would have it, she didn't. Instead, she found Archie with his head in the oven and a suicide note on the kitchen table."

"Yikes," I said.

"Yikes indeed," Laurence Baxter agreed, taking a slow sip from his drink.

"That poor woman," Harry said quietly.

"I didn't even know he was dating anyone," De Vries added. "Very private type, Archie Banks. Secrets within secrets, that sort of thing."

"I never met her, but he claimed she was quite a looker,'" Angus confided to me quietly. "He said she hailed from Australia, you know, down under. Met her on a cruise gig or some such thing. But, if you ask me, I think it was just a cover."

I looked over at him, not fully understanding his words.

"Wouldn't have been surprised," he said, his voice getting even lower, "if Archie worked both sides of the street, if you get my meaning." This was followed by a very deliberate wink.

"He blamed us all," Roy Templeton said loudly, pulling me back into the main conversation. Roy switched off the television.

"He steals from us, and it's *our* fault he gets kicked out of The Magic Circle? Preposterous!" De Vries said, and I wouldn't have been surprised if he had added an indignant "harrumph" to the end of his statement.

"I'm not saying his feelings were reasonable," Roy replied. "But he was essentially blackballed by the industry and couldn't work."

"A man like that, without honor, he does not deserve to be a magician," Borys said, setting his teacup down.

"No honor," Hector agreed. "No honor at all."

We all sat silently for several minutes. Some of us were doubtless considering the sad fate of Archie Banks.

However, nothing that profound was occupying my mind.

I was thinking about inventive and painful ways to kill Jake North.

* * *

The old guys were longtime drinkers, professionals really, far more skilled than me. So I don't think any of them were surprised when I excused myself early, begging off for some much-needed sleep.

"We'll figure out a plan of action in the morning, don't you worry," Harry said as I got up to leave. "Jake won't get away with this."

This statement was greeted with echoes of agreement throughout the room, and I was pleased this kerfuffle with Jake—annoying as it was—appeared to have taken my uncle's mind off his current standing as suspect number one with Scotland Yard. While I appreciated his concern, my issue with Jake was small potatoes compared to a potential murder charge. I vowed that the next day—in addition to tracking down Jake and telling him off in the strongest possible terms—I would make some progress on clearing Harry of any and all charges.

As I made my way through the massive house toward the sleeping quarters, I was reminded of Harry's earlier comment to our host about the need to leave a trail of bread crumbs to find your way back to your room. The layout wasn't all that byzantine, but it was dark, the path was a bit twisty, and I had consumed enough port to be feeling its effects on my already jet-lagged motor skills.

This was, of course, really no excuse, but it did help explain why I yelped like a frightened dog when I rounded a corner and found myself face-to-face with the daunting Miss Hess.

"Looking for your room?" A simple enough phrase, but it came out of her mouth with such a wave of menace I could feel the hairs on the back of my neck stand up. Not only stand up but start to pack their bags and update their passports.

"Yes. I mean, no. I mean, I know where it is. Just headed there now," I added, as I sidestepped around her. "Thanks, have a good night. See you in the morning," I added for some inane reason.

"Be careful in the dark," she said as she turned the corner. "We wouldn't want any accidents, would we now?"

* * *

I was surprised Megan wasn't in our room when I finally found it, but she showed up minutes later as I was beginning to get dressed for bed. I recognized instantly she had consumed much more alcohol than I had.

"Did you have any idea how much Roxanne hates Laurence Baxter?" were the first words out of her mouth. I jumped up from the task of removing my shoes and rushed to shut the heavy door behind her before she could head any further down that particular train of thought.

"I mean, she loathes him," Megan went on, not adjusting her volume despite my obvious steps to minimize just how far her voice might carry.

"I've suspected as much," I replied quietly, hoping she might get the hint and modulate her volume. "She jokes about it, but there's always a bit of a bite behind those jokes. There are a number of the Magi who she doesn't seem to care for, but she's saved the strongest vitriol for poor Baxter."

"Tell me about it," Megan said, sitting on the bed a little harder than she had anticipated. "What did he ever do to her?"

"I think it has more to do with what he may or may not have done to her husband," I said, again demonstrating a volume level I was hoping she would imitate. "Early in their careers, they were both up for some of the same gigs, and Laurence always seemed to be the one to get them."

I sat down in a nearby chair and continued the process of removing my shoes.

"Which happens all the time with magicians," I said. "I mean, there are only so many jobs to go around."

"However," I continued, struggling with an obstinate shoelace knot that refused to come undone, "Roy Templeton and Laurence Baxter's acts are so radically different, I find it hard to believe they were ever really going head-to-head. But there is no denying Baxter's level of success has clearly eclipsed Roy's—and everyone else's for that matter."

I achieved victory with the knot on the left shoe, and it looked like the right shoe wasn't going to be nearly as difficult. Until it was.

"I think it's true of all the Magi, because they were all coming up around the same time," I said, tugging at the lace, which only made things worse. "They were all young and hungry and jostling for the same opportunities. Some people did better than others. Resentments were formed. Jealousies developed. And a few of them have held onto their bitterness longer than others."

The last of the troublesome knots finally unfurled, and I pulled off both shoes, feeling like I had won a contest of some kind.

"Of course," I went on, "Harry has always said if he had lost all the jobs he got in his career and had gotten all the jobs he'd lost, he would basically have had the same career. I guess things just work out the way they work out."

Sadly, Megan missed these last meaty morsels of wisdom. When I looked up from my completed task, she was sleeping soundly on the bed, blissfully uncaring that both her shoes were still firmly on her feet.

I removed her shoes with envious ease and then repositioned her on the bed so her head was at least in the vicinity of her pillow.

Then I covered her with a blanket, got into my pajamas, and fell asleep moments later.

I woke up once in the middle of the night, and the house was dead quiet. I wouldn't realize until morning what an apt description that turned out to be.

CHAPTER 8

The "casual" lunch Laurence Baxter had offered the day before had me anticipating what breakfast might be like from the moment I woke up. I doubted the traditional English breakfast atrocity I had undergone at Fawlty Towers would be duplicated in these more posh surroundings. And, once again, Baxter and his staff did not disappoint.

When we found our way to breakfast, Megan made a beeline for a cup of coffee, as she was still feeling the effects of her late-night girl-chat session with Roxanne. Uncle Harry, Hector, and De Vries were all seated around the table, each working on breakfasts in various stages of completion. I was just pulling up a chair when Laurence came in, dressed like the country gentleman he was (or at least, had become), a newspaper folded neatly under his arm.

"Ah, the dead awaken," he said with great cheer when he saw me and Megan. He placed the newspaper at the head of the table and walked to the swinging door to the kitchen, opening it just enough to speak into it. "Two more for breakfast, Gwen," he said and then turned back at the sound of other people entering the room—the Templetons and Angus Bishop, all looking to be in about the same shape as Megan. "Strike that, five more," Baxter said. "And more coffee, by the looks of it. Lots more coffee."

For a moment I tried to picture what it would take to fit a

crowd of this size for breakfast in my small apartment and realized I easily could accomplish it, as long as guests were willing to eat in shifts of two at a time. Baxter's table was set for twelve, and even with nine of us in the room, the space didn't feel the least bit cramped.

"Gwen will be out in a moment to take your breakfast orders," Baxter said as he took his place at the head of the table. "As you can see," he continued, gesturing at the folks already eating the food in front of them, "Cook can throw together just about anything your heart desires."

He looked more closely at what Harry, De Vries, and Hector were eating. "Anything from steak and eggs...to a traditional English breakfast...to...I'll just say it's something Spanish involving eggs and cheese, am I right Hector?"

Hector was in the middle of chewing, but he nodded enthusiastically.

I glanced at Harry's steak and eggs—which would never have been allowed back home in Franny's kitchen, given his cholesterol levels—and then stole a peek at De Vries' traditional English breakfast. I was prepared for the worst, but unlike the freak show I'd been served earlier in the week, what I saw on his plate not only looked edible but actually quite enticing.

The eggs were poached perfectly, the bacon looked crunchy and inviting, the toast was browned impeccably, the tomatoes looked appealing, and even the dollop of baked beans didn't seem entirely out of place on the fine bone-china plate. The contrast with my first encounter with the traditional English breakfast could not have been starker. The version Baxter was serving looked like it had been created for a high-end gourmet cooking show. The one I had been served earlier in the week was more suitable for a horror film.

My decision made, I took a seat and poured myself some orange juice. Then, when the young maid, Gwendolyn, asked me what I would like for breakfast, I happily announced to one and all that I would like the traditional English breakfast, thank you very much. This was, as it turned out, a bigger deal to me than anyone else, and soon the conversation turned to that night's show at The Magic Circle.

"My understanding is we are safe to continue our week-long Magi Festival this evening," Baxter said as he buttered a piece of toast taken from an odd device on the table in front of him. It looked to be made of metal, and it secured each singular piece of bread in its own tiny toast corral. As he was the head of the club's board, I sensed this decision to resume the shows was actually his to make. But I guessed he wanted to give the impression he was just one of the guys, and no one seemed to want to contradict him on this, even though everyone knew he wasn't.

Gwendolyn, at the door to the kitchen, scanned the room to see if anyone needed anything. Hector raised his coffee cup, and Gwendolyn returned and took it from him with a big smile, heading to the coffee urn on the sideboard to refill it. He watched her do it and then glanced to me with a playful wink. Despite his advanced years—or perhaps because of them—his eye for the ladies, which was legendary within the group, had apparently not diminished.

"We essentially lost Saturday, Sunday, and Monday nights," Baxter continued. "So I think the simplest solution would be to move those missing acts to our remaining four evenings and simply shorten everyone's stage time. Does anyone have any objection to this idea?"

"I do three tricks and three tricks only in my show," Angus said as he reached out a stubby hand and nabbed one of Baxter's toast slices. "The whole mess can either take forty minutes or twenty minutes. In a pinch, I can do it in ten minutes, but I once did stretch the whole thing out to ninety. Pretty proud of that. So, I've no problem cutting back my time."

Although it sounded like an odd boast, it was actually not uncommon for comedy magicians to be able to expand or contract their acts at will, still doing all the same tricks but simply adding more or less comedy and audience interaction. While I had some tried-and-true comic lines I could add to my act on the fly, I felt a little jealous about their ability to change the length of their shows on a whim. To make my standard show longer would require either adding a moderated Q&A segment or a handful of knock-knock jokes.

"The less the merrier as far as we're concerned, right hon?" Roy said, turning to Roxanne for confirmation. "Cut us to twenty, ten, whatever works for you."

"My husband is one of the few performers I know," Roxanne said to Megan, "who actually prefers *less* time on stage."

"Always leave 'em wanting more," Roy said, smiling broadly.

"If he had his way, his act would consist of an introduction and a bow."

"One never wants to overstay one's welcome," Roy added. "Although encores are always appreciated."

"All I ask is that the complete act takes at least as much time as I took to put on my makeup and pour myself into my Spanx," Roxanne said with a laugh.

"In that case, we would probably need to add an intermission," Roy said. "'Cause your prep is taking longer and longer every year."

"If only other things got longer every year," she said in a loud stage whisper.

After an awkward moment of silence, Roxanne and Roy burst out laughing. I really couldn't tell if this was a practiced routine, a new ad lib, or simply a veiled argument taking the form of playful banter.

While they all continued to discuss their willingness to shorten their shows, I noticed Megan was trying to get my eye. I gave her a quizzical look, and she glanced down at her hand, indicating one of her rings. She then pointedly looked at each of the older gentlemen at the table, her scrutiny falling on each of their hands. She then looked back to me for a silent explanation.

Just as I had done when I first met Laurence Baxter, she had recognized that the ring we always saw on Uncle Harry's finger was not nearly as unique as we had perhaps thought. Each of the magicians at the table sported the same ring.

Upon hearing the name "Jake North," I mouthed the words "I'll explain later" to her and turned my attention back to the conversation.

"I'm sorry?" I said.

"We need to sort out this business with Jake North," Baxter said. "I can't say I want him on our stage if he's pilfering from other magicians. That sends a bad message, if you ask me."

"I'm just saying, I think we should hear his side first," De Vries said quietly.

It looked like Baxter was about to reply, but something caught his eye across the room. He got up quickly, carelessly tossing his perfectly folded napkin on the table. I turned to see where he was headed and was surprised to realize Miss Hess had entered soundlessly and was standing, statue-like, behind me. She and Baxter exchanged a few words so quietly that, even at my close range, I couldn't discern a sound. They were breathing louder than they were talking. Seconds later, Baxter left the room. Miss Hess surveyed the group around the table for a moment and then followed him, leaving as noiselessly as she had entered.

"He oughta put a bell on that one," Angus said, taking Baxter's sudden exit as an opportunity to snatch two more pieces of toast from his holder.

"*Ella me asusta,*" Hector said, shuddering visibly. While my Spanish failed me, his body language did a good job of translating.

"As I was saying," De Vries said, "before we land on anything definitive, I would love the opportunity to talk to Jake North and see what he has to say for himself and his actions. It could have been a simple mistake."

"A simple mistake?" Angus said, just about to chomp into the toast and stopping in mid-bite. "Like, what? He accidentally did Eli's routine like a monkey accidentally typing out *Hamlet*? Not bloody likely."

"Where I come from, you are innocent until proven guilty," De Vries said, pointedly turning his attention back to his breakfast.

"Yeah, where I come from, that sort of behavior will get you twenty stitches and a nice long stay in hospital," Angus replied, crunching his toast defiantly.

"I'll talk to Jake, and we'll sort it out. He may end up with only a couple stitches," I joked quickly, hoping to diffuse the tension in the room, if only a little.

"One time, in Vegas, a magician stole one of Roy's routines verbatim, word for frickin' word," Roxanne said, again addressing Megan directly. "You know what Roy did? He got on a plane, flew to where the guy was working, knocked on his hotel room door, and Roy punched him square in the mouth. Broke the jerk's nose and took out two teeth."

"I also bruised a knuckle, which later got infected and still bothers me to this day," Roy added, flexing his right hand to demonstrate an unseen issue with flexibility, "but she leaves that part out, because it tends to suck the wind out of the story."

"Case in point," Roxanne agreed, jerking a thumb in Roy's direction.

"You flew to where he was working?" Megan said, clearly not sure if they were putting her on or not.

Roy shrugged. "I had frequent flyer miles that were about to expire. I figured we could take a trip to Hawaii, or I could settle a score and screw up my hand."

"Ever the romantic," Roxanne said. "But the word got out—don't get on Roy Templeton's bad side."

"So, did that stop the magician from stealing material?" Megan pressed.

Roy shook his head. "Sadly, no. He never stole from *me* again," he said. "But that type never stops, really. They just change their methods. Of course, no one has ever been as blatant as Archie Banks when it came to out-and-out ripping people off."

"His rule of thumb," Harry said as he set his knife and fork down, "was if he could figure out how you did a trick, then it was fair game. Which is why I always told him all my secrets whenever I got the sense he was eyeing one of my bits."

"That stopped him stealing from you?" I asked.

Harry shook his head as he dabbed at his mouth with a napkin. "No, but it did act as a bit of a speed bump."

This phrase produced a questioning grunt from Hector, who was also just about finished with his breakfast.

"*Qué?*" he asked.

"He still stole from me. It only slowed him down," Harry explained. "I don't think anything could have stopped him."

"Oh yeah? I think the gas stove did a pretty neat job of it," Angus said with a grim chuckle.

"Yes, well, there was that," Harry agreed.

"Back to Jake North," De Vries said, clearly wanting to get the debut of his new illusion settled as quickly as possible. He looked at me directly. "How soon do you think you can talk to him?"

I wasn't entirely certain, as I had no real idea how to get in touch with Jake. I had his email address, if he was still using that account. And somewhere I had his cell phone number, but I wasn't sure if it had made the migration from my old phone to my new one. To check, I pulled out the phone and opened the contacts app. But before it had even launched, everyone at the table turned to the archway that separated the dining room from the massive front hallway.

Laurence Baxter was standing there, his hands fluttering at his side, as if he had no idea what to do with them. He was as pale as he had been when Oskar's body had been discovered on stage at The Magic Circle, and it quickly became apparent why.

"The staff has informed me," he said, a slight hitch in his voice, "and I have verified they are correct. Sadly we've had a death in the house overnight."

Everyone looked around the table, quickly mentally sorting who was there and, more importantly, who was missing. Baxter answered our question before anyone could raise it.

"Borys," he said. "Borys is dead."

CHAPTER 9

I thought it would be tough to make Laurence Baxter's large house feel crowded, but the police accomplished the feat in record time.

What started with a call to the British equivalent of 911 and the arrival of their version of EMTs, blossomed quickly into a full-blown police investigation. I recognized a couple faces from the team that had been on hand at The Magic Circle, including Detective Inspector Matthews, with whom I'd had a frustrating conversation about Harry's connection to the death of Oskar. That seemed like a very long time ago, although it occurred to me it had only been three days and not even three full days at that.

After Baxter's announcement of Borys' death, a quiet dread fell over the usually voluble group. So, by the time the full contingent of police had arrived, most of us were still seated. Angus Bishop had disappeared into the hallway a few times to press Baxter for more details, each time returning with a morsel or two. The first piece of information was that Borys had been discovered when one of the maids—young Gwendolyn, who had helped at breakfast—entered his room to make up the bed and discovered a corpse in it. The second was the EMTs suggestion that, based on their review of the body and the level of rigor, the cause of death may have been poison. The third was that the police were concurring with this initial assessment.

Although they continually refilled our coffee cups, our plates had been silently carried away by the household staff, who I could hear whispering away in the kitchen. They were silenced immediately upon the appearance of Miss Hess, who moved slowly and ominously through the dining room and into the kitchen, the swinging door making more noise than she had.

A verbal exchange of some kind took place on the other side of the door, but all I could hear were muffled female voices and then the hiss of Miss Hess as she said loudly, "Second girl, you come now."

A few moments later, she returned from the now-silent kitchen, ushering Gwendolyn in front of her. The young girl looked pale and shaken.

Hess and her charge passed Angus on their way out of the dining room. He turned and waited until they were out of earshot before turning back to the group.

"They are questioning the staff to see if anyone brought Borys any food or drink last night," he said, "but the consensus seems to be it's likely something he had before he retired to his room."

"Which means it could have been something we all had as well," Roy Templeton offered.

"Except none of us is dead," Roxanne said.

"Declining, yes. Dead, no," Roy agreed.

"The tea," Davis De Vries said suddenly. "Wasn't he the only one to drink tea last night?" He looked around the table, and we all agreed, but Angus shook his head.

"He brought his own tea, always did," he said. "No way to get poison into his tea."

"But he didn't bring his own hot water," De Vries countered. "And no one else used it, right?"

"He offered me some tea," I said, "but I didn't have any. I'm not a big tea drinker," I added, in case my refusal of the tea would somehow indicate some hidden involvement in the crime.

94

"Hence, they're talking to the staff," De Vries concluded, as if the matter had been settled.

Turns out, it wasn't as settled as he thought it was. A few moments later they started pulling each of us out of the dining room for individual interviews.

* * *

Detective Inspector Matthews began her questioning of me by assuring me this was "all routine."

"Really?" I said. "Two magicians dead in seventy-two hours, both probably murdered? That's routine?"

"The situation is abnormal," she said, her mixed English and Indian accent having lost none of its charm. "It is the act of questioning which is routine."

I couldn't argue with that, and so I answered her questions as fully as I could, recapping the previous day's events. Particular emphasis was placed on the late-night drinking session in Laurence Baxter's den, where I was asked to recount—to the best of my ability—everything that had been said or done while I was in the room.

My strongest memory of the evening's session had been the inadvertent discovery of Jake North performing my card routine on a late-night chat show; the rest of the details were fuzzy. I related my version of who was drinking what, the arrival of the hot water for Borys' tea, his offer to share said tea, and my polite refusal. As for the particulars of the conversations that didn't concern Jake North's thievery, I had to admit I was a bit fuzzy.

"There was a long discussion about which magician was the fastest at calculating the numbers for the Magic Square," I offered. I could tell from her expression that more explanation was required. "It's a popular magic trick that requires some quick arithmetic," I added for clarification.

"And was a consensus reached," she asked, "about the maths and who was the best?"

I shook my head. "Hardly. A consensus is a difficult thing to come by with magicians," I explained. "A few of the guys lobbied hard for a magician named Richard Leigh. Everyone else was split, often along national lines. Then, as is often the case, the conversation drifted into other topics.

"You see, late night conversations with magicians are always similar and tend to revolve around the same subjects," I continued. "It's always about a new technique that is either much better or much worse than an old technique, with heated arguments on either side. Or it's about a particularly heinous gig or booker or green room or stage set-up. Or an audience member who confounded every out we have for a particular routine. Or what we would have said in a certain situation, but we didn't want to lose the gig." I stopped and took a breath, realizing that despite the length of my list, I had neglected a number of recurring subtopics. "Some of the specifics change, but that's the general outline of every conversation with a group of magicians."

"Yes, well, it is the specifics that interest us this morning," Detective Inspector Matthews said quietly. "Tell me, what are the dynamics of the group?"

"The dynamics?"

"Who's in charge? Who likes who? Who bears a grudge?"

"Well, they all bear grudges," I said with a wry laugh. "They're performers."

Her expression suggested I dig deeper, so I thought about the people assembled in the room the previous evening.

"Well, obviously, Laurence Baxter is the most successful," I began, gesturing around the room, which appeared to be one of an abundance of small sitting rooms. If I had the number of closets in my apartment that Baxter had sitting rooms, I'd be a happy renter.

"I mean," I said, "of the original group, he's the one who really hit it big."

"The original group?" she asked, consulting her notes.

"The Magnificent Magi," I explained. "They all started around the same time, helped each other get started, competed for gigs. They all wear the same ring," I added, helpfully gesturing at my hand for some reason, even though I don't wear a ring.

"And they were all assembled here last night?"

"I think so," I said, trying to remember the photo Laurence Baxter had pointed out at The Magic Circle. "I mean, obviously Oskar Korhonen wasn't here."

"Obviously," she agreed.

"And there was at least one other member," I continued, trying to remember the name. "But he died, I guess. Years ago."

"Do you know the circumstances?"

"Archie Banks," I said a little too loudly, pleased my memory had finally kicked in. "His name was Archie Banks, and they said he died of suicide. No, that's not the right way to put it, he was a suicide. He killed himself," I finally said, glad to have gotten that all sorted out.

"Archie Banks, suicide," she repeated as she added to the page of notes I had helped her generate.

"Yeah, he stole a lot of magic routines from all of them and then killed himself," I said, watching as she scribbled down my words. She looked up at me.

"He stole from them. And then he killed himself," she repeated.

"Yes," I said, thinking back on Harry's explanation of the event. "But I believe, at the time, it was felt he was only making an attempt at suicide and had really not wanted to kill himself. Apparently, he attempted suicide a lot. It was sort of a thing with him."

She looked up from her notes, waiting to see if I had anything useful to add to the story.

"At least, that's what they told me," I finally said.

"All right then," she said as she closed her notebook. "Let's see what they have to tell me."

* * *

When I returned from my interview with Detective Inspector Matthews, I found that most of the dining room's earlier occupants had been moved to different areas in the house for their own bouts of questioning. I was surprised Uncle Harry had finished his interview before I had and even more surprised to see he was sharing a cup of coffee with his old friend, Henry McHugh.

"How did it go?" Harry asked as I entered. He pushed a new coffee cup across the table toward me as I returned to my original seat.

"I was just going to ask you that," I said, reaching for the coffee urn. It was nearly empty, but I poured what was left into my cup. I nodded a greeting at McHugh as I poured, and he gave me a welcoming nod in return.

"A friend in the service alerted me to the situation," he said. "I thought I might be able to lend a hand. Or an idea."

"I was just telling McHugh that their questioning of me seemed, at best, perfunctory," Harry said. "He suggested a longer, more in-depth interview is in my not-too-distant future."

"That would be the traditional approach," McHugh agreed. He was dressed in the same tweed jacket I'd seen him in before, and his trilby hat was in its apparent permanent position on his head. "Harry is still their key suspect from the murder this past week-end. So they will note your reaction at this new interview and then compare and contrast how you behave after you've had some time to sort yourself out. And what about you?" he said, turning back to me.

Before I could offer reflections on my interview, Laurence Baxter entered, escorting Megan. He pulled out a chair for her by force of habit, but he was clearly distracted.

"This is a morning I could have done without," he said.

"No one expects to wake up with a corpse as a house guest," McHugh agreed.

"Well, clearly someone did," Baxter said. He stopped, surprised to see this new figure in his dining room, and then seemed to wave it off as all part of the surreal morning he was having. He reached for the coffee urn and cursed quietly when he recognized that it was empty. He carried it to the swinging kitchen door.

"Can we have some more coffee, please," he said, holding up the empty urn as physical evidence of his displeasure at the current state of household affairs. He waited for a moment, then turned back, looking exasperated. "No one there. Of course, they're all being questioned. I suppose I'll have to make it myself."

Baxter stomped into the kitchen, and we could hear him banging around as he began what appeared to be, for him at least, the arduous process of making coffee.

"If he gets this upset over a lack of coffee, how is he likely to react when we tell him the cream pitcher is empty?" McHugh suggested with a smile.

"Everyone reacts to stress differently," Harry said quietly. "He's got to deal with all the special shows this week at The Magic Circle, a house full of bothersome guests, and now a dead body and a police invasion. I think he's allowed a tiny crack in his famous British reserve."

"Yes, a murder investigation is always an interruption to even the best-planned garden party," McHugh agreed. He turned to me, leaning across the table and lowering his voice. "So, tell me about the tea."

As I had done with Detective Inspector Matthews, I explained how Gwendolyn had brought in the tea service, accompanied by Miss Hess, and how Borys had offered me some tea. McHugh asked a couple questions about the timing of the delivery and the exact location of each person in the room, and then sat back and considered what I had recounted.

"If the poison was in the kettle, it could have been added at any point after the afternoon tea," he said slowly. "So, basically, anyone could have put the poison in the kettle at any point during the evening."

"If, in fact, that was how the poison was delivered," Harry offered, and McHugh nodded in agreement.

"And, if what you told me is correct," McHugh said, turning to Harry, "the odds are quite good Borys would be the only one in the group who would drink tea last evening. Is that correct?"

Harry nodded. "Yes, given the choice between Baxter's high-end liquor cabinet and tea, this group could be counted on to always choose free booze."

"Except for you two," McHugh said, pointing at me and then at

Megan. "Someone may have had prior knowledge of Borys' habits, but you two were both unknowns in that regard."

"I would have taken tea if it was offered," Megan said. "But Roxanne dragged me off to her room for girl chat. And alcohol. Too much alcohol," she added, slowly rubbing her temples with her forefingers. I looked over at the kitchen to see if Baxter had made any progress with the coffee.

"What about you, Eli?" McHugh asked. "Are you a tea drinker?"

"If you'd asked me a couple years ago, I would have emphatically said no. But Megan has introduced me to the pleasures of a warm cup of Earl Grey." I turned to her, and despite her headache, she flashed me a smile. "However, Angus made such a strong argument against the tea last night, I decided to give it a pass."

"Did he?" McHugh said thoughtfully. "Interesting. Or not."

"A wise and fortuitous move on your part," Harry said gravely. He looked to McHugh for agreement, but his old friend had settled back into his chair and was stroking the first of his several chins.

"This is so odd," I said to fill in the silence. "With the first slaying at The Magic Circle, the murderer was well aware his victim would be one of two people—Harry or Oskar. Did he care which one? We don't know. Was the wrong person killed? Again, we don't know.

"But the intended victim last night had to be Borys," I continued. "He was the only one who was sure to drink the tea. There was always the chance Megan and I might have had some tea as well, but Borys was—for lack of a better term—a sure thing."

"I think that is very likely correct," McHugh said. "There was always the likelihood of collateral damage," he added, "but I think it's clear Borys was the one who was scheduled to die."

"What does that mean?" I asked as Laurence Baxter banged back into the dining room, returning with the coffee.

"I can't speak to the quality," he said holding up the urn triumphantly. "But here's the blasted coffee."

McHugh was the first to hold up his empty cup. He turned to me as he did.

"What does it mean?" he repeated. "I have no idea. Let us have some more coffee and consider a few possibilities."

* * *

The conclusion of the questioning of guests and the household staff finally arrived about an hour later and coincided with the removal of Borys' body. While the staff had returned to the business of running the large house, the rest of us had wandered into the front foyer to stretch our legs and determine what to do next.

The low, somber hubbub of the group came to a sudden stop with the appearance of two EMTs at the top of the stairs, carrying a stretcher between them. Borys' body was encased in a black plastic carrier. All that was discernible was a small, inert shape encased within a terminal sleeping bag.

We all stood in respectful silence as they made their way down the stairs and past us toward the front door. Hector Hechizo made a quick sign of the cross as they moved by him, and McHugh took off his hat. I noticed both Roxanne and Megan were visibly crying, and even Angus Bishop wiped his eyes with a handkerchief, which then disappeared immediately into his pocket.

"You think of the strangest things at a time like this," Harry said quietly. "I'd always meant to ask Borys about the center tear he developed. It was remarkable. Never get the chance now, I guess."

"Aye, that secret dies with him," Angus agreed quietly. He was normally so upbeat and talkative, it was interesting to see this more subdued side of the glib old magician.

"Yeah," I said. "I kept meaning to ask him to translate a Russian phrase I heard at the hotel we were at earlier this week. Never got around to it."

"Not to worry. He likely wouldn't have been able to do it," Angus said. "Borys wasn't Russian, he was Ukrainian."

"You mean Romanian," Laurence Baxter corrected.

"Romanian, Ukrainian, same difference," Angus grumbled.

Detective Inspector Matthews had followed the grim procession down the stairs and watched closely through the open front door as the body was loaded into the coroner's van. She made a note of the time and then turned to the group, doing a quick head-count to ensure we were all present and accounted for.

"Thank you, all of you, for your cooperation this morning," she said in her clipped British-Indian hybrid accent. "As I mentioned to some of you, we may need to follow up at a later date for a more in-depth conversation. I understand those of you who are not British residents are staying on for at least a few days?"

"Yes," Laurence Baxter said, speaking for the group. "We have a series of shows at The Magic Circle through Saturday," he said as he looked around the group. "I'm guessing we will cancel tonight's show, because of this...most recent tragedy. But you're all staying on, correct?"

"*Si*," said Hector.

"Absolutely," said Roxanne, and Roy nodded in agreement.

"Where she goes, I go. Marriage is just long-term stalking, really," he said brightly, and then realized humor might not be the best response in this situation. He quickly switched to a more appropriate somber expression.

"Of course," De Vries added. "I can stay as long as required."

"I've got nothing booked for a fortnight," Angus Bishop said. "Maybe longer."

Everyone turned to Harry. "Obviously I'm not going anywhere," Harry said quietly.

The group reacted sympathetically, but there was a palpable feeling in the room—and there had been since the announcement of the discovery of Borys' body—that the group's built-in sense of unity was beginning to ebb. Two members of the group were dead, and while no one had voiced any actual suspicion of Harry, I was getting the sense it was beginning to bubble up from under the surface.

I scanned the lined faces of the Magnificent Magi assembled in the lobby. I knew Harry was not the killer—that line of thinking was a non-starter—which meant that if it was someone from within the group, they were standing with us right now.

I suddenly realized—looking at all their unhappy faces—that

they were all staring right back at me. I had forgotten we were all expressing our availability to Detective Inspector Matthews. I turned to her. "We're here for as long as you need us," I said.

Baxter turned back to Detective Inspector Matthews. "And, of course, I'm at your disposal."

"All right then," she said. "We will be in touch."

With that, she stepped through the door, and Baxter closed it behind her. The group was still unusually quiet as he turned back to us. He sighed, clearly searching for the right thing to say at a time like this. However, as with the rest of us, Baxter wasn't really schooled for times like this.

"Well, that one plays things close to the vest, doesn't she?" Baxter said with a forced chuckle. "Hard to tell what she's thinking."

"Not at all. She is thinking someone in this house is a murderer."

We all jumped at the sound, looking around to see where it came from. It was the unmistakable voice of Miss Hess, who we discovered standing at the top of the stairs. She glowered down on the group, her gaze landing on each of us for a tad longer than we might have liked.

"And I, for one, am inclined to believe her," she added, before turning slowly and disappearing down the second floor hall.

CHAPTER 10

The surprising and sudden death of Borys had thrown all of us into a sort of limbo, not sure what to do with ourselves or where to turn next. I was itching to do something—anything—to clear Harry's name, but I feared the additional murder had pushed my uncle further up Scotland Yard's list of suspects. I felt helpless in my inability to do anything productive to lower that ranking.

Megan and I puttered around for a while, tossing out ideas of how to spend our day. I was thinking a trip back to The Magic Circle was in order to revisit the scene of the first crime and see if it triggered any new avenues of pursuit. Megan was game, but our impromptu plan was cut short when Davis De Vries cornered me about contacting Jake North so we could sort things out.

Clearly De Vries was anxious to get his Catherine Wheel illusion successfully launched this week and felt Jake was the linchpin who could make it happen. So I set aside the plan to head to The Magic Circle and made some attempts to contact Jake, trying all the contacts I had for him. Sadly, after about twenty fruitless minutes, I didn't have much positive news to report.

"The cell number I have for him has been disconnected," I explained. "So I sent him an email, and I got a generic reply telling me to click on a link, which took me to his website. On that site, I was given the opportunity to join his mailing list, but it didn't offer any other contact options, although I was entered into a drawing to win an official signed Jake North t-shirt, with the slogan 'What Are You, Blind?' emblazoned across the front. Fingers crossed on that one. But otherwise, I think I've reached a dead end."

De Vries pursed his lips thoughtfully. "Not much to report on my end, either. I left a message with his publicist," he said, "and haven't heard anything back from her. She was slow to respond last time, but the indication I got was he was interested in premiering the illusion this week because it would take place at The Magic Circle, his schedule permitting. I followed up the phone call with an email and a text to her but still nothing."

I felt badly for him. I didn't have any other ideas on how to contact this now reclusive star—ironically, the same actor who would have attended the opening of a grocery store in his earlier days of semi-fame.

"Is she British?" Harry asked.

De Vries and I were standing in front of the house, and I hadn't realized Harry and McHugh had planted themselves nearby in patio chairs that offered a fine view of the heath.

"Is who British?" De Vries replied.

"Jake North's publicist," Harry said.

"Yes, I believe she is," De Vries said.

"Then have Baxter call her," Harry suggested. "He's the closest thing magicians have to royalty, at least in this country."

McHugh nodded in agreement. "I concur. A call from Laurence Baxter will be returned at lightning speed. Faster than a call from the Queen herself, I suspect."

We didn't have the resources to perform a double-blind experiment to prove McHugh's hypothesis, but we did have Laurence Baxter, and he was more than happy to place the phone call.

We all stood around him while he did it, listening to his polite-to-a-fault message for the publicist, filled with "sorry to bother you," "hope I'm not intruding," and the devastating *coup de gras* "Anyway, again, this is Laurence Baxter, and I do hope to hear back from you if you have time. Thanks so much, and have a lovely day."

She clearly had time and a "last number called" button, because the phone rang just as Baxter was handing it back to De Vries. Obviously recognizing the power of the resource he had at his disposal, he immediately handed the phone back to Baxter, who navigated through the conversation with consummate skill. The end result was an agreement that her client, Jake North, would in fact premiere the new illusion, and he would also, incidentally, love to have a chat with his dear old friend Eli Marks.

And, as luck would have it, he suggested the meeting take place at The Magic Circle.

* * *

The precise arrangements for that conversation rivaled the cinematic meeting between Michael Corleone and Virgil Sollozzo, minus the hidden revolver (I'm guessing) and bloody dénouement. Finally, it was decided this casual conversation would take place the next morning in the Executive Director's office at The Magic Circle. The agreed-upon participants would be myself, Jake North, and his publicist. Laurence Baxter would act as my second, and the whole thing would be overseen by Executive Director, Gareth MacKenzie—the man who I had seen on the first night giving pre-show instructions to my uncle Harry and the not-long-for-this-earth Oskar Korhonen.

In addition—although he wasn't officially part of the proceedings—Davis De Vries would be allowed to stand in the hallway and listen in on the conversation, with the understanding his role was to be strictly a silent one.

This was only the second time I had seen Gareth MacKenzie and both times he had been a mass of nerves; I wasn't sure if this was a permanent condition or a reaction to two stressful situations. Although he was dressed in a different suit than the one I'd seen him in on Saturday, this one looked equally baggy. His bald head sported several rivulets of sweat, despite the fact his office—and the entire building—was excessively cool.

Speaking of cool, Jake's publicist was an unflappable brunette who introduced herself to Laurence Baxter as Stephanie Milbury. In contrast to Gareth MacKenzie, her suit was tailored to perfection, and her hair and makeup were equally coiffed. Her intensity and forced cheer suggested she was fishing for a new client and Baxter—no stranger to his impact on the general public—did nothing to disabuse her of this notion, at least for the time being.

Baxter and I were on time, which allowed Jake to make a showy entrance five minutes later, all handshakes and smiles, as everyone in the Executive Director's office pretended this was the most casual of encounters. Once greetings and introductions had been covered, MacKenzie took it upon himself to introduce the topic under discussion for this hastily called meeting.

"The motto of The Magic Circle," he began, "is *indocilis privata loqui*, which translates from the Latin as 'not apt to disclose secrets.'"

"A closer translation might be 'incapable of speaking of private things,'" Laurence Baxter added, and then recognized correct Latin translations were not the primary concern of this meeting. He nodded at MacKenzie to continue.

For his part, MacKenzie's cool attitude toward Baxter from the moment we had arrived showed no signs of thawing. As the President of the Board, Laurence Baxter was technically MacKenzie's boss; however, this seemed to have no dampening effect on his manner toward Baxter, which could be best defined as just this side of pissy.

"Yes, well, the gist of it," Gareth MacKenzie said as everyone turned their attention back to him, "'is that magicians—regardless of whether or not you're a member of this organization—have a sacred duty to protect secrets. And while that is generally perceived as keeping the inner workings of our illusions out of public scrutiny, it also means one magician shall not take the secrets of another and call them his or her own.

"My understanding," he continued, looking from Jake to me and back again, "is there is the suggestion that Mr. North may have presented one of Mr. Marks' illusions as his own on a television broadcast, without prior communication or consent."

I looked over at Jake, who had a puzzled look on his face.

"Say what?" he said. Despite his recent success and increased level of fame, he had lost none of his California "dudeness." In fact, it may have intensified.

"Jake, you did my Ambitious Dog routine on TV this week without my permission or any credit," I explained.

"Oh, that," Jake said, breaking into a wide smile. "That was just, you know, an accident."

"You accidentally did his trick," MacKenzie repeated slowly. "And how, exactly, would such an event come about?"

Jake shrugged. "Things were going really well on the show, and the crowd was loving me. Then the host asked me to do one more trick, and I was already running on empty. You know how it is," he suggested, looking around the room. MacKenzie said nothing, while Laurence Baxter provided the slightest of nods in agreement at the notion.

"So you did my trick, just on the spur of the moment?" I asked.

"Absolutely. Never planned to do it. It's your trick, man," he added jovially, falling just short of giving my arm a playful punch.

"Then I can't see there is any objection on moving forward with Mr. North presenting my new illusion here this week," Davis De Vries declared from his position in the hallway, as if the matter were entirely wrapped up to everyone's satisfaction. Jake and his publicist started to get up, but Gareth MacKenzie held up a hand to stop them.

"One moment, please," he said, summoning his most authoritative voice. It fell short of truly commanding the room, but it did succeed in preventing a sudden exodus. He turned to me. "Mr. Marks, are you satisfied with this explanation?"

"Not entirely," I said, looking up at Jake, who was poised to make a quick exit. "The trouble with doing my Ambitious Dog routine on the fly, as it were, is it requires a very specific gaff." I recognized, with the publicist in a room, I couldn't go into any detail on the nature of the device. "Let's just say it requires a unique and special item, which one would be unlikely to have on one's person. Unless they intended to perform my Ambitious Dog routine," I added, deciding I had used the word 'one' enough for the day.

"I admit to being unfamiliar with the workings of your illusion," MacKenzie said as Jake reluctantly sat again. "But you're saying it is not an impromptu effect and that it requires deployment of a special element or device?"

"Yes," I said simply, feeling the Executive Director had covered all the salient points.

MacKenzie nodded, and then looked to Jake. "Mr. North?"

There was a tense moment, and then Jake broke into a big smile. "What can I say, I love the bit. I do it all the time for people, and I always have the gaffe on me," he added, turning to me and increasing the intensity of his grin. "Believe me, I always tell them it was created by my old pal Eli Marks. I always give credit where credit is due. This one time I forgot to say it, and for that, I'm sorry. It won't happen again."

He put out his tanned hand, and I looked at it for a long moment before extending my own paler version. We shook hands, and as we did, I heard a small muffled whoop from the hallway. De Vries, still standing in the doorway, was grinning widely as he glanced down at his watch.

"Excellent," he said. "So glad you two were able to bury the hatchet and put this behind you. We are good, correct?" He looked over at Gareth MacKenzie for confirmation.

"That depends." The Executive Director turned to me. "Mr. Marks, are you satisfied with Mr. North's explanation?"

I felt all the eyes in the room were on me, with De Vries giving me the most intense scrutiny. I considered my options.

"Sure, I guess," I finally said.

"Excellent," De Vries said quickly, once again taking a look at his watch. "Then why don't we all go up to the theater and steal a quick peek at the Catherine Wheel?"

Jake jumped up and slapped me on the back. "Come on, dude, let's take a look at this sucker," he said with more exuberance than might have been necessary. He followed De Vries and his publicist out of the room. I looked to Laurence Baxter, who smiled back wryly.

"I guess that settles that," he said, gesturing me toward the door.

I grunted in agreement, still not sure what we had actually accomplished.

"You joining us, Gareth?" Baxter said warmly over his shoulder on his way out.

I turned back to see if Gareth MacKenzie was following us, but the small, bald man in oversized clothes was staring at Laurence Baxter as he headed down the hallway.

His expression was hard to read, but it felt anything but warm.

* * *

Once we made it to the theater, it quickly became apparent why De Vries had been so antsy, continually checking his watch during the meeting with the Executive Director. As it turned out, *someone* had summoned the press, and consequently, we all walked into an impromptu press conference. A small contingent of media people had arrived and were set up by the front of the stage for the unveiling of the Catherine Wheel, which was currently safely out of sight behind the red velour curtain.

"I'm so happy to be here today to unveil Davis De Vries' Catherine Wheel," De Vries continued once he had carefully stepped up on the stage. "It's an illusion years in the making, and it will, I hope, join the ranks of other stunning illusions I've designed and created in my long and happy tenure within the magic community."

He then segued into a not-so-quick recap of his career as the designer and builder of iconic magical illusions—most of which were connected, in the public's eye, not to De Vries but to each magician who had originally performed the illusion. At the conclusion, a reporter raised a hand.

"So, Mr. De Vries, with the Catherine Wheel—"

De Vries cut him off immediately. "Sorry, but I should nip this in the bud right away," he said with a quick laugh which almost sounded convincing. "The correct name for the illusion is 'Davis De Vries' Catherine Wheel,' which I should also point out is trademarked." He ran his hand through his perfectly coiffed white hair and then gestured to the reporter to continue with his question.

"Looks like De Vries is making a last grab for posterity with this one," Harry growled under his breath to me. I'd discovered him seated in the back row of the theater, along with Angus Bishop and Roy Templeton, all of whom were waiting for some much-needed tech rehearsal time on the stage. But that would have to wait, it appeared, until after De Vries made a pitch for his fifteen minutes (or more) of fame.

"Difficult to blame him," Angus whispered. "He's worked bloody hard for forty years, made others famous with his designs, and yet no one knows who he is, the poor bastard."

Roy clucked his tongue. "Poor my bloodshot eye," he said a bit too loudly, and then continued in a heavy whisper. "Have you seen his place in San Diego? It gives Baxter's Folly a run for its money. He's not hurting, believe you me."

"It's not always about the money," Harry said.

"Most of the time it is, mate," Angus countered.

"Yes, but not always," Harry continued. "Sometimes it's about posterity. About leaving a legacy."

"Well, if debts can be considered a legacy, then I'm golden," Roy said, giggling quietly at his own joke as we settled in and waited for the highly scheduled, yet seemingly spontaneous, press conference to wrap up.

With the last of the official questions out of the way, Davis De Vries moved into performance mode and stepped to the center of the stage. Although he looked every inch the confident designer and inventor, after hearing his peers remarks about him, I wondered how thin that veneer was and how deep his resentments might run. Did he have any possible grudge against Borys, who never used large-scale illusions like the ones he created? Or against the one-armed Oskar Korhonen? Or, for that matter, against Harry?

"Now it is my very great pleasure to introduce to you the performer who will inaugurate the Davis De Vries' Catherine Wheel," he continued, "although, frankly, no introduction is really required. Please welcome magician, television star, and accomplished actor who is currently selling out on a nightly basis in the West End theatre district...the incomparable Jake North."

He gestured to the wings and Jake stepped out as video cameras rolled and cameras snapped photo after photo. The sound of all the activity drowned out the snickering in the last row, although I'm not entirely sure if we were all laughing at the same thing. It was either De Vries' statement that Jake was both a television star *and* an accomplished actor...or the use of the phrase "selling out on a nightly basis." Either way, the old guys in the back row were suddenly enjoying the show.

I wouldn't say what followed was technically a disaster, but it was clear Jake had not been completely prepped as to the nature of his commitment. To begin with, every time he mentioned the Catherine Wheel, he called it "the Cathy Wheel." This would require an interruption and clarification from De Vries, which definitely put a crimp in the flow of questions. Try as he might, the full name "Davis De Vries' Catherine Wheel" did not appear to have the cachet he had been hoping for.

Once it became apparent Jake wasn't really helping the cause, De Vries took a new tack and jumped ahead to the actual unveiling of the illusion. Whatever rehearsal this program had gone through looked like it had been for naught, as bombastic introductory music came blaring out of the sound system squarely in the middle of his introduction. De Vries finally conceded to its louder volume and waved to someone backstage who wisely pulled the ropes that jerkily opened the curtain, finally revealing the device in all its glory.

Despite the hiccups along the way, this reveal had clearly been worth the wait.

Even after hearing Harry's earlier description of the illusion, I had to admit the first sight of the Catherine Wheel—that is, Davis De Vries' Catherine Wheel—was stunning. It was imposing and enormous. This impression was enhanced by the small size of The Magic Circle's stage, but I suspect it would have looked massive just about anywhere.

The thing darn near sparkled like an exploding star when the stage lights hit it, so much so that even the jaded press took a step back and delivered a collective 'ooh' and 'ahh.' The wheel's spokes jutted out from a hub, which appeared to be encrusted with rubies, sending red reflections bouncing around the room. I'm not sure what the material was—it looked like a mix of chrome and solid gold—but this was no PVC-pipe basement workshop creation. This was stunning, more work of art than standard stage illusion.

Of course, the reaction of the three magicians next to me in the back row was one you would expect from seasoned pros: Awe mixed with practicality.

"That thing fits in two travel cases?" Roy Templeton hissed once the room's first reaction to the illusion had settled. "Two cases?"

"Plus he says it can be put together by one guy," Harry added. "With no tools."

"It's like pulling back a screen and discovering the Holy Grail," Angus Bishop whispered reverently. "You hardly even need to do a trick with the bloody thing, just open the curtain and stand back."

Jake appeared to be equally awed. He stepped back to get a better view of the device and might have backed right off the stage if a couple reporters with quick reactions hadn't reached up to steady him. As he regained his balance, two young women dressed in matching sparkly cocktail dresses appeared from the wings and grabbed Jake's arms, positioning him next to the illusion. Each of the women then struck a pose on either side of the slightly dazed actor.

"Yes, ladies and gentlemen, this Saturday night will see the first public performance of Davis De Vries' Catherine Wheel," De Vries said, trying to sound dramatic and almost succeeding. It was clear he was a man accustomed to watching from the wings and not commanding center stage. "Performed by Jake North and," he continued, gesturing toward Jake and the two women and then clearly forgetting their names, so he quickly added, "with the trusty aid of these two lovely assistants."

This was evidently the key photo op portion of the press conference, and the media folks wasted no time capturing image after image of Jake in front of the towering wheel, flanked by two smiling models.

I noted that the large-scale illusion's placement was exactly where the deadly chair that had taken Oskar Korhonen's life had been situated. I was sitting way in the back, and although the theater has great sightlines, I had to squint a bit to see the expression on Jake's face. I leaned forward once I determined what it was to make sure I was reading him right.

Despite all the hoopla going on around him, Jake North looked like he might be physically sick.

And, as it turned out, I was absolutely right.

CHAPTER 11

"I s *this* your card?"

In the first five minutes I spent in the the Club Room after leaving the press conference in the theater, I would guess I heard that phrase, or slight variations on it, nearly a dozen times. As it turned out, today was an open club day, which meant members gathered to swap ideas, practice their moves and geek out over new tricks. It was a popular event, so much so that the room was overflowing with magicians and wannabes of all ages—mostly male—trading secrets and absorbing new ones.

As I snaked my way through the crowd, I spotted Hector Hechizo, holding court at a table, demonstrating one of his impossibly complicated card routines. Three members sat around him at the table as he took each of their decks of cards, shuffled them, cut them, and then spread them out on the table into a messy tableau. With every move the piles got messier, which seemed to delight Hector. He laughed as he rattled off his patter, a charming and surprisingly decipherable mix of Spanish and English. The three young magicians did their best to keep up with him, following his instructions as best they could, each getting hopelessly confused about what they were doing and why.

I peered over the crowd that had gathered to watch, amazed at

115

Hector's ability to create what appeared to be a disaster on the table but which would ultimately prove to be a miracle.

"He makes Lennart Green look like a neat freak, doesn't he?" a voice said next to me. I turned to see that, as he had done at our first meeting, Laurence Baxter had appeared silently beside me. He was watching the card artistry with unbridled admiration.

"I don't know how he keeps track of the cards," I said quietly.

"He lost me five moves ago," Baxter said. "But fear not, he is always in complete control. Hector is the definition of *sprezzatura*."

As if that were his cue, Hector quickly straightened each of the three different decks, squaring them up and handing each back to its proper owner. Then, on his command, the three young magicians turned the decks over and spread the faces so everyone could see.

Every deck was now in new deck order, each suit separated and in sequence. The crowd around the table roared in surprise and then burst into applause. Hector nodded humbly and gestured to his three subjects, as if it were they who had accomplished this miracle and not him.

"Do you think he'd ever tell me how he did that?" I said, turning back to Laurence Baxter. However, he had missed the conclusion of the trick and had moved several feet away. He was giving instructions to Gareth MacKenzie, who looked tense and uncomfortable—like a school boy who has found himself suddenly being reprimanded by the Head Master.

"Gareth, it's bloody freezing in here. Be a good fellow and get the temperature up to something above arctic wasteland. And look into refilling the nut bowls, we've run low on cashews." Without waiting for a reply, Baxter moved into the crowd, giving a cheerful wave to a small group who had assembled across the room.

Despite the urgent tone of the request, MacKenzie stood immobile. His face remained expressionless, but his jaw moved slowly, suggesting he was grinding his teeth. A small vein in his temple pulsated in time with his jaw. He noticed me and recognized I must have overheard the exchange.

"Treats me like I'm on his bloody domestic staff," he said, spitting out the words. "Plus he insists on bringing in his own servants to muck around the place, so I have to deal with that lot as well. Acts like The Magic Circle is his own, personal in-town apartment."

I shrugged. "He *is* Laurence Baxter," I said, not sure if this qualified as an answer or why, for that matter, I felt the need to apologize for Baxter's officious behavior. "And President of the Board."

"For now," MacKenzie said with a harrumph, turning to watch as Baxter glad-handed some arriving attendees.

"Do you also perform magic?" I asked, hoping the change in topic might alter his mood.

MacKenzie shook his head. "No, I don't have much of a taste for it," he said grimly. "I had an uncle who tortured me with childish magic tricks when I was a lad. Soured me on the whole enterprise."

"Given your experience, you have picked an interesting career path," I suggested.

"We go where life takes us," he said, still glaring at Baxter across the room.

I heard him mumble something indecipherable as he skulked away to adjust the thermostat, add cashews to the nut bowls, or simply ignore Baxter's requests in the privacy of his office.

* * *

Harry was still upstairs rehearsing, so I spent the next forty-five minutes wandering the room, watching magicians as they ran through routines and sought advice and counsel from their peers. From time to time I tossed in a thought or a comment. Once it became apparent this interloping American had a pretty solid handle on the basics of magic, folks starting coming up to me to ask questions they might have been too shy to address to Laurence Baxter, Hector Hechizo, or any of the other high-profile magicians who moved in and out of the room.

I helped one young lad with his top change, using many of the same words—although with a warmer tone— that the legendary

Dai Vernon had used on me the one time I met him at the Magic Castle in Los Angeles. At the time, I was about the same age as the kid I was currently assisting.

"The thing about the top change," I said as I quickly demonstrated it, "is that it's a ballsy move which often requires more guts than actual skill. You just have to dive in and do it. Plus, if you're able to distract them with a larger move while you do it, they don't even notice the smaller move."

I did it for him twice more and then offered some tweaks while he demonstrated it back to me. By this time a small group had formed around us, consisting of magicians from about twelve to twenty, running the geeky gamut from "just a little" to "oh my, yes very."

Satisfied he had the understanding he needed, the kid with the top change question turned away and was replaced by another young magician who lamented he was having trouble with audience management.

"For this trick, they're supposed to hold two cards facedown," he said, the level of distress obvious in his tone. "But they keep turning the cards over and revealing them before I want them to."

"That's a tricky one," I agreed, taking the two cards from him and holding them facedown between my thumb and forefinger, just as the audience member would do at that point in the trick. I went through the phases of the illusion in my mind, forming a response to his question. However, before I could get the words out, another voice took over.

"Oh, luv, it's all in the eyes. You can control their every move with your eyes and just the slightest touch."

I looked over to discover the female magician I had seen here on my first night had stepped in and was taking over. She wasn't dressed for a performance, but her attire still had a vaguely steampunk Victorian vibe to it. Big hair, big eyes, and a big smile. Before I could pull her name from my memory, she did it for me.

"Angelika," she said with a broad smile. "We met the other night. Mind if I weigh in with my two pence worth?"

I nodded my acquiescence, but she was already moving full

speed ahead.

"So, you want them to keep the cards—and their hand—down until you're ready, right?" she asked the kid who had posed the question. He seemed a bit bowled over by the force of her personality, but he had enough wits about him to nod his head in agreement.

"Piece of cake," she said, suddenly turning to me. Since I was still holding the two cards, I unexpectedly took on the role of the audience member in this demonstration. "Once they have the cards in position, just place two fingers lightly on the back of their hand."

She did just that, barely touching the back of my hand with two fingers. I looked up and saw she was staring right into my eyes.

"Look 'em in the eyes, smile, and while you do that, gently push down on their hand. Doesn't take much pressure, just enough to make them lose the desire to hold the hand up."

She did exactly that to me, and I had to admit it killed any inclination on my part to hold the hand up. The move was subtle but effective.

"Once you've done that, you're good to go," she said to the kid, then turned back to me. "You don't want to hold your hand up until I tell you to now, right?"

"Absolutely," I agreed, looking down at my hand holding the two cards. While I still had complete control of the hand, the idea of lifting it up—and revealing the cards—was nowhere in my mind.

"Brilliant," the kid said with a big smile, snatching the cards from my hand as he and his friends scampered off to try out what they'd just learned. Angelika watched them go.

"Were we ever that young?" she said wistfully.

"If I was, I have no memory of it," I agreed.

"Silly gits," she said, then she pivoted and turned her full attention to me. "So you're Harry Marks' nephew, right? Sorry, had no idea when I met you the other night. Harry's a bit of a legend, don't you think?"

"Depends on when you ask me," I said. "Somedays yes, somedays no.

She nodded in understanding. "Family, you gotta love 'em," she agreed.

"No, but Harry's great. He's always been very supportive, and I've been exceedingly lucky to have him as a mentor."

She took two small steps toward a nearby wall and leaned on it expertly, producing a pack of gum from seemingly out of nowhere. She offered me a piece. I wasn't sure if the offer was genuine or if I was being pulled into an impromptu trick, so I shook my head."

"No thanks."

"What was the best advice he ever gave you?" she asked as she unwrapped a piece and popped it into her mouth.

I thought about this. Several nuggets of wisdom floated across my consciousness, and then one jumped forward.

"I was young—in my twenties. I'd been working for a while, but Harry had never really seen my act, you know, in front of an audience. So I invited him to a gig I thought would show off my best stuff. He brought my Aunt Alice. I did the show, got a great response, and we all went out to eat afterwards."

I smiled at the memory, which was so strong I could actually remember the smell of the steak I ordered and every other detail, down to the color of the wallpaper at Axel's—a local restaurant we always saved for special occasions. And the popovers, I could smell the popovers.

"Aunt Alice cooed about how much she loved it," I continued, "about how well I did, how proud my parents would have been. You know, on and on. Harry, however, was abnormally quiet. So I finally had to ask him, 'So, Harry, what'd you think?'

"Harry thought about this for a long moment—a way-too-long moment, it felt like. And then he said, 'Eli, tonight I saw a wonderful magician perform. Talented, skillful, in all ways delightful. But I never saw *you* up there. I never saw Eli. I saw a generic magician—dexterous, yes. Funny—you bet. But I think you're doing your audience a disservice not to let them see Eli while you're up there. Because, in my humble opinion, I think Eli's pretty terrific.'"

I smiled at the memory. We stood quietly for a few moments as young magicians jostled past us, talking and laughing.

"You're a lucky one," Angelika said, clearly not getting the same joy out of the story I did. "Imagine being a lass, in your early twenties, and telling your mum you're leaving school to become a full-time magician. That got me an earful, I can tell you."

"No daughter of mine, that sort of thing?" I suggested.

"Throw in plenty of profanity and you're halfway there, luv," she agreed. "Of course, on the plus side, the magic community welcomed me with open arms..." Her voice dripped with sarcasm.

"A woman's place is in the box?" I offered.

"I've heard that one and more, believe me." She crumbled up the gum wrapper and tossed it into a nearby waste can. "It was a bit of a tussle, believe me. This profession has historically put women in boxes. And then cut them in half."

"Or thirds. Or quarters. Or thirteen pieces," I added, thinking of Davis De Vries' Baker's Dozen illusion. "And I'm guessing you didn't want to take the less-satisfying path of becoming a magician's assistant?"

"A box jumper? Not on your life, mate. My mind was set. My mum, of course, wanted me to stay in school, follow in her footsteps, and be a nurse or some such thing." She shuddered at the thought.

"Not for you?"

She shook her head. "I gave it a go, but in the end I couldn't stomach the idea the rest of my life would consist of emptying bedpans and yanking out catheters."

I involuntarily winced at her use of the word "yanking" in conjunction with the word "catheter," but I nodded in understanding. "The heart has its reasons, which reason knows nothing of," I said, just a little too sagely.

"Well," she smirked, "aren't we just the little fortune cookie message generator today?"

"I don't know who said it," I said, trying to cover my tracks. "But it felt appropriate."

"Pascal said it, mate, and when he said it, he at least had enough class to say it in French," she replied, clearly enjoying watching me squirm. "And you only quoted the first half, Yoda. He went on to say, 'We know the truth not only by the reason, but by the heart.'"

"You clearly know that one by heart," I said.

"You live it, you learn it, that's my motto," she said. "What's yours?"

She had put me on the spot, and all I could think of was "No shirt, no shoes, no service," which hardly seemed appropriate.

"I'm not sure I have one," I admitted.

She stepped closer to me, a little closer than I might have expected. "Every man needs a motto," she said with a wink. "You oughta get yourself one, luv."

She reached up and gave my nose the slightest of tweaks, laughed, and stepped away, quickly disappearing into the crowd. I leaned against the wall she had been using for support, feeling a sudden and surprising need for it. Once I got settled, I turned to see Henry McHugh standing next to me. He had been apparently been waiting patiently for my conversation with Angelika to conclude. He still sported his trusty trilby.

"Are you all right, my boy?" he said with concern. "You look a touch wobbly."

I straightened up quickly, if not convincingly. "We were talking about mottos," I said by way of explanation. "She wanted to know mine, but I couldn't come up with one. But I just remembered a saying my Aunt Alice used all the time that would have been the perfect response."

McHugh smiled at the mention of my late Aunt. "Ah, the divine Alice. What pearl of wisdom did she gift you with?"

"She said, 'If you don't want to slip—'" I began, but McHugh was ahead of me.

"If you don't want to slip, don't visit slippery places," he said, finishing a piece of advice I had heard from Alice on way too many occasions, each time due to my own errant behavior.

"Wise words, my boy," McHugh said as we both turned and watched Angelika flirt her way across the room, catching the eye of nearly every man as she moved past. "Wise words indeed."

CHAPTER 12

I quickly learned McHugh had not turned up simply to act as my personal Jiminy Cricket during my encounter with Angelika, as indispensable as his presence might have been. He had come to talk to Harry and let him know the British police were ready to have their longer interview with him, and in McHugh's opinion, sooner would be better than later.

"Look, I know you're anxious to head back home," McHugh told Harry once we'd tracked him down in the auditorium. He had finished his technical rehearsal and was packing his gear into its worn but solid traveling cases. "So the sooner you talk with them, the sooner they will no longer need to talk with you, as it were."

"I'm still stunned by all of this," Harry said as he locked one of the cases. "First Oskar, then Borys. But, of course, I will talk to them. When do they want to see me?"

"Now," McHugh said, glancing down at his watch. "And I told them I'd be happy to act as your escort."

This sudden change in plan required a quick call to Megan, who had intended to meet us for lunch at The Tate, which Harry had earlier recommended for its fine view of the London skyline. When she was informed Harry and I were headed back to the police station, she was eager to join us there, but I suggested that some other activity—virtually any other activity—would prove to be a more interesting and worthwhile way to spend her afternoon.

"Well, I can always spend some more time in the greenhouse. Plus, Roxanne did say something about shopping at some place called Neal's Yard," Megan said. She tried to sound like this option was a poor second to spending the afternoon in a dreary police station, but she wasn't quite pulling it off, so I tossed her the life preserver she needed.

"I think I remember McHugh saying that was a great place," I lied. "Why don't you go check it out, and we can both go back there later if you think I'd like it."

This plan was agreeable to her, so we decided to reconnect at dinner, with the hopes of getting our romantic London getaway at least partly back on track.

"What did I say was a great place?" McHugh asked as I pocketed my phone.

"Neal's Yard, but I made that up so Megan wouldn't feel obligated to spend her afternoon waiting with us during Harry's interview," I explained. We had made our way down the vertiginous spiral staircase and headed out The Magic Circle's front door.

"Oh, but she'll love Neal's Yard," McHugh said as we hit the street. "If she likes tea, there's a shop just down from Neal's Yard which I can recommend to her without hesitation. They offer a stunning selection of teas, and not just from India and the West Indies and China but from locales where you'd never expect to find tea at all, let alone outstanding tea, but believe me..."

He was still telling me about the shop and its varieties of tea long after we'd flagged down a taxi and began our short ride to the police station.

* * *

Somehow Laurence Baxter had gotten wind of Harry's impromptu police interview and had arranged for his solicitor, Simon Wexler-Smith, to be waiting for us when we arrived. The large man was once again decked out nattily in a three-piece pinstripe suit. With his white walrus mustache, drooping eyes, and dense, silvery eyebrows, he looked the perfect cliché of a British attorney of a certain age.

Harry waved off the need for an attorney to accompany him into the interview, clearly annoyed at the idea of needing any assistance. However, a few quiet but determined words from McHugh seemed to turn the tide, and a few minutes later Harry and Wexler-Smith started to make their way down a long hall. At the far end of the corridor, Harry turned and gave me a short, upbeat wave before he was swallowed into a distant conference room.

McHugh and I settled ourselves into the lobby's hard plastic chairs. I checked my watch, forgot what it read, and immediately had to check it again. That was as good an indication of my current mental state as any. Two murders and Harry as a key suspect was not what I had signed on for when I offered to accompany my uncle to London. I had been hoping for a nice week abroad with my girlfriend, and yet once again, I found myself within the bowels of a police station.

McHugh smiled over at me. "Don't get too concerned about the timing, my boy. Might take ten minutes, might take two hours," he said. "And we can't draw conclusions from either end of that spectrum. There are wheels within wheels. New evidence, old evidence, it all plays a role."

"New evidence?" I said, perking up at the notion. "Have you heard anything?"

"I've heard many, many things, barely a fraction of it useful," he said, folding the newspaper he had started to read. He looked up at the ceiling thoughtfully. "They've produced a more thorough forensics report on the unique chair that so effectively placed a knife in the back of your Mr. Korhonen."

"What did they learn?"

"They learned how little they actually know, sad to say," he said. "They believe the device may have been oiled recently, but they also pointed out it could actually have been years. Not too helpful, that."

"They can't tell something as simple as a recent oiling?" It seemed like a pretty straightforward deduction to me, but I realized I had no idea how you would actually determine such a thing.

"Back in the day," McHugh said slowly, "I had occasion to escort a prisoner of some reputation to a dental appointment, of all things. Not sure why, but I pulled the short straw, and there I was, cooling my heels while a bright young hygienist cleaned the devil's teeth. While in the course of her exam, she asked the fellow —as I gather she inquired of all her patients—just how long it had been since he had last given his teeth a thorough flossing."

McHugh, who had been gazing across the room at nothing in particular while recounting this, turned to me.

"He was a bit of a smart aleck, this one, and so he turned the question back on her. 'How long do *you* think it's been, luv?'" McHugh shook his head. "Poor thing, bad enough she has to clean the teeth of this hooligan, now she has to play Ask Me Another? She hemmed and hawed, finally saying she thought it might have been six months, perhaps at most a year. The fellow looked as ecstatic as a man serving a long and well-deserved sentence can look. He said, 'Wrong, ducky. It's been twenty-seven years, if it's been a day.'"

McHugh punctuated this last sentence with a quick slap of his folded newspaper against his knee, shaking his head at the memory, before opening the paper and returning to his reading. I waited a few moments, not sure if I had missed a key element of the story or perhaps suffered a quick bout of short-term amnesia.

"So, you were saying about the forensics and the chair and then...flossing?" I offered tentatively.

McHugh snapped back from his reading, once again folding the newspaper. "Yes, of course, the chair," he said quickly. "The point is, even the experts never really know about these things. That chair could have been sitting patiently for years and years, like a rusty mousetrap just waiting for the right person to sit on it at the wrong time.

"The other point of interest," he said, turning toward me, "was what they discovered while going through Borys' effects. You know the zippered case he carried on his person, the one with his special blend of tea?"

"I do," I said, remembering how Angus Bishop had chided him about it and Borys' explanation that he needed to safeguard his tea because other magicians keep pinching from his stash while he was on stage. "I saw him take a teabag out of it the night he died. He offered me one as well."

"And a good thing you didn't accept the offer," McHugh said with a grim smile. "Yes, well as it turns out, he had eleven teabags in the pouch when his body was found. The lab ran tests, and five of those teabags tested positive for poison."

I considered the implications of this. "So, it wasn't the water that was poisoned, it was the teabag."

"Apparently."

"And whoever put the poisoned teabags into his pouch could have made the switch at any time. It wasn't necessarily someone at Laurence Baxter's house that night."

"Just so," McHugh said. "It was a time-released murder, a trap set to go off at some undetermined but deadly point. So I'm hoping this new development will help to take some of the—I believe the word is *heat*—off of our Harry."

"That would be nice," I agreed. "Regardless, though, don't you think the deaths of two magicians in just three days of each other is sort of an odd coincidence?"

McHugh shrugged. "I believe it was G.K. Chesterton who called coincidences 'spiritual puns.' That sounds suitably intellectual, although if pressed, I would have to confess I don't entirely understand what he meant. Of course, he also said 'The reason angels can fly is they take themselves lightly,' which may be one of my favorite quotes of all time."

Since he appeared to be in a relatively chatty mood, I put a question to him I had been pondering since tracking him down the previous Sunday night as he led his popular Jack the Ripper walk.

"How was it you and Harry met?" I said. "I mean, you've been friends for certainly as long as I can remember."

"Nearly as long as I can remember as well," he said, setting his newspaper on the empty chair beside him. "It was years ago, of course. I was on the force and had just been promoted to Detective Inspector in the homicide division, a proud moment indeed. And one of the first cases I was assigned to was the death of Harry's friend, Archie Banks."

"I thought it was a suicide," I said, not understanding why this would involve the police, let alone someone from homicide.

"Anything outside of natural causes triggers a police investigation," McHugh explained. "Strictly routine in this case, as there was a detailed suicide note and no evidence of any possible cause of death but suicide. And since the note went into some detail about Mr. Banks's dissatisfaction with his fellow magicians, Harry was one of the chaps I had to speak to."

"So you interviewed all these guys when they were younger?" I found the idea fascinating, trying to picture this venerable group as young up-and-comers.

"I did indeed," McHugh said with a smile. "Characters one and all, Harry being one of the most remarkable. Our thirty-minute interview turned into dinner and then an evening-long chat."

"What about?"

"Well, he was fascinated with true crime at the time," McHugh said.

"He still is," I said, thinking of the hours Harry had spent in deep conversation with my ex-wife, an assistant district attorney, about her current and past cases. He was so ardent in his fascination, she often chided me for not being as interested in her day-to-day work as my uncle. I was never sure if she was kidding or not, which was an ongoing issue, on many levels, in our short but combustible union.

"And I've harbored a life-long fascination with magic and magicians," McHugh continued. "Just loved it, always have, dating back to listening to The Piddingtons on BBC." He looked to me, and my quick head shake told him I was in the dark on that one.

"They were a married couple who performed a mentalism act on the radio," he explained. "Big stuff at the time, quite sensational. An amazing couple—the things they got away with. Stunning. It's amazing the tricks you can pull as a double act. Anyway, I found what Harry did to be enthralling, and he felt the same way about police work, and we quickly became fast friends."

"And where does Jack the Ripper come into all this?"

McHugh laughed. "As with most significant occurrences in one's life: unplanned and from out of nowhere. The short version is I was asked to speak on police procedures at a Jack the Ripper conference. I read some books before the presentation, just to have a basic understanding of the case. And then, before I realized it, I found myself digging through files at Scotland Yard and working out my own perspective on all the clues, real and imagined. There is some fine work being done in that field by exceptionally bright people. But there is also considerable chaff mixed in with the high-end wheat. So I eventually wrote my own book to set the record straight, as it were. And I've traveled around the world with it ever since. Of course, I did more of that after Cora died, as she didn't care for traveling. More of a homebody was Cora."

He grew silent for a moment, and I successfully resisted the urge to fill the silence. He then sighed and looked over at me with a sad smile.

"That was when I started the walking tour, which I did much more frequently back then, sometimes five nights a week. I guess it's safe to say I found immersing myself into the world of Victorian London more comfortable than my present-day reality."

I nodded slowly. "And now, with these murders, we have our own Jack the Ripper to deal with."

McHugh shook his head and held up a hand. "No, I don't think so. I believe all of Jack's victims were truly random—crimes of opportunity, with the poor unfortunates in the wrong place at the wrong time." He glanced down the hall, and I followed his gaze. Harry and Wexler-Smith were slowly making their way toward us.

McHugh turned to me and finished his thought. "These murders, if they are the work of a single person, are just as calculated and brutal, but they are also far more focused and, I think, actually quite personal."

With that, he got up and moved toward Harry and the solicitor. I considered what he had said about the personal nature of the murders and wondered if that might be the key clue to crack open the whole affair. Then I got up and followed him, anxious to hear how the police interview had gone.

* * *

"Well, that was a complete waste of my time and theirs," Harry said, not for the first time in the past few minutes. We had said our goodbyes to McHugh at the police station and, with Harry acting as navigator, we were deep within the London subway system on our way back to Laurence Baxter's house in Hampstead Heath.

"So you said," I responded. "McHugh said it was strictly routine."

"Strictly nonsensical, if you ask me," he said with shake of his head. "The same five questions as the last interview, just reworded and in a different order. This is us," he added as he got up and headed toward the doors of the subway car.

The train was just pulling into Charing Cross station, where—if I was understanding the quick itinerary Harry had spouted as we walked into the tube station—we would switch to the Northern Line. I couldn't quite get the geography right in my head, but Harry did it with ease. He moved smoothly from line to line and always knew which train we were looking for and which one not to step into. He had already kept me from walking into two different express trains in the few days we had been here. Since then, he'd kept a close eye on me as we bustled our way through the busy stations.

"Charing Cross," he said suddenly, as if surprised by where the train had landed us. "We're so close it would be silly not to take a quick detour and drop in on Davenport's."

Davenport's was a famed London magic store, much older than our own magic store in Minneapolis, which was a relatively new kid on the block in comparison. Although I didn't know the particulars, my understanding was Davenport's had been around since the Victorian era. As with everything else in London, Harry seemed to know exactly where it was, and so I did my best to keep up with him as he zigged and zagged his way through the underground maze that was Charing Cross station.

"Word on the street is they have a set of the linking rings used by Ching Ling Foo in the early 1900s. I've always wanted to take a peek at them." Talking about the magic props clearly excited Harry because the more he talked, the faster he walked.

"Is it wrong of me to say I've always found the Linking Rings, I don't know…" I said, looking for the right word. "Sort of boring?"

This comment produced a raised eyebrow from Harry but did nothing to break his stride.

"Wrong to say it?" he repeated as we turned another corner. Charing Cross station seemed to be structured like an octopus, with arms heading out in several directions. "No, not wrong. You just have never seen it done right, apparently. When we get home, I'll show you a video of Jay Marshall, simply a classic version. Tina Lenert has a lovely new take on the illusion. And Mike Caveny turned the whole routine on its head by using clothes hangers." He looked over at me and smiled, happy to be back in mentor mode. "Eli, like a lot of supposedly 'boring' magic tricks, if you can get it into the hands of the right people, it becomes new and amazing and a thing of beauty."

We turned one more corner, and Harry let out a small yelp of victory.

"There it is, just where I left it," Harry said with a laugh. We passed several other small establishments in this bizarre, nearly deserted underground shopping mall and then pushed open the glass door to Davenport's magic store.

As we stepped inside I realized that although I had spent the better part of my life in a magic store, I had actually been in remarkably few *other* magic stores. Consequently, the feeling as I entered Davenport's was an odd sense of déjà vu, where everything felt simultaneously familiar and completely foreign. It was like we had been transported into an alternate universe in which all the elements of our store had been shaken up and reassembled by a stranger. The store was smaller than our shop, but they had many of the same tricks, props, and posters we did. However, enough of the elements were different to make the overall effect a bit mind-boggling.

Harry, of course, felt none of this and had immediately approached a clerk behind the counter.

"I understand you have a set of linking rings used by Ching Ling Foo," Harry said. "Since we were in the neighborhood, I thought I would stop by and see if it was possible to take a look at them."

This seemed to be news to the clerk, who was obscured from my view by Harry. After rephrasing his original question several times, it finally became clear the answer would be found with a higher authority, and so the manager was summoned. While this transpired, I busied myself looking at the products in the glass cases, more curious about how the merchandise had been laid out for presentation rather than what they were selling.

For years, Harry and I had been waging a silent war in our shop. The skirmishes all involved the proper method for displaying magic tricks. Harry preferred, in my opinion, to jam the cases so full of products it became a jumbled mess. My preference was a more spare presentational style, which I felt helped to feature each illusion and make it stand out. In Harry's mind, this made it look like we didn't have any products to sell, and so he would quickly restock the display as soon as my back was turned. It was an ongoing and ultimately unwinnable battle, with both sides convinced they were fighting on the side of the angels.

Soon the manager arrived, recognized Harry immediately, and quickly ushered him into the back room for a special viewing of the century-old metal ring set. As I moved my inspection from one display case to the next, I glanced up and realized I knew the clerk behind the counter. He saw me at the same time, and we both studied each other, briefly puzzled as to how we knew one another.

"You're Eli Marks, I met you the other night at The Magic Circle," he finally said before I came to the exact same, albeit tardy, conclusion.

"That's right. And you are...Lee," I said, taking a stab in the dark. I mentally acknowledged the irony of this phrase, as he had been the stagehand who had moved the deadly chair to center stage. But my first memory of him had been his dazzling display with cards.

"Liam," he corrected. "Liam Sutherland."

"Yes, you were doing the...the thing with the cards," I finally said, not sure how to describe the acrobatics he had put the deck through.

"Cardistry," he said.

"Excuse me?"

"Cardistry," he repeated. "I'm a cardist."

"A cardist?"

"I specialize in card flourishes," he explained. He picked up a deck of cards from the counter and quickly demonstrated a series of fans and one-handed cuts, essentially juggling the cards in the air in front of me. "You've seen this sort of thing before, right?"

"I have, I just didn't know it had a name beyond calling it card flourishing," I said, getting a little hypnotized as the cards danced in front of my eyes.

"Oh, it's the next big thing, mate," he said as he concluded what I had to assume was a presentation which had taken him months, or maybe even years, to master.

"Is there a lot of call for that here?" I asked, looking around the shop at all the traditional magic illusions on display.

"Sadly, not so much," he admitted as he slid the deck of cards back into its box. "I spend my days demonstrating Svengali decks and self-working Three Card Monte routines to the tourist trade and geeky kids."

"You don't get to demonstrate anything other than cards?" I asked, looking at all the fun options around the room. He shook his head, rolling his eyes at the other effects.

"I'm a card man," he said with finality that seemed premature,

133

as he probably wasn't yet even eighteen. "I don't bother with that other twaddle."

"Okay, card man," I said, glancing at the door to the backroom and realizing it was likely Harry would not return for a while yet. Since I was in a rare competitive situation, I figured I should use the time constructively and pick up whatever selling tips I could. "What's your favorite card trick to demonstrate?"

"Oh, that's easy," he said, reaching into the display case for a deck of cards. "Hands down, this is my favorite. It's a killer, a mind-blower."

"Will it fool me badly?" I added, using a favorite phrase among magicians, who are never merely fooled but only "fooled badly." He nodded in rabid agreement as he pulled the deck from its pack.

"Let me ask you this, mate," he said, and I recognized the practiced tone and cadence of the opening phrases of well-worn patter. "I've always believed there is a real connection between cards and dogs.

"For example," he continued, looking up at me and clearly not recognizing the growing look of dismay on my face, "Dogs travel in packs and so do cards. Dogs do tricks and so do cards. And there are those who say dogs pick their owners, and I believe the same is true of cards. So, go ahead, pick a card, whichever card you'd like."

He had spread the deck, face up, toward me, gesturing that I could pick from any of the visible cards for my selection. I gamely reached out and pulled a card from the spread.

Liam then proceeded to perform my Ambitious Dog routine, virtually word-for-word the way I had done it for years—long before I demonstrated it to Jake North at our fifteenth high-school reunion. He showed me how I had picked the only blue card in a red-backed deck and then walked me through the sequence where the magician helps the spectator attempt to get the card to change back to its original color. When that didn't work, he revealed that —because my card was the leader of the pack—the entire deck had instead changed color.

From there, he took me through each of the other phases in my routine, finally concluding with the card doing its final trick—like a dog, this card could roll over—revealing it was now the only reversed card in the deck. He looked up at me, waiting for the enthusiastic response he was sure was coming.

"That's...that's, um, great," I said as I tried to come up with the right words. "Did you see that on TV the other night?" I continued, trying to take all the stress out of my voice. I don't think I succeeded. "I mean, you saw it on TV, right?"

Liam shook his head, puzzled either by my stammering questions or my complete lack of amazement at what was clearly a stunning card trick.

"No, never saw it on the telly," he said, trying to read my expression—which I guessed was an odd mix of rapidly changing emotions. "Bloke taught it at a magic lecture a couple weeks back. Brilliant trick, dead simple to do, been getting great reactions here in the store."

"I see, I see," I said, trying for casual nonchalance in my efforts to extract information out of the kid. "So someone taught it at a lecture. Who did he attribute the trick to, if you remember?" I tried to make this last question sound off-hand, but I don't think Liam was paying particularly close attention to my tone.

"He didn't credit anyone. The impression I got was it was his own trick. Really a nice piece of work. Let me see, I have his lecture notes here somewhere," Liam said as he turned and opened one of the drawers in the large cabinet behind him. "He demonstrated it and sold it and the gimmick at the end of the lecture. You know how they do."

I nodded, because I did know that. I knew lecturing magicians often sold the tricks they demonstrated, along with the gaffs and gimmicks that made the tricks work.

"So he sold the trick and the gimmick," I repeated. "At this lecture. This trick he created."

"I have to tell you, he was just a so-so magician, but when I saw this trick, I knew I had to have it. We all did," he added as he turned around. He was sorting through a handful of brochures and pamphlets. "Oh, here it is!"

135

He pulled one pamphlet out of the stack and tossed it in front of me. A smiling magician was pictured on the front. At the top of the cover were the words "Lecture Notes." Under the photo was the name of this so-so magician who was selling my trick as his own.

The name was Jake North.

CHAPTER 13

"Breathe."

    "I am breathing."

"Honey, I think you *think* you're breathing, but to me it looks like you're hyperventilating."

Megan and I were in the midst of a whispered debate about my alleged inhalation and exhalation skills standing behind the last row of seats in The Magic Circle's small theater. A chaotic rehearsal was taking place on stage, with De Vries overseeing the final touches on the Davis De Vries Catherine Wheel before one lucky magician got to give the trick a spin, as it were.

That lucky magician was Jake North, and I'd made a point of avoiding him so far. I needed to maintain some distance, as I was unsure what might come out of my mouth when we finally came face-to-face. Sensing my volatile emotional state, Megan had suggested she come along with me to the rehearsal to provide moral support. I thanked her but reminded her she would, during the course of such a rehearsal, likely see how the trick worked, which was something she always hated to discover.

"Don't worry," she cheerfully replied. "Knowing me, I'll forget the whole thing the next day."

I had to admit this was a fair assessment of her retention abilities, at least as it related to magical secrets. And I had to admit I

137

was pleased to have her by my side during these first few moments when I might be encountering Jake. She had been supportive since the moment I had told her about Jake's latest betrayal.

"Why would he bother doing a lecture?" Megan had asked after I recounted my experience at Davenport's Magic Shop.

That thought had not, until that moment, occurred to me. Leave it to Megan to, once again, find the most pertinent question inside a thorny situation.

"He certainly doesn't need the money," she continued as she mused on the topic.

"No, he certainly doesn't," I agreed.

"Maybe he does it to make himself feel like a big-shot magician," she suggested. "I mean, back at home, when you sponsor lectures at the magic store, it's usually with only the best magicians out there, right?"

"That's right," I said, mentally running down a list of some of the amazing performers who had graced our small back room, offering precious secrets to a handful of local magicians gathered around in folding chairs.

"So maybe Jake figures if he does a lecture, he must be a big-shot magician," she concluded, and I found no reason to argue with her logic.

"Tell me again about the karmic wheel," I asked.

"It always turns," she said warmly, and I immediately felt better, if only a little.

After learning about the depth of Jake's deceit at Davenport's magic shop, I opted to keep the information close to my chest, at least for the time being. I recognized De Vries was counting on making a splash with his new illusion, and I figured I could put off my inevitable confrontation with Jake until after the big premiere on Saturday night. So, for the time being, Megan and I stood in the back of the house and observed the chaos on stage.

"People, we need to make some progress here," De Vries said to everyone and no one in particular. "What's preventing us from running this, top to bottom? What's the hold up people?" He

138

looked at the two stage hands who had finished positioning the large wheel, the two female assistants who were practicing their handiwork with a large silk, and then at Jake North, who was leaning against a pillar and checking his phone. Jake glanced up and saw the look on De Vries' face.

"What's the hold up, people?" Jake repeated, pocketing his phone and stepping to the center of the stage. His semi-celebrity status seemed to carry more authority than anything De Vries was doing, and everyone snapped to immediate attention. "Are we ready to try this sucker?"

This was followed by general sounds of assent, and moments later, music began to blast out of the speakers as lights shifted on stage and everyone took his or her place. The volume of the music then jumped up several notches.

"Why does it have to be so loud?" Megan practically yelled in my ear.

"In magic, music is either loud to help build energy or to cover a sound that might give away how the trick works," I explained. "Or more often than not, both."

Unable to hear me, Megan just shrugged, and I nodded that I, too, thought the music was a tad too loud. I turned back to the stage, to see that Jake had already positioned himself on the wheel and the two female assistants were in the midst of securing him to the structure. I felt a presence to my right and turned to see Angelika had taken a position next to me to observe the rehearsal. She had a scowl on her face, which may have been directed at the large-scale illusion or at the two scantily clad women currently tying a willing magician to it.

She turned to me and said something I couldn't quite decipher. "What?"

She must have taken my one-word response as a suitable answer, for she continued on with what appeared to be—without being able to actually hear it—a short but passionate diatribe.

I didn't make out most of it, but I did catch "bloody box jumpers" before she turned and headed toward the theater's rear doors, clearly disgusted by the traditional gender stereotypes being exhibited on stage. She would have made a solid, dramatic exit if someone hadn't stepped into the theater just as she was attempting to step out. It was Miss Hess, who defiantly did not step aside, forcing the younger woman to snake around her in order to get through the doorway. Once again, I couldn't hear what Angelika had to say, but the tone of her short exchange with Miss Hess came through loud and clear via body language and harsh facial expressions.

Miss Hess turned and glared at her and then, perhaps because the object of her scorn was no longer visible, she turned her glare on me. I quickly returned my attention to the stage. A few moments later, when I felt it was safe to sneak a look back at the doorway, I was relieved to discover the scary old woman was no longer standing in the entryway. A cold finger gave my shoulder a hard stab, and I turned to see she was now standing directly behind me. Whatever sound of surprise I made was probably drowned out by the earsplitting music; however, I suspect it was so high that only dogs would have heard it anyway.

"Have you seen Herr Baxter?" she asked. Surprisingly, her voice cut right through the cacophony and I had no trouble under-standing her. Puzzled by the physics of that, I shook my head dumbly.

"I saw him earlier, backstage," I shouted. "But not lately."

"His presence is requested in the Executive Director's office," she said, her voice again cutting directly through the music.

I shrugged impotently, and she gave me a look that suggested, at least to my mind, she had never before encountered a more incompetent fool. She then turned and moved slowly out the door. If anyone was ever to deserve the title of living ghost, it was Miss Hess. I waited a moment for my gooseflesh to subside and then once again returned my attention to the rehearsal.

The music had reached a fever pitch and so had the spinning of the Catherine Wheel, sparks flying out of the ends of its spokes. The two box jumpers each climbed on a small step next to the device and, in shaky unison, held up a large, eight-foot-square opaque silk with as much drama and panache as they could muster for this first rehearsal. Jake, who was just a blur now on the spinning wheel, was obscured behind the thin silk, disappearing from our view.

Although I only vaguely understood the principles of the trick, I knew this was when all the action was happening behind the over-sized silk. Somehow, Jake was getting off the wheel, while from the audience's perspective, it still continued to revolve and spark at a furious rate. The glitzy assistants would soon drop the silk, revealing an empty, spinning disc. And then, moments later, Jake would appear triumphant somewhere else in the theater. I glanced around, curious to see what location they had chosen for this surprise manifestation.

The spot for Jake's return turned out to be a surprise to everyone, not the least of whom were the two young ladies holding up the silk. One moment it was parallel to the Catherine Wheel and the next it was ripped from their hands as Jake stumbled face forward, collapsing with a hard thud upon the stage.

He lay there motionless, the wheel and its flashes of flames spinning crazily behind him as the two assistants stared down in shock at the prone figure sprawled in front of them. Both stagehands rushed toward the body, then stepped back several feet from the crumpled form, clearly unsure of what their responsibilities were in this new situation.

Any fear that he was the latest magician to come to an untimely end was quickly abated, as Jake painfully pushed himself up off the floor onto his elbows, confirming to one and all he was still alive.

And then, to drive his point home even further, he proceeded to vomit all over the stage. Repeatedly. With great volume and gusto. As performances go, it was one for the record books.

Megan, always squeamish about this sort of thing, turned to me as the music and the flaming wheel came to a screeching halt. People began to run to his aid, then stepped back, not sure he had finished his impromptu show stopper.

"Remember what I said about the karmic wheel?" she said.

"I do."

She looked down at the stage and the writhing, sickening and sick mess which was Jake North.

"It always turns," she said with a smile the Cheshire Cat would have been proud to call his own.

* * *

Rehearsal was suspended while the stage and Jake were cleaned up. At the same time, a search went out for another eight-foot silk, the current one being considered an utter loss.

News of the fiasco traveled quickly and soon two of the Magnificent Magi who were hanging out at The Magic Circle—Roy Templeton and Uncle Harry—joined Megan and me in the back of the theater to offer their respective two cents on the recent turn of events. We all looked down the aisle at Davis De Vries, who paced in front of the stage, running and rerunning a hand through his crisp, white head of hair.

"Poor man can't catch a break," Harry muttered.

"This will definitely hurt sales," Roy said in a matching somber tone. "I mean, who wants to buy an illusion that requires the front two rows to wear rain ponchos? Although," he added, brightening, "it worked for that comedian Gallagher back in the '80s."

"He was sledgehammering watermelons," Harry said.

Roy nodded. "Yes, I suppose that's an easier sell than tossing cookies like Linda Blair."

Megan moaned at the image as Roy, now on a roll, stepped forward and spun around, facing the small group. He rubbed his hands together excitedly.

"I've got the solution," he said. "All he has to do is rebrand it. Instead of the Catherine Wheel, he simply needs to call it The Wheel of Nausea. Wait, strike that," he said as another idea occurred to him. "It would be the Davis De Vries Wheel of Nausea. It is trademarked, after all."

We all said nothing, for experience had taught us there was no stopping Roy once he got going. And the more you tried to stop him, the worse it got. Silence was our only weapon, and we used it.

"Or The Davis De Vries Vomitorium," he continued. "That one has a classical ring to it with some nice alliteration. Or the Puke-a-Nator. The Tilt-a-Hurl." Harry held up a hand and pushed past him, silencing Roy if only for a few moments. Harry extended his hand to De Vries, who was just coming up the aisle.

"Doctor, how are you holding up?" Harry asked.

De Vries shook his head. "Doctor, I am at my wit's end," he said quietly. "I know the damn thing will work, and it will be brilliant, but roadblocks keep popping up out of nowhere."

"That last one looked more like road kill," Roy said. We all suppressed anything resembling a chuckle, so Roy quickly switched to a more somber attitude. "Sorry, Doctor," he said, patting De Vries' back. "Rough business, I know."

De Vries sighed and then straightened up, squaring his shoulders and holding his head up high. "I guess the only thing to do is to talk to Baxter about canceling the premier. If what happened this afternoon were to happen in front of a paying audience, can you imagine what those jokesters down there," he said, gesturing to the meeting room on the main floor, "can you imagine what names they would be calling the Catherine Wheel?"

"Everyone is sympathetic to what you're going through," Harry said, pointedly looking at Roy Templeton, who had suddenly adopted an expression of great contrition. "And it's not like you to give up. You've run into problems with new illusions before, and you've always powered through them."

"I was younger then," De Vries said.

"Nonsense," Harry said, putting his arm around his old friend's shoulder. "Who was it who said, 'The best idea is often the next idea?'"

"Dai Vernon?" Roy said quickly. "Charlie Miller? No, it was Alex Elmsley. Or maybe Ganson."

"It was you," Harry said emphatically to De Vries, but even he couldn't help crack a smile at the antics of the old jokester. And then Harry's smile helped coax a smile out of De Vries, and soon the old friends were laughing about the situation and offering ways to put a positive spin on it.

"Look pal, just because that Hollywood hack has a sensitive tum-tum is no reason to put a fork in the Catherine Wheel," Roy said, giving De Vries a playful punch on the arm. "It's frickin' brilliant, and the world needs to see it! You can't give up after one untimely barf."

"You and I both know this city is teeming with magicians who would give their eye teeth for a chance to be the first to publicly perform a Davis De Vries illusion," Harry said. "You don't need a, quote, unquote, 'big name' on your device," he added, gesturing toward the gleaming disc on stage.

"That's right, because there already is a big name on the wheel," Roy said, picking up Harry's pep-talk tone. "And that big name is Davis De Vries. Cue the orchestra!"

Roy held up De Vries' arms and waved them from side to side while making the sound of a cheering crowd. To help out, I offered some audio back-up, producing a quick series of whistles and cheers. Our general boisterousness seemed to be pulling De Vries out of his funk. Harry and Megan couldn't help be drawn into the spirited mix, adding their own laughter and applause.

Then, one by one, they each grew quiet. I was the last to realize something was up by the looks on everyone else's faces. I turned to where they were looking, and my last shout was cut off in mid yelp.

Laurence Baxter was standing just inside the theater's main entry, Gareth MacKenzie at his side. Behind them I recognized Detective Inspector Matthews and two other similarly dressed and serious men.

De Vries lowered his arms and straightened his suit coat, running a quick hand through his unruffled hair. The rest of us stood frozen, waiting for the announcement Baxter was clearly poised to make. Megan took my hand and squeezed it, and I wrapped my other hand around hers.

"I'm sorry to report," Baxter said, his voice not coming out as strongly as he thought it would, "there is more bad news, I'm afraid." He turned to Detective Inspector Matthews and then back to us.

"There's been another death," he finally said, although by that point the pronouncement was hardly a surprise. "And there is a thought I may, in some way, be involved. I am leaving with these fine folks, for some questioning. Sorry to miss the rest of the rehearsal."

With that Baxter turned and was escorted out of the theater by the police.

* * *

"Baxter a murderer? Impossible!" Davis De Vries spat out the words. "You might as well say Harry is a murderer."

Harry smiled wryly. "Actually, the police hold that same suspicion," he replied quietly. "Makes me wonder why they took Baxter this time and not me."

Although I didn't say it out loud, I had wondered that same thought. I was not proud of the relief I was taking now that Baxter was apparently the focus of the investigation, if only because it took some of the interest off of my uncle.

The rehearsal had been abandoned, at least for the time being, and there appeared to be no immediate answers available on who had been killed or why Baxter had been taken in for questioning. So our small group made its way down the block and around the corner to Shah Tandori, an Indian restaurant much beloved by members of The Magic Circle. We were early for lunch and appeared to have the restaurant to ourselves. At the sound of the door opening, the waiter peered out at us from the kitchen, surprised to see customers arriving so soon.

Moments after we were seated, Roy Templeton, who had been pacing in front of the restaurant, rejoined us, holding up his cell phone triumphantly.

"Got ahold of Roxanne," he said, relief evident in his voice. "She's alive and well out at Baxter's Folly. She said she'd do a quick head count to see who may be missing out there on the Heath."

At that moment I realized how nervous he must have been, given the open-ended nature of Baxter's pronouncement. I had not gone down the same mental path about my own loved ones, as both had been with me all morning. And, for that matter, both were seated on either side of me—Megan looking through the large menu and Harry checking a text on his phone.

"McHugh is either on his way or he is here," he said to the group, and as if the universe had set out to prove him right, McHugh chose that moment to walk through the front door. As the only people in the restaurant, we were easy to spot. He moved toward us, and Harry pulled a chair over from a nearby table to add him to our party. All conversation at the table stopped as he settled in. Harry asked the key question we all had.

"So who was murdered?"

McHugh started to say something but stopped as the waiter approached the table and put a glass of water in front of him. When asked if he wanted anything else to drink, McHugh ordered tea and then turned his attention back to us.

"I just got off the phone with a friend of mine at the Yard," he said, stopping for a moment to take a sip of water. Somehow this seemed to inspire Davis De Vries and Roy Templeton to also take a quick drink from their own glasses—ice tea for De Vries and a dark ale for Roy.

"I'm sorry to report Hector Hechizo was found dead this morning in a hotel about three kilometers from here," McHugh continued.

McHugh's statement produced a series of overlapping questions from the group—How was he killed? When was he killed? Why is Baxter a suspect?—and he waited patiently until all of our questions had been expressed.

"The method of the killing suggests a perpetrator with a more than rudimentary understanding of medical procedures," he said slowly. "It appears Mr. Hechizo was killed via what I can only term as something akin to blood-letting. That is, a series of—in this case, hundreds—of small cuts, covering the entirety of the victim's body."

"Like being nibbled to death by ducks," Roy said quietly, and McHugh nodded at the analogy.

"That's not far off. It was the sheer number of cuts which resulted in enough blood loss to cause death. And what's most unsettling about the procedure," he added grimly, "is there is every indication the victim was conscious and aware the entire time."

"How is that even possible?" De Vries said. "Was he bound and gagged?"

McHugh shook his head. "The preliminary report suggests a paralytic drug of some kind was used. Such a drug would, essentially, freeze all the muscles in the body, allowing the victim to be awake throughout the entire ordeal, regardless of how long it might have taken. And the police believe it took a good long while indeed."

"But," De Vries said, leaning forward. "The lungs, the heart, breathing—"

"Exactly," McHugh said. "For the patient to survive while under the effects of such a drug, he would have to intubated with a breathing tube or device of some kind."

"Well, I can see how that would suggest someone with a medical background," De Vries said. "But Baxter hasn't practiced in over thirty years."

"Forty if it's a day," Roy added. "He gave up medicine virtually right after he got out of school."

"Be that as it may," McHugh said as the waiter set a cup of tea in front of him, "it is the shiny object which currently has the attention of the force and until something shinier comes along..." He took a long sip of tea.

"Hundreds of little cuts," Harry repeated almost to himself. McHugh looked over at him.

"Well, that's the thing, Harry," he said, setting the cup back in its saucer. "That was how it was first described to me. But the second time my contact said it, he referred to it differently. He said, and I quote, 'It must have been a thousand cuts.'"

This phrasing clearly brought Harry up short. He blinked at

McHugh, started to say something, stopped, and then started again. "That was the phrase, 'a thousand cuts?'"

"It was indeed. Taken on its own, that's a unique expression. But when you put it into context with the other two murders..."

He let his words hang in the air as Harry processed what he was hearing.

"A stabbing. Then poison," McHugh continued slowly.

"Are you thinking what I'm thinking?" Harry finally said.

"Often," McHugh replied and then turned to the group. "Harry and I have the amusing habit of occasionally landing on the exact same thought at the exact same moment. And, unless I miss my guess, we have done that again. Am I right?"

Harry nodded slowly, and the two men considered this silently for what felt like a long time. Finally, I couldn't take it anymore.

"So what the heck are you two are thinking?" I said, making no effort to temper my exasperation.

Harry looked over at me and then at the group. He was clearly choosing his words with great care.

"We're thinking the evidence suggests the possibility our murderer might be none other than Archie Banks."

This produced a shocked reaction from everyone around the table. I mean, actual gasps, jaws dropping, the whole nine yards.

"But Archie died over thirty years ago," Davis De Vries finally said.

"Yes," McHugh said, looking over at Harry, who nodded in agreement. "That is presently the one sticking point in our theory."

CHAPTER 14

As tantalizing as this bizarre statement was, both Harry and McHugh declined to elaborate further until, as McHugh explained obliquely, "We do a quick check of the paperwork."

Instead, Harry insisted that, since we were already seated in a fine Indian restaurant, it would be borderline criminal not to partake in some fine Indian food. This argument was met with annoyed grumbles, but once the food began to arrive, the primary sounds from the table were simple, satisfied sighs of contentment. Once we were all sated, McHugh sat back, wiped his face with the cloth napkin, and suggested we all accompany him to his flat for some coffee, tea, and much-needed explanations.

"All will be elucidated," he promised.

Megan, De Vries, and I were all for it, but Roy Templeton opted out of the plan almost immediately.

"Thanks for the invite, I'm as intrigued as the rest of you," he said to the group as we assembled in front of the restaurant. "But I left Roxanne alone out there at Baxter's Foll—" He caught himself before completing his traditional dig at Laurence Baxter's estate and, in deference to his host's current situation, took a decidedly kinder tone in his remarks. "She's alone out there at Larry's, and I think she'd like some company. When I called and told her news about Hector, it hit her hard. To be honest, it's still settling in on

149

me. Let me know what comes of this whole Archie Banks thing. And be sure to give me a call if you find Elvis as well."

With that final attempt at humor, he flagged a passing cab and was gone. I put out a hand to signal another taxi for our group, but McHugh waved it away.

"We're two minutes from Euston station, and it's a six minute tube ride to my flat. Trust me, in today's traffic, we'll be better off on the train."

With that he led us to the nearby station, and less than ten minutes later we were exiting a different station, one which deposited us into a charming London neighborhood known as Camden Town.

Upon seeing the sign announcing the station, I realized my only other experience with Camden Town had been that it was my sole spoken line in a high-school production of *A Christmas Carol*. Due to the large number of characters in the show, a wide net had been cast for supporting players, a net which eventually captured me and a handful of other non-theater geeks. My one line came near the climax of the performance, when—as The Poulterer—I was dragged on stage to confront a recently transformed Ebenezer Scrooge, who instructed me to "Take this bird to Bob Cratchit: 15 Bagshot Row, Camden Town!"

At that point, I would utter my one line ("Camden Town?"), which would then propel Scrooge into a longer spiel about how the bird was too large and how I needed a cab and so forth. Even at the time, it seemed like a lot of effort for very little payoff. I had to arrive at the theater an hour before the show, sit around in an itchy wool costume for two hours, and then wander on stage to say two words, which, in reality, weren't truly required to move the plot forward. To prove my point, one night I decided to skip my line altogether, which produced only a momentary pause on Scrooge's part as I stared back at him blankly. Unflustered, he launched back into his monologue, and the show continued as if nothing had gone astray.

If I had to pinpoint the one moment that determined why I became a magician instead of an actor, that would it.

Ironically, the role of Ebenezer Scrooge in the production was performed by none other than Jake North, who was routinely handed all the key male roles throughout his sunny high-school theatrical career. This, in turn, made him very popular with the girls. However, I took solace in the fact that—while Jake was getting all the girls—I had, by the age of sixteen, nearly perfected the Erdnase Diagonal Palm Shift. Turns out self-delusion is a strong force, at any age.

Remembering *A Christmas Carol* got me thinking of its famous opening line ("Marley was dead: to begin with. There is no doubt whatever about that."), which returned me to the purpose for this sudden expedition to McHugh's flat: The amazing suggestion that the three murdered magicians had been struck down by a man thought to be dead for over thirty years.

Dead as a doornail, as the saying goes. Or not.

"I will readily confess to—during the course of my career—squirrelling away copies of the occasional official ephemera that passed across my desk and piqued my interest," McHugh said as he pulled open one of several file drawers in a cramped alcove off his small sitting room. "I have, over the years, winnowed the file considerably, but I believe the document in question is one that I held onto. For reasons I hope will soon become apparent, as it is, at the very least, an interesting read."

The four of us—Harry, De Vries, Megan, and I—were in his sitting room, sipping tea and nibbling on the sugar cookies McHugh had placed out for us before he began his deep dive into his filing system. Although "system" might have been too strong a word. Small filing cabinets were loaded on top of other larger, mismatched filing cabinets, with stacks of papers resting precariously on top of these equally haphazard cabinet towers. While I couldn't distinguish any sort of organizational structure, it only took him about five minutes and what appeared to be two incorrect drawer dives for him to put his hands on the piece of paper that he was searching for.

"I have seen my share of suicide notes over the years," he said as he turned toward the group. He held the paper up to the light to check it was, in fact, the one he was hunting for and then turned back and closed the drawer from which he had extracted it. "But this is one of the few I made a copy of, because it was—and I suspect, still is—endlessly intriguing.

"And I think," he continued, as he lowered himself into the remaining empty chair, "it may offer some insight into the events of the last five or six days." He gave the paper one last look and then handed it over to Harry.

Harry glanced at the faded piece of paper while he patted his pockets, trying to determine the location of his glasses. From where I was sitting, I could see the note was hand-written and appeared to be a photocopy of the original. Harry finally gave up on his search and looked over at me.

"Eli, I can't find my glasses. Do you mind?"

He handed the paper to me and sat back in his chair, rubbing his beard thoughtfully. I looked down at the document. The photocopy was a bit smeared; however, the handwriting was so neat and precise that it was still easy to read, despite the poor quality of the copy. I read the single sheet out loud.

To whom it may concern:

This is the only way out I can see. No other options remain. You know who you are and what you have done to me. You stabbed me in the back and poisoned my reputation. I am already dying a death of a thousand cuts, so I might as well go ahead and compete the job you started. You have drowned my dreams, pushed me over the edge, and I am at the point of no return. I hope you can live with that. While my career goes up in flames, you ride high on success, fueled by the failure you heaped upon me.

This may be my death, but my blood is on your hands.

AB

I finished reading and turned the paper over to ensure I hadn't left anything out. Confident I had completed my assignment, I handed the paper to Davis De Vries, who took it gingerly, as if it possessed heretofore-unknown explosive properties.

"Oh my," he said, holding the document at arm's length. "He really did blame us for the nosedive his career took, didn't he?"

"It was his own fault," Harry said firmly. "It was a bizarre fiction back then, and it is equally bizarre under today's circumstances. There is honor among magicians. If you steal from your brethren, I think you shouldn't be surprised when they give you the boot. He blamed us for everything bad that happened to him, when in fact he had no one to blame but himself."

"I really can't," De Vries said, stammering as he looked up at McHugh and Harry, "I really can't fathom what you are thinking. Are you, are you actually suggesting Archie Banks has come back from beyond the grave and is killing us, one by one? Are you suggesting that?"

Harry greeted this short outburst with a warm smile. "Oh, no, Doctor. I don't believe we're suggesting anything of a supernatural or other-worldly explanation for the events of the last few days."

"Absolutely," McHugh said, and I realized for the first time he was still wearing his trilby hat, which laid to rest any question I had about him ever taking it off. I had assumed it would come off at home, which was not the case. "However," he continued, "the specific wording of this suicide note, coupled with the circumstances of the three recent deaths, are too analogous to be ignored."

De Vries had passed the note back to me, and I read part of the note aloud. "'You stabbed me in the back and poisoned my reputation.'" I looked up at the small group. "Well, that certainly describes what happened to Oskar and Borys."

"Coincidence," De Vries huffed, clearly not getting on board with this train of thought.

"Absolutely," Harry agreed. "That certainly could fall under the heading of a common coincidence. However, it's the other phrase, 'I am already dying a death of a thousand cuts,' which, I think, moves this out of the realm of coincidence and into..." He looked around the room. "Well, I'm not entirely sure where it moves us."

"Archie Banks is dead," De Vries said, clearly getting annoyed at where the conversation was headed.

"Yes, that is the most likely premise," McHugh said, standing up and moving across the small sitting room. The entire flat, with the exception of his office alcove, was neat and tidy and had the feel of a woman's touch in the small details. I suspected the apartment had seen very few changes since the death of Cora, McHugh's wife. Harry's apartment offered the same, museum-like setting to the memory of his own late wife, my Aunt Alice.

"And, if you follow that line of thinking," he continued, moving to the window and pulling back a curtain to let more light into the room, "then someone is using the suicide note as a blueprint of sorts to exact a revenge on Archie Banks' magical peers."

"And, so far, doing a bang-up job," Harry said.

"Indeed," McHugh said, returning to his chair.

"The next line in the note," I said, glancing down to confirm my memory, "is 'You have drowned my dreams.' Since, so far the killer has been going in order, I'm guessing that would be the next likely line of attack.

"Of course," I added, thinking back to the large estate which was currently housing the Magi, "there aren't a lot of opportunities for drowning at Baxter's mansion. He's got a great fitness room but no pool. I didn't see any lake out in the Heath, unlike Minnesota, where you can't turn around without stepping into a body of water of some size. Other than a birdbath in the garden, I'm not sure where he—or she—would find the opportunity."

"Well, the killer got Hector into a hotel room, so I don't think we should confine the area of concern to Hampstead Heath," McHugh said. "There are plenty of bodies of water—including the Thames, which has seen its share of drowning victims—to choose from, I'm afraid."

"You're afraid," Harry said with a bit of a growl. "The only thing you need to be afraid of is the possibility of being collateral damage."

McHugh stood behind his chair and placed his hands on top of it, straightening a small white doily which lay across it. "Admittedly," he agreed. "However, our first step must be to take this information to the fellows on the force, so they can follow up on our line of thinking: that a person or persons unknown are bringing Archie Banks' words from his suicide note to life, as it were. As well as explore the other, less likely path."

De Vries narrowed his eyes at McHugh and then looked to Harry. "And what is that other less likely path?"

"The other line of thinking, as absurd as it might be to consider, is to question a fact we always thought was beyond reproach," Harry said.

"And the fact is?" De Vries pressed as he folded his arms across his chest.

"That Archie Banks may not actually be dead." Harry said.

He turned to McHugh, who nodded in silent agreement.

* * *

"This is nonsense," De Vries said when we stepped back out onto the street an hour later. I sensed from his mood he was an unlikely subway candidate at the moment, so I began to scan the street for an available taxi.

"I would not say nonsense," Harry said. "Bizarre, yes. Implausible, by all means. But this is a deadly business, and it cannot be treated lightly."

De Vries harrumphed and took up his own search for a cab, looking down the street in the opposite direction from where I was looking. I wasn't entirely in his camp about Archie Banks at this point, but I was also far from convinced by the events of the last hour.

McHugh had spent a good deal of that time on the phone with Detective Inspector Matthews, suggesting in which file she could find the original copy of Archie Banks' suicide note and offering several possible directions in which the investigation could head. Most seemed reasonable to me but one felt absolutely gothic.

"And they are actually considering *exhuming* Banks' body?" De Vries said, turning back from his cab search. "Literally digging up the past?"

"That would put one of the theories to rest," Harry said quietly.

"Nonsense," De Vries repeated and returned to his taxi search. "Let's get back to the Heath and see how Baxter is holding up."

One of the pieces of information McHugh had gleaned in his phone call was that the police had finished their initial interview with Laurence Baxter, and he had been released without any charges being filed.

"What's so odd about this," I said, ignoring De Vries' pique, "is how all the murders implicate Baxter. But at the same time, they don't."

"What do you mean?" Harry said.

I could see De Vries had turned slightly so he could listen while still pretending to be deeply engrossed in the hunt for transportation.

"Well, he is the President of the Board at The Magic Circle, but he was not particularly involved in the set-up or rehearsal for the event which took Oskar Korhonen's life. And he was the host for the house party where Borys was poisoned, but it was determined Borys' teabags were likely tampered with long before he arrived at Baxter's Folly."

I stopped myself, a little ashamed of having adopted Roy Templeton's term for Baxter's estate. "And finally, a third house-guest of his was found murdered, using techniques that require medical expertise. However, it didn't happen in his house but instead at a hotel miles away."

Harry considered what I had said. "And what does all that mean?"

I shook my head. "I actually don't know. It might mean nothing at all."

De Vries had succeeded in hailing a cab and was ushering us toward its open rear door.

"Well, here is one thing I do know that is absolutely true,"

Harry said before we climbed into the taxi. "I really wish I had packed more than this one pair of shoes."

I looked down at his feet, sporting a fine pair of black, Italian leather shoes, which were as polished and pristine as the day he had bought them.

"Why is that?"

Harry turned and looked up at McHugh's flat.

"Because if I know my friend, I would imagine in the next day or so I will be wearing these very shoes while we traipse and trample through a muddy cemetery in search of a ghost."

He was partially correct in his prediction, but as it turned out, it was my far-less-expensive pair of Jack Purcell sneakers that were about to do all the traipsing.

CHAPTER 15

Dinner that night was intended to be a celebration of Laurence Baxter's speedy release from custody. However, the grim events of the previous days succeeded in putting a damper on any festivities, and it quickly devolved into a dour affair, albeit a dour affair with top-notch food.

There were eight of us at dinner, with three empty chairs acting as constant reminders that we'd lost three magicians and friends—Oskar, Borys, and Hector—in just about the same number of days.

Ever the attentive host, Laurence Baxter made several well-meaning attempts at benign conversation starters ("Looks like we'll have a full moon tonight." "Cook tells me tonight's squash is direct from our garden." "Have I mentioned Dame Judy Dench is practically a neighbor?"), but none of these topics really took hold, each dying out with barely a response. Instead, we enjoyed the excellent food in relative silence, with the household staff noiselessly bringing in new courses while mutely removing the remnants of the last.

Roy Templeton, who I had never seen be so quiet for so long, was clearly stressing out at the lack of verbal interplay, and finally, he could take it no more.

"I see the tabloids had a field day with your afternoon under lock and key," he said with a forced casual air. "Many classic headlines, I must say." He began to list some off. "'Is Prison Time in the Cards for Baxter?' 'Magician Hopes to Make Charges Disappear.' 'Escape Artist Unable to Escape Police Incarceration.' Did you have a favorite?"

Laurence Baxter's expression suggested that, no, he did not have a favorite tabloid headline. "It wasn't precisely an incarceration," he said quietly. "I was brought in for questioning but not charged or held."

"Absolutely. But not according to the tabloids," Roy said with an overdramatic shake of his head.

"Bloody tabloids," Angus Bishop said in a low growl. "You oughta sue them for candor."

There was a quick exchange of looks around the table.

"Candor?" Davis De Vries said slowly.

"I think he means slander," Roxanne offered, and Angus nodded in agreement. "Well, in that case," De Vries said, "in this instance the correct term would be libel. If anyone cares," he added, because it was pretty clear no one did.

"My solicitors are currently looking into pressing action," Baxter said, not looking up from his food. After a long moment, he set down his fork and sighed. "I'm ashamed to say that I'm also concerned about the impact this may have on upcoming bookings. This is not the image I've cultivated, after all. Bound to feel the effects at the box office."

"Not to worry, back home, being a police suspect invariably has a positive impact on the crowds," Roy offered cheerily. "Many's the time I've suggested to Roxanne we'd be far better off, professionally, if she could manage just one juicy indictment. Nothing big, just a felony among friends."

"Sorry to let you down, hon," she said, giving his face an affectionate pat. "So what are the police doing with the Archie Banks suicide note your friend dug up?"

Harry looked up from his meal. "They are looking into it. And, difficult as it may be to believe, they're also looking into digging up Archie Banks himself."

"Waste of effort, really. I doubt we'll recognize him after all this time," Roy said, doing a poor job at suppressing a chuckle. He turned to Roxanne for support. "Get it, we won't recognize him?"

"Nice one, hon. But I wouldn't recognize him regardless," Roxanne said. "I never had the pleasure of meeting the man."

This brought Roy up short. "You knew Archie Banks," he said, the confidence draining out of his voice as he spoke.

Roxanne shook her head. "Not on your life or, for that matter, his. I didn't meet up with you and this gangrene gang until at least a couple years after he kicked it."

"I could have sworn you were there," Roy said. "I guess the memory is the first thing to go."

"That's what I hear," Roxanne said. She waited a practiced beat and then added, "What's the first thing to go?"

"I forget," Roy said, which sent them both into a fresh wave of laughter.

All eyes turned to our host to see his reaction to the comic duo's latest round of playful banter. It took a few seconds, but finally, the stupid joke made Baxter chuckle and once he broke, the rest of us followed suit. The remainder of the meal didn't have the same energy as earlier gatherings around this table, but—at least for the time being—Roy and Roxanne had succeeded in lifting the pall which had come over the group.

* * *

I don't know if we were conforming to gender norms, but the men once again spent the rest of the evening chatting away in Baxter's study while Roxanne and Megan went off on their own for "some quiet girl time," as Roxanne coyly put it.

"Well, in that case, you're going to need to find yourself a quiet girl. Let me call around," Roy suggested, but his riposte came too late, as the two ladies had already disappeared toward the second floor.

Fresh decanters of alcohol were delivered by Gwendolyn under the watchful eye and silent glare of Miss Hess, who directed the young maid with sharp jerks of her head and low, almost predatory growls. The nature of the interaction was such that all conversation ceased while we observed the tense encounter. Once the vessels had been set and rechecked for errors of placement, Miss Hess gave Gwendolyn a silent nod, and the girl scuttled out of the room like she had just encountered a particularly aggressive spider.

Miss Hess surveyed the room and then made her own measured exit, turning to close the study's large, double doors behind her. This task took what felt like a full minute as she slowly pushed the heavy oak doors into place. It wasn't until we heard the reassuring snick of the door latch that any of us felt safe to breathe, let alone talk.

"That one really sucks the air out of a room, doesn't she?" Roy finally said, breaking the silence. "Where did you find her, Gorgons-R-Us?"

"I think she's basically just shy, actually," Baxter said in response, and if all of us had been drinking at that moment, the room would have experienced a giant, simultaneous spit take.

"Yes, like Mussolini was shy," Angus Bishop said, getting up and helping himself to a cocktail.

"I would have said Goering, but you're on to something there, Doctor." Roy agreed, joining him at the drinks table.

"Poor Hector," Davis De Vries said quietly, immediately shifting the mood of the room. "As they say, what a way to go."

"What a way for all of them to go," Harry said, nodding to Roy who had appointed himself the designated bartender. "Ghastly, just ghastly."

"And to what end, really?" De Vries continued, also nodding at the offer of a drink from Roy. "A hack magician dies thirty-odd years ago, and now this?"

"Unless it's all just an elaborate scheme designed as a cover for something else," I suggested as the thought occurred to me. I turned to Harry. "You always taught me, in magic, a big move covers a small move."

"Indeed it does," he agreed, taking the drink Roy handed him.

"But what small move, if any, is being covered by this killing spree?"

"The question always comes back to who benefits from this?" De Vries said, sipping his fresh drink.

"Follow the money," Roy said emphatically as he returned to the drinks table. His task of serving drinks complete, he was ready to pour one for himself. He looked up and was greeted by a roomful of blank faces. "Sorry. I have no idea what that means in this context," he admitted sheepishly. "It's just something they always seem to say in criminal investigations. Follow the..." His voice trailed off and he returned to mixing a drink for himself.

"Well, in the case of Archie Banks there was precious little money, as we all know," Baxter said. "But, for that matter, which of us hasn't held a grudge against one or the other at some point in our careers?"

I turned to Harry, who was silently musing with his drink in his hand. "What are you thinking?" I asked.

"A big move covers a small move," he repeated thoughtfully. "Maybe we're looking at this all wrong. Maybe it's a small move covering a big move."

"What do you mean?"

He shook his head. "I have no idea."

"Here's what I know," Roy said, drink in hand as he settled into a chair. "And you can take this to the bank: when you look at a question using rose-tinted glasses, all of your herrings are going to appear red."

He held up his glass in a quick "cheers" motion and took a sip, while the rest of us considered what—if anything—that statement meant.

* * *

For being such an old house, Baxter's mansion was unexpectedly free of the peculiar creaks and groans you might anticipate hearing in an old English manor home. Which is why it surprised me to encounter an odd, high-pitched whimper as I made my way back to my room later that night.

Ever the drinking lightweight, I had left the rest of the crew of old magicians in the study, none of them giving the slightest indication the evening's end was anywhere near. I said my good nights and made my way upstairs, hoping to avoid another sudden and surprising encounter with the spooky old housekeeper.

Instead, upon reaching the second floor landing and turning the corner, I was surprised to nearly collide with the young maid, Gwendolyn. She was leaning against the wall, a delicate handkerchief to her eyes. She had clearly been the source of the whimpering I had heard.

"Oh, excuse me, sir," she said quickly, straightening up and giving her face one last pass with the handkerchief. "Sorry, so sorry."

"Oh, that's fine. Is everything alright, are you okay?"

She glanced around to ensure we were alone. "Oh, it's that dreadful old woman," she said, her voice a cracking whisper. "Nothing I ever do is right. It's always, 'Second girl, pay attention,' or 'Second girl, where are your brains?' It's endless. Simply endless."

"There is nothing worse than having a bad boss," I said sympathetically, thinking of some of the clients I had done shows for in the past but would never agree to work for again. The kind of people who, if they walked in front of your car, you'd really have to think about whether to hit the brake...or the gas.

"The thing is, I need this job and can't let her scare me out of it. Plus, what kind of reference am I likely to get from the old crone if I quit?"

I nodded supportively, not sure what the correct response was in this situation. And, to be frank, I was also a little terrified the silent old crone would suddenly appear out of nowhere.

"Do you want me to talk to Mr. Baxter?" I suggested. Her eyes went wide, and she began to shake her head vehemently.

"Oh no, that would get me sacked for sure," she said, the tremor returning to her voice.

"I wouldn't have to name names," I said. "Just, you know, man to man, tell him I thought he should know Miss Hess isn't treating some of the household staff with the sort of regard he would expect. That sort of thing."

She continued to shake her head. "She'd know," she said in a hoarse whisper. "She knows everything that goes on around here. Simply everything." She dabbed at her eyes again and pushed past me. "I'm sorry to have troubled you, sir. I must get back to the kitchen. I am behind my time."

She rounded the corner, and I could hear her running down the stairs. Moments later, I heard her shoes on the marble floor as she crossed the foyer.

And then, once again, all was quiet.

CHAPTER 16

As my uncle had predicted, McHugh persuaded the London police to exhume Archie Banks' grave. This, it was felt, would set to rest any fears that Archie might have somehow faked his death and was now exacting a murderous vengeance on the magicians he felt had wronged him. It was a long shot, and McHugh was the first to admit it.

"But," he had gone on to say, "experience has taught me there is value in leaving no stone—or, in this case, grave—unturned."

Consequently, a small band of us found ourselves seated in a surprisingly cheery pub just a stone's throw from the lovely but remarkably creepy Highgate Cemetery. We were eating a traditional pub lunch while waiting to hear the results of the nearby grim excavation. Baxter, of course, sat at the head of the long table with Harry and the Templetons taking up one side, while Megan, Angus, and I sat on the other.

Once again Baxter's celebrity status paid off, as the barman himself provided table-side ordering and delivery, a rare occurrence "you're not bloody likely to see repeated at other pubs" Angus was quick to point out. Our food had been served and we were all in the midst of eating when the door swung open and McHugh entered. He spotted us and made his way across the room.

"What have they found?" Harry asked as he stood and reached for another chair. McHugh waved it away and gestured for Harry to sit back down.

"Nothing as of yet," he said, looking over our small group. "The earthmover has just been loaded off the truck. I told the Yard I'd be right back, I just needed to pop over and pick up my assistant."

We all looked around, wondering where in the bar this new colleague might be seated, and then noticed McHugh had trained his gaze upon me.

"My eyes are not what they once were," he said. "And so another pair might be of help. Plus, I'm guessing your friends here would appreciate a play-by-play. Grab your phone, your sandwich, and follow me."

I did as I had been instructed, and moments later, we were walking through the ancient arch that welcomes you into the sprawling confines of Highgate Cemetery.

* * *

"Can you folks hear me okay?"

"Red Six, we read you loud and clear. What's your twenty?"

I recognized the voice as Roy Templeton's. "Just a few feet from Archie Banks' grave," I said quietly as I adjusted my Bluetooth earpiece's position in my ear. "They're just getting ready to fire up some of the heavy equipment."

At McHugh's suggestion, I was talking to the group back at the bar via my mobile. They were all huddled around Megan's phone, which was on speaker.

"Have a little respect," I could hear Roxanne shushing Roy. "He's surrounded by dead people."

"Just like a regular Wednesday matinee for me," Roy answered. This was followed by a small yelp from Roy, which was probably the result of a punch on the arm from his long-suffering wife.

The location of Archie Banks' grave was easy to spot, at least today, as it was surrounded by various police officials—from

166

uniformed Police Constables to Detective Inspector Matthews and her compatriots. DI Matthews was conferring with what appeared to be the leader of a group of groundskeepers, one of whom sat atop a small earthmover, waiting for the official word to get started.

"How did McHugh get permission to do this so quickly?" Megan asked quietly in my ear, as much to the group gathered around her as to me.

"Apparently, Archie Banks had no heirs, so there was no family to deal with," Angus said, trying to match her quiet tones.

"If he had no heirs, who did he leave his estate to?" she said, clearly puzzled.

"Given the state of his career before he died," I distantly heard De Vries say, clearly several feet from Megan's phone, "I would be very surprised if he had anything resembling an estate to leave to anyone."

"At the time, there wasn't even enough to pay for the funeral," Angus said. "It was Baxter who kicked in for the cemetery plot. The rest of us pooled our money and bought the coffin."

"That was very considerate of you," Megan said.

"Yes, I suppose it was," De Vries agreed.

All was quiet for a few moments, which was a relief for me, as the voices in my head were making it hard for me to focus on whatever it was McHugh had brought me along to focus on. I looked over at the gravesite, their comments about paying for the funeral still—literally—ringing in my ears.

"So who bought the headstone?" I asked, gesturing to the weathered gray stone surrounded by brambles and weeds. I then realized that, for the audience I was speaking with, gestures were at best superfluous. And to anyone in the cemetery, I looked a tad loony.

Silence at the other end of the Bluetooth suggested the group had been stymied by this innocent question.

"Hello?" I asked tentatively.

"They're all shrugging their shoulders and shaking their heads," Megan explained. "I'm surprised you can't hear the rattling of our brains and the creaking of our limbs," Roy added, followed by another of his famous explosive laughs.

The headstone looked like all the others around it, although newer than most. Thirty-plus years in the ground made Archie Banks a relative newbie at Highgate Cemetery, so the lettering on his gravestone lacked the worn and nearly illegible quality of many of the others nearby. Along with his name and the years of his birth and death, the stone also featured an engraving of a single flower, positioned directly above his name. Since the earthmover had not begun to excavate, I stepped closer and snapped a photo of the grave marker.

"What was that?" Megan asked.

"Just snapping a photo of the gravestone," I explained. "In addition to the lettering, there's also an engraving of a flower."

"What's it look like?" she asked.

The workers wanted me out of the way, so I stepped back and consulted the photo on my phone.

"It's round and puffy, with lots of small petals."

"Hang on."

I heard murmuring in the background, and several seconds later, Megan returned.

"Roxanne thinks it's a marigold," she said.

"The marigold is a symbol of grief and mourning," Roxanne yelled in the background.

"Did you hear that?"

"I could have heard that even without the phone. Thanks, Roxanne."

Any further conversation was drowned out by the earthmover, which roared to life as it began its task.

* * *

"What we have here is a brilliant illustration of exceptional dirt displacement and management," McHugh was telling me as the workers created a larger and larger pile of earth next to the headstone. "First rate work, really. My hat's off to the team, very nicely done."

I looked to McHugh to see if this was a joke, but he seemed genuinely impressed with the efforts of the groundskeepers. I had to admit his admiration was well-founded, as they had done a remarkable job of unearthing Archie Bank's grave while keeping the surrounding graves and path clear and unobstructed.

The team was just in the process of pulling the coffin from the ground using ropes and a pulley. I whispered this progress to the folks listening back in the pub.

"It will be interesting to see the level of decay after all this time," Angus said, his voice quiet and serious.

"Oh, I would expect complete decomposition of everything but skeletal matter," De Vries said. "After all this time, I mean."

"You think so?" Angus said.

"Most definitely," De Vries replied.

"Well, it depends on the type of wood used for the coffin, doesn't it?" Roy said, as the three men warmed to their morbid chat. "And if the body was embalmed. In an oak coffin, for example, I believe it can take decades for thorough decomposition to occur."

"And, of course, you have to take into account the local water table," De Vries added.

"As well as the type of soil," Angus said.

There was a loud grumble from the machinery, and I turned to see the coffin had been extracted from the grave. It was being lowered, rather shakily, onto a nearby plot of cleared land. McHugh followed the small cadre of police as they moved toward the dirt-encrusted box. I steered clear of them and instead made my way up a slight incline to the right of the gathering. After I reached the top of this small hill and turned back, I realized I had discovered the perfect position to see into the coffin when the lid was removed. I alerted the folks in the pub to my new position.

"Just what are they expecting to see when they open the bloody box?" Angus whispered. "No body, just a note saying 'Off to kill some old mates, back in a bit?'"

"Best case scenario is the casket is empty, proving Banks is still around and they now have a perfect suspect," Davis De Vries said.

"Second that," Roy agreed.

"Short of that, finding a body which, via forensics, turns out to be someone *other* than Archie Banks would be a significant outcome," De Vries continued.

"Dental records, that sort of thing?" Roy said.

With all the old guys whispering in my ear, it felt like I was listening to a morbid AARP golf tournament.

"Most likely. With no heirs, not sure how DNA would enter into the equation. They will most likely rely on dental records," De Vries said. "Isn't it wonderful how the police procedurals on television have made quasi-experts of us all? I feel I could speak intelligently on this topic for hours."

Before I could agree or disagree with that assessment, the sound of wood splintering signaled the coffin was being pried open. Moments later, the top had been removed and, as I had thought, my vantage point gave me a bird's-eye view of the coffin's interior.

A quick shout-out to Hollywood horror films. For all their failings, apparently they do get at least one thing consistently right: the way a body looks in a coffin after it's had years and years to decompose. The sight before me could have been a perfect, if low-key Halloween decoration on any suburban front porch. An assemblage of pale, gray-white bones poking out from the remains of a dark gray suit. A stark skull, with a fixed and crooked smile. Boney hands protruding from the sleeves.

I made a sudden deep intake of breath and stepped back. "Oh," I said. "It just occurred to me I don't think I've ever seen a body in such a state."

"Isn't it what you expected?" Angus asked in my ear.

"I guess so," I said with a shudder. "But it just makes me feel, I don't know—dirty, I guess. I think I may have to take a good long soak tonight."

"Good thought," Angus agreed. "I may do so as well."

"What else do you see, Eli?" This was from Harry, who had

been strangely silent throughout.

"Well," I considered, looking at the pile of bones in the box below me. "The suit still looks pretty good. It's gray, double-breasted."

"Hey, I think I remember that suit," Roy said suddenly and a little too brightly. "I had one just like it. Probably still do."

"It's not the suit that interests us," De Vries said. "I'm more interested in what is on—or not on—his right hand."

As if to answer him, one of the detectives stepped away from the coffin, widening my range of vision. And there it was: the red ruby ring worn by all the members of the Mystical Magi was wrapped around a thin third finger on the skeleton's right hand.

"Yep, he's wearing the ring," I reported via my Bluetooth.

"Then that's clearly him. Good thing we never made him give the damned thing back when we tossed him out of The Magic Circle," De Vries muttered. I began the slow climb down from my vantage point while the police tech people began the process of removing Archie Banks' remains from the decaying coffin.

"That's funny," I heard Roy say as he turned away from the phone. "I thought we did get the ring back."

* * *

"This is really lovely," Megan said as she stopped to admire a large, worn statue of an angel marking one ancient grave.

The skeletal remains of Archie Banks had been removed and the excavation team had finished refilling the now empty grave. McHugh and I gave our short report to the folks in the pub, and while everyone else dispersed to points unknown, Megan and I had headed back to the cemetery for a more complete tour of the grounds. Harry had been correct in his suggestion that we should add the ancient cemetery to our tourism short list, as the graveyard was well worth a longer expedition.

I looked up at the large statue, which stood at a slightly askew angle over a worn and illegible gravestone. "I'm always amazed at the lengths people go to when it comes to commemorating death," I said.

"Or celebrating life," she suggested as we ambled on.

"Leave it to you to put a positive spin on a cemetery," I said, giving her hand a quick squeeze.

We walked for several moments in silence and rounded a corner, suddenly facing a long row of large mausoleums of Greek or, more likely, Roman derivation.

"Do you want to be buried when you die?" she asked. This was certainly a reasonable location for such a question, but nonetheless, it took me a bit by surprise.

"I haven't given it a lot of thought," I said. "But it seems sort of silly to go to all the trouble. And expense."

"You're interested in saving money after you die?"

"That might be the only time I can," I offered. "Particularly if I have a coupon. How about you?"

She stopped at an iron gate marking the entrance to an impressive stone vault, peering into the murky darkness.

"I used to think I wanted to be cremated, with my ashes spread over the flowers at the Rose Garden by Lake Harriet. Like I did with my grandmother."

"I didn't know you were allowed to do that."

"You're not," she said. "There's some sort of silly law against it."

"A law against distributing human remains at random locations throughout the city? Give me the petition to strike that one from the books, I'm ready to sign."

She laughed. "It's a garden; what's the big deal?"

I had to admit, in reality, it didn't strike me as being such a big deal. "So you were told you couldn't spread her ashes?"

"Yep."

"And you went ahead and did it anyway?"

"Well, not all at once. Anytime I was going to visit the rose gardens, I'd open her urn and pour some of Grandma into a baggie. Then, when I was walking through the garden, I'd flick a bit here and there."

"Like the POWs in *The Great Escape*," I suggested. "Although, they were dumping dirt to cover up their tunnel building, but the concept is the same."

"Anyway, it didn't take long," Megan continued. "She wasn't a large woman."

"So that's what you want done with your ashes?"

She shook her head, grabbing onto the bars blocking entry to the tomb and giving them a bit of a shake. "It was until today. Now I think I want a tomb. A mausoleum. Something big and impressive that will last forever."

"Like the library at Alexandria?"

She cocked her head to one side. "I suppose 'forever' is a relative term."

"I suppose it is."

Megan started suddenly and turned around. She scanned the row of tombs across from us, and then looked back the way we had come.

"What's up?"

She shook her head. "I just had the sudden feeling we weren't alone."

I gestured to the row of vaults, many of which held multiple generations. "We aren't alone. There could easily be a hundred people entombed within just a few feet of us."

"No, not dead people. I've got no problem with dead people," she said, still surveying our surroundings. "It's the living that can give me the creeps. You ever get the feeling someone is watching you?"

"Not until you just mentioned it," I said, feeling the hairs stand up on the back of my neck. "Have you seen enough tombs for the time being?"

"I have."

* * *

Once we got away from the long row of mausoleums, I could sense Megan begin to relax, which in turn helped me to calm down. We spent the next few minutes looking at really old tombstones,

173

remarking on how disturbing small statues of cherubs actually are ("Those freaky, fat baby angels," as Megan preferred to call them), and enjoying the impromptu nature walk.

The paths were twisty and the landscape covered with trees, so it didn't take long for us to get lost. Not hopelessly lost, just lost enough. Megan has no real sense of direction, and so it often falls on me to keep us headed on the right track. After several turns, I was beginning to feel I was doing my job quite badly. I did keep a lid on feelings of panic, because I recognized we were inside a fenced enclosure and eventually had to end up somewhere. After a few tense minutes, I was very relieved to round a bend and see Laurence Baxter standing in front of a grave marker.

"Oh, Eli, you'll find this interesting," he said when he saw us, not in the least surprised. He waved us over as if we'd just wandered in from another room at a ritzy cocktail party. "This is the grave of David Devant."

"Who's that?" Megan asked as we approached. The name rang a bell, but I couldn't provide anything resembling an actual answer. Luckily, Baxter, still in host mode, was already on top of it.

"Devant was a predecessor of mine, after a fashion—he was the first president of The Magic Circle."

I nodded in agreement, as if that had been the answer I intended to give.

"In fact," he continued, "the room where Eli and I met at the Circle is named for him—the Devant Room."

"Of course," I agreed.

"Quite the legendary magician was our David Devant," he went on, brushing aside some leaves from the grave marker with his foot. "You know about his egg bag routine, of course."

"Of course," I lied.

"What was his egg bag routine?" Megan turned to me, and I feigned I was about to answer, then gestured to Baxter as the greater authority.

"Oh, a high water mark indeed," he began, as I turned my attention to studying the grave marker. It was a very simple tombstone. Besides the name and the birth and death dates, there was

174

not much to hold my attention. Not even a nice flower engraving like on Archie Banks' tombstone.

"And they say the routine even made the Queen laugh during a Royal Command Performance, which is no small trick," Baxter said as he finished his explanation of the egg bag illusion. Based on what I had overheard, it was just the normal egg bag routine—with an egg continually appearing and disappearing inside a cloth bag—but was taken to new heights with Devant's performance skills.

"So, while others of note are buried in the East section of High-gate," Baxter continued, "Karl Marx, George Eliot, Anthony Shaffer, and the like, I always make a point to visit the West section and the grave of Mr. Devant when I'm in the neighborhood."

He turned and began to saunter away, so we joined him. I assumed if he knew where David Devant's grave was, he would also know how to get us back to our starting point.

"As it turns out, there is an interesting point of connection between David Devant and the late Archie Banks," he continued as we walked along side of him. "Both were ousted from The Magic Circle. In Devant's case, twice!"

"So, apparently they took Devant back at least once," I said.

"Oh, they did both times," Baxter laughed. "They would hardly name a room after him if they didn't."

"What did he do wrong?" I asked. "Was he stealing material like Banks?"

"Nothing so brazen, no," Baxter said, stopping to right some flowers that had tilted to one side in front of a gravestone. "They claimed he divulged magic secrets in two books he penned. It caused quite the uproar at the time, outrage at the shocking expo-sure and all that."

"Imagine if they saw all the exposure on YouTube these days," I suggested.

"Indeed," he agreed. "It would induce a mass panic, if not collective embolisms. Anyway, I always felt a special connection to old Devant. That was one of the reasons I wanted a house in Hampstead. It was his old stomping grounds."

And so it went, the next few minutes consisted of an amiable guided nature walk with Baxter pointing out some unique vegetation found in the cemetery.

"And that one there is a hearty little beast," he said. "Although, I have had absolutely no success getting one to thrive in my greenhouse. Just infuriating."

"I think some things can only survive in the wild," Megan suggested. "People and plants. They just don't like restrictions."

"Well put, my dear," he said as we made one more turn, revealing the cemetery's entrance in the distance. "Anyway, given how this all shook out, I'm not sure it was worth everyone's time to come all the way out here today,"

"Did you think for a minute the coffin would be found empty when they opened it?" I asked.

Baxter shook his head. "No, and I'm pretty certain the dental records will prove it is, in fact, Archie Banks in the box. Of course, we won't know for sure for several days," he added. "But I agree with McHugh, every avenue should be explored."

He looked toward the cemetery's main gate, and I recognized one of his cars idling, with a driver standing by patiently.

"Can I give you both a lift back to the Heath?" he asked, gesturing expansively toward his car.

"I'm sure Megan would appreciate it," I said. "I'm going to take the tube down to Leicester."

"Another West End visit?" Baxter said as we neared the car. The driver had moved to the passenger door and swung it open.

"I have to settle some business with Jake North," I said. "I made an appointment, via his publicist, to chat with him in his dressing room before the play tonight."

"Well," Baxter said, giving me a warm pat on the back, "as we say in the theater, 'Break a leg.'"

I chuckled dryly. "I think Jake can consider himself lucky if that's all I break."

CHAPTER 17

"Fifteen minutes, Mr. North."

"Yeah, okay." Jake's response to the assistant stage manager's short statement was mumbled and morose. She looked over at me, and I nodded, as if to say, "I'll make sure he gets on stage on time." Or perhaps the nod meant, "Yes, he is sort of a jerk, isn't he?" The annoyed headshake she gave in response told me all I needed to know about her relationship with the play's current star.

I had quickly discovered that while the onstage antics at *A Pretty Taste for Paradox* were all high-energy fun and fancy, life backstage was anything but. From the moment I had arrived at the stage door for my scheduled pre-show meeting with Jake, everyone I'd encountered seemed edgy and annoyed—either with the production as a whole or with my old high-school chum. Or both.

Upon my arrival at his dressing room door, Jake's enthusiastic greeting was cut short when I held up the lecture notes Liam, the kid at Davenport's magic shop, had given me. He stared at the photocopied booklet for a long moment before taking it from me and stepping back into his dressing room. I followed, letting the door swing shut behind me.

Jake sat heavily in his chair in front of the makeup mirror,

177

letting out a long sigh as he absently paged through the pamphlet. I debated whether I should stay standing and present a position of power or sit down as a symbol of appeasement. The arrival of the assistant stage manager for her short announcement about the impending start of the show pushed me away from the closed door. So I split the difference and sat on the arm of the worn couch on the other side of the small room.

"Do you know what the expression 'dead to rights' means?" Jake finally asked, looking up at me for the first time.

"I think it means being caught red-handed," I said with some authority, although in reality I don't think I had never used the expression and was a bit fuzzy on its actual meaning.

"Yeah. That's what I thought," Jake said, setting the brochure on his makeup table. "It's in one of my lines in the play, but I hardly ever say it, because I'm not entirely sure what it means."

I considered asking why there were no dictionaries on his planet but decided this might start us down a path of hostility I was really trying to avoid. I was also curious about his casual relationship with the text of the play but felt it was a discussion best left for another time. He picked up the lecture notes again.

"Sorry about this," he said quietly. "You've got me dead to rights."

"Thanks, but the more times you apologize, the less meaning it has," I said, thinking back to our tense, mediated conversation in Gareth MacKenzie's office at The Magic Circle.

He nodded in agreement. "It's my fault. I never should have tried to do the whole magician thing. My experience on that vomit wheel certainly proved that. It's like that Houdini quote."

I raised an eyebrow at this, as Jake's grasp of magic history had never been what one might call robust. "Houdini quote?" I repeated.

"You know, about actors being magicians being actors. Or something."

"You mean, 'A magician is an actor playing the part of a magician?'" I said.

"That's the one."

178

"That was Jean Eugene Robert-Houdin. Not Houdini."

"Whatever," he shrugged. "Being the famous actor who does magic all the time is hard. They always want something new. It never ends. Everywhere I go, it's gotta be something new. And once you do a trick on TV, forget about it. You can't use that one again. It's back to the freakin' drawing board."

I smiled in spite of myself, recognizing Jake's complaint as being a common one among genuine magicians.

"So I'm always paying a fortune to hire some guy to teach me something new or busting the bank to buy some fresh illusion or being forced to use whatever is at hand," he said, once again gesturing at the lecture notes as if they were Exhibit A in a courtroom trial.

"So you're an actor playing the part of a magician playing an actor playing a magician?" I suggested.

Jake nodded. "That's about it. And I gotta tell you, I'm exhausted."

"Well, I'm here to offer you a lifeline," I said, reaching into my coat pocket. "Not that you deserve one." I pulled out a folded sheet of paper and handed it to him. Jake took it and opened it, sighing as he did.

"What's this, a summons?" he asked, his voice tinged with resignation. For a moment I almost felt sorry for him, then remembered who he was and that feeling immediately vanished.

"It's a letter you're going to post on your website and your Facebook page," I explained as I watched his lips move slowly as his eyes scanned the single sheet. "It's telling your fans that you're retiring from magic."

His lips formed the words 'retiring from magic,' and I wasn't sure if he was repeating what I'd just said or if he'd just hit that portion of the short letter.

"What does that mean?" he finally said. "Retiring from magic?"

"It means that you are no longer the famous actor who does magic. Now you're just the famous actor."

He nodded at the concept and looked up from the note. "And if I don't post this?"

I pulled another sheet of paper from my pocket. "Then I post this on my website, on the magic chat boards, and as a full-page ad in *Genii* magazine telling the world that you not only stole my effect but that you went so far as to market it and charge for it. With photos and links to the evidence, which is—as we're both aware—abundant."

I dramatically held up the folded sheet, which in reality was the hotel bill from the *Fawlty Towers* Megan and I had checked out of a few days before. But Jake didn't need to know that.

Jake sat quietly for a moment, then he sat back and once again sighed. For someone who was about to go on stage in a high-energy farce, he looked very tired.

"Okay," he finally said. "That seems fair."

Another long pause. I fought the impulse to fill the conversational void, but I soon lost that battle.

"Well, at least you have this play to do," I offered, gesturing to the stage on the other side of his dressing room door.

"They hate me here," he said, shaking his head. "Everybody in the cast hates me. I hate this play. I hate London."

This was a surprising admission, so I felt the need to push further. "Why does the cast hate you?"

Jake waved the question away as he got up and began to put on his missing costume pieces—a striped tie, a suit coat, a pair of cufflinks.

"They're all a bunch of sticklers for saying every line in the damned script. Like it's written in stone or something," he said as he started to put on the cufflinks. "I've always been great at ad libbing, you know that, and they aren't, and so it bugs them. I mean, where's the famous 'Yes, and...' attitude I keep hearing about in the theater? 'Yes, and my ass' is more like it."

I was going to point out while "Yes, and..." was a staple of improvisational theater, it wasn't a frequent factor on the legitimate stage, but I was too intrigued to quibble.

"You ad lib. During this play? This mystery play?" I asked.

"Sure," he said. "Toss in a new clue here and there. Spice it up. Keep people guessing."

The cufflinks weren't behaving as planned, so he shoved his wrists in my direction. I gave him a you've-got-to-be-kidding look, but it didn't register, so I dutifully began to insert the cufflinks into the cuffs of his starched white dress shirt. While I did that, he looked over at a hand-written list crookedly taped to the inside of the dressing room door. He leaned back to read it while I worked on the links.

"Well, at least it looks like I'm the murderer tonight. So I've got that to look forward to."

I glanced toward the list and then back at him. "What do you mean? You already know who the murderer is before the audience has even voted?"

He smiled his trademark wicked grin. "It's rigged," he said, adding an unnecessary wink. "I had them put it in my contract."

"You had them put in your contract that you would be chosen as the murderer at every show?" I was beginning to get a more complete picture of why the cast hated him.

He shook his head like I was talking nonsense. "I'm not an egomaniac," he said reassuringly. "I'm hardly ever picked as the murderer. Only like, nine out of sixteen times."

"How did you land on that figure?" I had abandoned my work on the cufflinks. "Being the murderer nine out of sixteen times?"

"I've got good lawyers," he said with a shrug, gesturing that I needed to finish up my work with the cufflinks, as he had a tie to attend to. "I said I wanted to be the murderer in just a little more than half of the shows. You know, give the other guys an occasional crack at it."

I returned to the work, finishing up the left cufflink and starting on the right. "Nine out of sixteen," I repeated softly. "Well, that *is* just a little over half."

"Like I said. Good lawyers."

* * *

Cufflinks, tie, and suit coat were all finally in place when the assistant stage manager returned, swinging open the door to bark,

"Places," and then moved quickly away to spread the word to the rest of the cast. I started to say my farewells, but Jake seemed to take no notice. He headed toward his backstage entrance. I gamely followed.

"You know," he said, making no attempt to speak at a level more appropriate to the backstage area like everyone else was doing, "I'm thinking—instead of being the famous actor who is also a magician—I might have better luck being the famous actor who is also a singer. You know, the guy who suddenly surprises everyone by putting out an album of his emotionally revealing but catchy hit songs. Nobody ever gets mad at a singer for doing the same song twice on television."

"Are you a songwriter?"

He shrugged. "I have some poems," he said, but then a new thought hit him. "Or I could up the ante and be the famous actor who also has his own band. You know, doing surprise gigs all over the place. 'Can you believe it, Jake North just showed up at The Cabooze with his band?' that sort of thing. I should look into booking a tour..."

"Well, there might be more to it than that," I began, but he was off on another thought.

"Or, you know what, I could be the famous actor who plays poker. You know, go on one of those TV poker shows and people will be like, 'Hey, I didn't know he's also an amazing poker player.'"

"Well, sure," I began "Or, here's a thought. You could be the famous actor who's also a philanthropist, using his new-found wealth to spread good works all over the world."

He seemed to consider this for a moment and then snapped his fingers in excitement. "I'll be the actor who is also a stand-up comic. You know, on the side. Edgy but accessible."

"Doesn't it usually work the other way—they start as a comic and then get into acting?"

"That's why this is brilliant."

I was about to tell him I needed to leave, that I had to get up at an unnamed hour for an unspecified thing, but the assistant stage manager saved me. She yanked Jake away and set him in front of the door that would swing open in a few moments and place him on stage.

"Remember," she whispered, but loud enough even I could hear it. "Your first line is 'Did anyone happen to see a man in a black coat ride by the house on a white horse?' *Black* coat. *White* horse."

Jake nodded disingenuously while the assistant stage manager held a hand to her headset, awaiting instructions. "Okay," she finally whispered. "Stand by."

I assumed "stand by" was going to be followed by its directional partner, "go," but Jake made no such assumptions. Without waiting for the final cue, he pushed open the door and stepped on stage. His sudden arrival cut into an actress' speech, but I couldn't hear if she even attempted to complete her lines, as the audience burst into wild applause at the arrival of the American star.

Jake waited for the applause to die away, pausing a few seconds longer than necessary, perhaps thinking it might spontaneously regenerate. Once he was certain his arrival had been properly acknowledged, he stepped forward with his first line.

"Am I nuts, or did a horse just go past?"

This was greeted by nervous laughter from the audience.

The assistant stage manager turned to me with a look so piteous, it nearly broke my heart.

"Good thing none of the guns in this show are loaded, huh?" I whispered, in a lame attempt to cheer her up.

"Don't be so sure," she shot back, and then turned and headed toward her next backstage cue.

* * *

As I sat on the subway, headed back to Hampstead Heath, I tried to remember how many days it had been since I took this same trip from Leicester Square and *A Pretty Taste for Paradox* to Laurence Baxter's estate. Four days? Five?

Last time, Harry had been fresh from his weekend in jail, under suspicion in the stabbing death of the one-armed magician Oskar

Korhonen. The eerie mentalist, Borys, had still been alive but was only a couple hours away from his fateful cup of tea. And the freakishly skillful Spanish card man, Hector Hechizo, was still several days away from his untimely and bloody end in a London hotel, which had led to Laurence Baxter himself being brought in for questioning.

This got me thinking about Harry's reaction to the play and his comments about the need for a mystery to be satisfying in order to succeed. This current mystery, I thought, was far from satisfying, with each new development—like the discovery of the suicide note and the disinterring of Archie Banks' body—adding little that was actually helpful. The correlations Harry and McHugh discovered between the murders and Banks' suicide note were fascinating but did little to crack open the case. In fact, in my mind, they simply added another level of confusion.

Not getting anywhere with this train of thought, I turned my attention to the lecture notes I still held in my hands. I wasn't sure why I had grabbed them as I left Jake's dressing room.

Paging through the photocopied brochure, I recognized immediately that—just like the training and the magic props he had paid handsomely for—Jake must have employed the services of a ghostwriter to create his lecture notes. And a pretty good ghostwriter, at that, I thought, as I read through the explanation of the first effect.

Intrigued, I turned to the write-up on my Ambitious Dog routine to see if the writer had captured the flavor and the nuances of the trick, such as they were. The unknown writer had done that and more. He presented the trick in clear, concise language, walking the reader through each phase and providing sharp direction at every turn. But the writer also added some thoughts on magic theory which made the trick—and, by extension, me—sound brighter than I had any right to expect.

The writer ascribed far more in-depth consideration to the routine than I had ever actually given it. He pointed out that the use of a surprising and stunning effect early in the trick—in this case, the realization the entire deck had mysteriously changed color—was designed to throw the audience off-track as to where the illusion was actually headed. This, he suggested, was a psychological ploy in the style of masters like Ascanio and Ortiz. High praise for a little routine I had stumbled into when I accidentally lost track of where I was while performing a traditional Ambitious Card routine for some drunken insurance underwriters.

I reread the notes on my trick, and one sentence suddenly stood out, although I wasn't entirely certain why. In referencing the phase in the illusion where—from the audience's point of view—the entire deck changes from red to blue, the ghostwriter had written: "It is important to remember: one wrong piece of information can color the entire trick in the minds of the viewers."

I think the writer might have been just playing with the word 'color' there. But the overall concept jumped out at me, and I immediately tried to put it into the context of the current situation with Archie Banks and the murders. Was there a wrong piece of information coloring our perceptions of the entire case?

I thought about all the pieces of information we'd gathered since Oskar's surprising death the previous Saturday night. The mysterious, murderous chair. The poisoned teabags, which may—or may not—have been switched with Boyrs' teabags at the Baxter estate. The slow bloody death of Hector and the implication the murderer had an association with the medical industry. Archie Banks' bizarre suicide note and its gory prediction of each of the murders. And finally, the body of Archie Banks (or was it him?), exhumed, skeletal and still wearing the Magi's signature ring.

Were any of these a wrong piece of information leading us seriously astray? And, on what felt like a related note, why did I keep thinking about that horrible English breakfast I had on my first day in London? I wasn't even hungry, but for some reason it kept popping into my head.

I was still pondering this as I left the train station and made my way up the lane toward Baxter's estate, enjoying the cool night air. The moon was almost full and provided more than enough light on the path, but that illumination paled by what I saw when I turned the corner toward the mansion. I was surprised to see both the inside and outside of the house were brightly lit up, the exterior illumination provided by the flashing lights from several police cars and an ambulance.

The ambulance was just starting to pull away from the house as I broke into a run.

CHAPTER 18

"They're saying it might have been an accident, but they're also saying it might not have been," Harry said, turning to McHugh for confirmation on this less-than-helpful assessment.

"In short, they are hedging, which is exactly what I would do given the circumstances," McHugh added.

We were standing in the mansion's large foyer, off to the side, observing Laurence Baxter as he wrapped up another of what I guessed had been a long and detailed conversation with Detective Inspector Matthews. She was patiently nodding and taking notes while he gestured to the staircase and then to all of his assembled guests. The crime scene team was upstairs in one of the bathrooms, and Megan was on the other side of the entryway, talking quietly with Roy and Roxanne Templeton. Davis De Vries stood off by himself, looking ashen.

The only guest who wasn't with us in the foyer was Angus Bishop, and the reason for that was simple; he was the one who had just left in the ambulance. The good news was he was still breathing when he left. The bad news was he was in a coma, and no one was certain if he was likely to come out of it. Or what shape he might be in when, or if, he did.

The facts I had gleaned so far were sketchy.

Apparently, one of the maids—poor Gwendolyn, who was two-for-two for finding bodies while simply doing her job—had discovered Angus unconscious in a bathtub in one of the several bathrooms on the second floor. Her screams summoned Roy and Roxanne, who were able to get the large man out of the water. First aid and mouth-to-mouth was attempted while an ambulance was summoned, and soon the professionals took over.

The sticking point, and the one element flummoxing the police —according to McHugh—was the amount of water on the bath-room floor. Gwendolyn said she distinctly remembered lots of water on the floor by the bathtub when she found the body. For their part, Roy and Roxanne had no memory of there being water on the floor when they came in the room. However, once they had managed to pull Angus' large form from the tub, Roy said the floor looked like "the engine room on the Titanic."

"So," Harry continued, "the water issue aside, it's possible Angus may simply have passed out while bathing and nearly drowned. Given the amount of alcohol he consumes on a regular basis, that hypothesis is not too far-fetched."

"Agreed," McHugh said. "However, more near-fetched is the issue of Archie Banks' suicide note. I don't have the exact wording on me, but it was something like, 'You drowned my dreams,' wasn't it?"

Harry nodded. "Yes, I think you're very close on that. However, if this was a murder attempt—"

"—which the lads, and lasses, on the force are hesitating to confirm," McHugh interjected.

"But if it was, then that means someone snuck into the bath and held Angus' head under water. Once he passed out, they assumed the deed had been completed."

"Or this person was interrupted. The room does have two forms of egress. Doors, that is," McHugh added for my benefit. I nodded in thanks.

"And let's not forget, our friend Angus was—is—a big fellow," Harry said. "I can't imagine it would be easy for one person, even a strong person, to subdue him, particularly in an environment as slick as a bathtub full of water."

"Certainly not the unfortunate Second Girl, Gwendolyn, who is building quite the CV in the discovery of murders and attempted murders," McHugh said. "I agree, it would require one exceptionally strong person or perhaps two people working in concert." He glanced over at the door, which Laurence Baxter was holding open for DI Matthews. "I would guess that's the direction this investigation will head."

While they continued to speculate, I crossed the foyer to check in with Megan, who had been comforting Roxanne. The older woman was both unnerved and still soaking wet from the effort of pulling an unconscious Angus out of the tub. She and Roy looked like cats left out in the rain.

"I think you both should take some ibuprofen before going to bed tonight," Megan said, turning to include Roy. "You're bound to be sore tomorrow."

"Good thought," Roy agreed, glancing up the stairs. "I'm just wondering if we're allowed to go back upstairs yet. I need to see a man about a horse."

"More like a pony," Roxanne said, and this crack made both of them snort, holding in a laugh they knew was not appropriate for the situation. "You're such a creature of habit. There's like four biffies on this floor alone." She took him by the hand and pulled him down the hall to a guest bathroom.

"Sorry I wasn't here for this," I said to Megan.

"Don't worry about it. I missed the whole thing. I was up in the greenhouse watching the sunset. I didn't know anything was going on until I heard the sirens and looked down to see an ambulance pull up to the front door."

I gave her a hug and was working on some warm words to go with it when Davis De Vries approached us. He still looked pale, made all the more so by his snowy head of hair.

"I'm going to get a drink," he said in what sounded like an invitation to join him. He moved past us toward the study but turned back and lowered his voice. "Just between us, I've come to the conclusion, late as it may be, that I'm really not enjoying my stay in this house."

"And then there were five."

Roy Templeton made this declaration in what turned out to be a pretty fair Vincent Price impression. We had been sitting in silence for several moments, and his sudden proclamation actually made me jump, if only a bit.

We were assembled in Laurence Baxter's study, most of us with drinks in our hands. I looked around and sensed everyone was doing some quick mental calculations in reaction to Roy's statement. McHugh had departed with DI Matthews, leaving just the core group of magicians sharing drinks, along with Megan and myself. I repositioned myself in the large, cushiony chair, trying to get comfortable and coming up short.

"Five? How do you figure?" Roxanne asked indignantly. She had joined the group wearing a bathrobe, quoting Robert Benchley about slipping out of some wet clothes and into a dry martini. Currently she was on her second.

Roy counted on his fingers as he spoke. "There's Baxter, Harry, De Vries, me, and you. That's five."

"Hold up there, Kemosabe. Don't include me in this morbid mob, I was late to the Archie Banks party, remember? I'm just the hired help. You know, the girl in the box." She took another long sip of her drink, finishing it. "You're the ones who got him drummed out of The Magic Circle."

"Yes, we all did, and now we're paying the price for it," De Vries said. He had been sitting quietly in the corner, sipping his second, or maybe his third, drink.

"But why? And, more importantly, who?" Roy said.

"I always tell my students the simplest answer is usually the right one," Laurence Baxter said as he got up and went to the bar. He glanced around to see who else might need a refill. When his eyes met mine, I gave a slight shake of my head, feeling I had already passed my meager limit.

I adjusted my position in the chair and realized that, while it was not the most comfortable seat in the room, it was the iPhone in my back pocket that was the real cause of my discomfort. I pulled it out, and the pain I had been experiencing vanished.

"Well, the simplest answer is that someone is enacting a revenge scheme for Archie Banks," De Vries said.

"I've heard revenge is a dish best served cold," Roy said. "But thirty-plus years? That's beyond cold. That's sub-zero."

"Unless it's Archie himself," De Vries said. His eyes looked a little glassy, and he was working hard on his enunciations. "From beyond the grave. Somehow." His voice trailed off. This idea, which earlier in the week he had scoffed at, was clearly becoming more palatable to De Vries. I was still resisting that explanation.

Baxter, at the bar, clucked his tongue. "Well, I can't speak for the rest of you," he said as he added ice to a fresh glass. "But I, as the saying goes, ain't afraid of no ghosts." He punctuated the phrase by tossing one final ice cube into his glass.

"I agree. Our situation, while extraordinary, is not likely to be supernatural," Harry said. He turned and smiled at Megan. "No offense to the believers in the room."

She smiled right back. "None taken," she said.

"Consequently, I think our time would be better spent focusing on the living and not on the dead. At least for the time being," Harry added, nodding to De Vries, who raised his glass in acquiescence.

"I for one," Baxter began as he moved away from the bar, and then he stopped. Miss Hess had appeared, silent as always, in the doorway to the study. She waited patiently while Baxter crossed the room to her.

Seeing that our host was otherwise engaged, Harry continued. "So, we have to ask ourselves, if not Archie Banks, then who? Who benefits?"

While we were all listening to Harry as he posed questions that needed answers, we were also doing our best to overhear the conversation between Baxter and his spooky housekeeper. As always, their conversation was so low it was virtually inaudible.

Baxter wrapped up the muted exchange and turned to the now-silent group. He set his drink on a nearby table.

"Excuse me for just a moment," he said, following Miss Hess out of the room.

"The issue we're running into," Harry continued, "and I've discussed this at length with McHugh, is the dearth of actual suspects in the case. Archie Banks is dead, has no heirs, and—on the surface at least—no one seems to benefit from these murders."

"Revenge is a mighty strong motivator, my friend," Roy Templeton said. "Sometimes blindingly so."

I could tell Megan had lost interest in the conversation. She leaned toward Roxanne and gestured toward the door.

"Did you hear what they said?" Megan asked the older woman.

Roxanne was listening intently to Roy, so it took a moment for her to realize Megan had put a question to her.

"What, dear?"

"I said, did you hear what those two said in the doorway?"

Roxanne leaned over to fill Megan in, and I turned to back to the group.

"Well, who was it who found Archie with his head in the oven?" De Vries asked from across the room. "We could start there."

"That's weird," Megan said, leaning toward me after she had stopped chatting with Roxanne.

"What is?" I asked, my focus actually on the main conversation.

"Roxanne said Miss Hess told Mr. Baxter she needed help moving the marigolds in the greenhouse."

I shrugged. "What's so weird about that? Given how frail she is, I would imagine she's not likely to be able to bench press even a small flower pot." I glanced down at my phone, wondering why I had a sudden strong desire to look at the photos. I flipped open the photos app, which took me to the last photo I had taken. It was of Archie Banks' tombstone.

"It was that girlfriend of his, wasn't it?" Roy suggested. "She came home late and found him. 'Honey, I'm home!' Nice surprise, that."

"Well, where is *she*?" De Vries asked. "Has anyone tracked her down?"

"She was from Australia," I offered, remembering Angus Bishop's comments to me about her. "At least, according to Angus." I looked over at Megan, but she was looking down at my phone and furrowing her brow in concentration. She took it from me and examined the photo more closely.

Roy shook his head and laughed. "Angus got that one wrong. Close, but no cigar. She wasn't from Australia. I remember she was from Austria."

I nodded, understanding that once again Angus Bishop had mixed up like-sounding words. I looked back to Megan, to see if she was following this, but her attention was clearly elsewhere.

"It's so weird. I spent a lot of time in the greenhouse over the last week," she said. "I can name every plant in it. And I don't remember seeing one marigold. But there is one here—on Archie's tombstone." She gestured toward the center of the photo as she handed the phone back to me.

Across the room, Roy continued on the subject of Archie Banks' girlfriend. "I know it was Austria, because I used to joke with Archie about her. I called her his version of Eva Braun."

"Austria?" Harry said slowly.

"Marigolds?" I said in reply, looking at the photo of the tombstone, with its loving addition of the engraved flower. The flower that symbolized grief. The flower that—according to Megan—would not be found in the greenhouse that Miss Hess was taking Laurence Baxter to this very second. The greenhouse on the roof. Four stories up.

Harry and I turned and looked at each other. I could tell—like he did with McHugh on occasion—we were having the exact same thought. Harry said it first.

"The suicide note."

"'You pushed me over the edge,'" I said quickly.

"'I am at the point of no return,'" he responded, finishing the line from the note.

"Austrian," he added.

"Marigolds," I said in reply.

I jumped to my feet and raced out of the room. Harry was right behind me.

"Eva Braun," Roy said, repeating his punch line weakly, looking after us as we ran out. He turned back to the rest of the room. "What? Too soon?"

CHAPTER 19

I took the steps to the second floor two at a time. I had left Harry at the base of the stairs, with instructions to call the police.

This sudden and unexpected cardio workout, combined with the one—or was it two?—glasses of wine I'd had, was making it hard to pull all the pieces together in my mind as I scrambled up the stairs.

The out-of-the-blue mention of a missing marigold—the same flower adorning Banks' tombstone—was one thing. Interesting, but not really earth-shattering.

But when you coupled it with the revelation that Archie's girlfriend had been Austrian, not Australian, it felt like things were centering on the creepy housekeeper.

I hit the second floor landing and, using the banister as a pivot point, rounded the corner on the stairs, heading up to the third.

The notion that the comically fragile Miss Hess was behind all the murders was, on the face of it, absurd. However, her connection to this house, Laurence Baxter, and, by extension, The Magic Circle certainly provided the access one would need.

But for some reason the words means, motive, and opportunity kept running through my mind as I neared the top of the stairs to the third floor. She certainly could possess the last two, but if I understood how the iconic phrase defined "means," I was thinking

Miss Hess would likely come up short in that department. She had trouble lifting a teapot, so holding Angus Bishop's head under the water for any length of time seemed too far outside her wheelhouse.

As I raced down the third-floor hall toward the spiral staircase, which led to the roof, I said the word "wheelhouse" out loud, suddenly doubting it was the right word, or for that matter, even a real word. Such was the current functioning of my brain cells. Before I could consider this further, I arrived at the black cast-iron spiral staircase.

The circular nature of this last climb made running impossible, and my feet almost slipped out from under me twice as I struggled up the steps, heading toward the doorway to the rooftop. My speed was significantly diminished, and so was my idea of bursting through the door in a dramatic fashion.

However, when I reached the door, it stood ajar, and I opted to keep moving rather than stop and catch my breath. I figured time was of the essence.

Stepping out onto the roof, I was immediately hit with a rush of cool air, which, given my unplanned workout, felt great. The sky was still clear, and the moon provided more than enough illumination. I looked first to the greenhouse on my left, which was dark and still. And then I glanced to the right and gasped. As involuntary as it was, it was also audible enough to give away my presence on the roof.

"Eli, stay back. She has a gun." Laurence Baxter's voice was full of tension.

He stood near the edge of the roof, his back to the four-story drop behind him. Miss Hess stood about ten feet from him and about equidistant from me. As he had warned, she had a small gun of some kind in her hand. It was pointed at Baxter. She glanced over at me, a scowl of annoyance on her face. She turned back to Baxter.

"Again, I give you the option," she said in her flat German—strike that, Austrian—accent. "You may jump and take your chances on the fall. Or I shoot and remove all doubt."

It immediately became clear what she was doing. Archie Banks' suicide note had included the phrase "you pushed me over the edge," and this appeared to be her intention for Baxter. I took a step forward, and she quickly turned the gun in my direction.

"No further," she snapped.

"Sure thing," I said, reaching for an unnecessary note of affability. "Whatever you say."

For some reason, I felt the need to hold up my hands, I suppose to indicate the truly minimal threat I posed. She turned back to Baxter.

"You jump. Or I shoot," she said, waving toward the edge of the roof with her free hand.

"The thing is," I continued tentatively, recognizing the lady with the gun had just told me to zip it, "if you shoot him, then his death won't match the wording in Archie's suicide note."

She turned to me, rolling her eyes at the level of annoyance I was providing.

"The suicide note said, 'You pushed me over the edge,' right?" I continued. "It didn't say, 'You shot me, and I collapsed on the roof, at which point you had to roll my dead body over the edge.'"

"I am no slave to symmetry," she said, turning her attention back toward Baxter.

"But—" I continued, not at all sure what might come out of my mouth next.

"You," she barked at me. "On the ground." She waved the gun at the grass in front of me, in case for some reason I didn't understand what "ground" meant.

I nodded in consent, still holding my hands high as I began to lower myself to the ground. My feet were standing on asphalt, but in front of me—and spreading across the rest of the roof—was a sea of green grass.

At that moment, I remembered what Baxter had told me about the pseudo-lawn that covered his mansion's roof. It wasn't grass at all but some form of Astroturf. He had said something about drainage issues precluding the use of real grass. As I got down on my knees, I glanced up and could see Miss Hess was watching me closely. I looked down again and was thrilled to see what I had hoped would be there: seams.

Like the sod it hoped to emulate, this fake turf had been laid out on the roof in long strips. I scanned the grass, looking from where I was about to kneel to where Miss Hess was standing. She was poised atop the same strip of grass that began right in front of me.

I was suddenly reminded of a favorite phrase of my Uncle Harry's, one he used anytime a trick did an outstanding job of fooling an audience. "I really pulled the rug out from under them!" he would say with glee. As this thought flashed through my mind, I also remembered that at one point in the midst of a dangerous situation, Harry had pulled an actual rug out from under someone and in so doing had saved his own life.

With that image fully formed in my mind, I followed Miss Hess' instructions and knelt down. I lowered my hands to the ground and, as unobtrusively as possible, gripped the edge of the fake grass, which easily peeled up from the asphalt. In this crouching position, I took a deep breath and then gave the fake strip of grass a strong and sudden yank.

If my goal had been to distract her, I was utterly and completely successful.

However, if my goal had been to pull the grass out from under her feet, I was less so.

Sadly, this had been my aim.

I yanked with all my might, and all I got for my effort was a handful of fake grass, which tore away from the main Astroturf like wet newspaper. This sent me sprawling backwards, and I crashed into the door to the roof, slamming it shut with a loud thud. My actions and the resulting tumble were bizarre enough to make Miss Hess actually turn toward me, almost taking a step in my direction as I struggled to get up.

This was just the distraction Laurence Baxter had, apparently, been waiting for. His hands, which had been stuck deep into his suit coat pockets, suddenly came out. One hand was empty. In the other he held a deck of cards.

I've been in my share of situations where a magician pulled out a deck of cards at an inopportune time, but this was one for the record books.

Peeling the top card from the deck, Baxter flung it with consummate skill and force directly at Miss Hess's head. She turned just in time for the hurtling card to strike her squarely in the forehead.

After it did that, the card fell to the ground. Unfortunately, the same could not be said of Miss Hess, the flying card having had no appreciable effect on its target.

In fact, Miss Hess looked down at the fallen card with the same look I've seen countless people give when they were on the receiving end of a lame card trick. Baxter, undeterred, continued to flick card after card at her, as if she were a watermelon that refused to play along.

She just stood there, with cards bouncing off her like bullets off of Superman. To be honest, it was so annoying and ineffectual, even I couldn't understand why she didn't just shoot him to put an end to it.

But Baxter's ploy accomplished at least one goal: it gave me the break I needed. I pushed off from my position on the ground and hurled myself at the old woman with all the force I could muster. I crashed into her at a full run, and the two of us slammed into the ground. Given her small size and general brittleness, I was convinced when she hit the grass she would explode into a cloud of gray dust.

Turns out, I was wrong.

Forget any notions of her being a fragile, weak wisp of a woman. She was a fierce and brutal fighter and was evidently determined to take me out at the beginning of round one. What little strength I possessed I put toward holding her gun arm at bay. But that was difficult, as she was using all her other limbs—and her teeth—in ways which would have given the Marquess of Queensberry an aneurism. In short, Miss Hess did not fight fair.

I'm not really sure what Laurence Baxter was doing during all this. For all I knew, he continued to flick cards at us in the hopes of producing a really intense paper cut. My focus was entirely on keeping this crazy old lady from killing me, and it was not a foregone conclusion that I would be successful.

She pounded a fist against the side of my head, while at the same time hammering me in the kidneys with a knee. I struggled to pull her pounding fist away from my head, and she took this opportunity to sink her teeth into my wrist. Just as I pulled my wrist out of her mouth, she head-butted me—smacking me hard in the nose. She must have done a good job of it, as I immediately saw drops of blood appearing on her face, apparently from my now-bloody nose. She head-butted me again, smacking me hard in the forehead, and this one really connected. I started to see stars, and my field of vision began to narrow. The only thing that kept me from passing out was another helpful hard slam from her knee into my kidneys.

In the midst of this struggle, I was reminded of my late Aunt Alice and some advice she had given me years before. At the time, I had been sent home from school with a note from the principal, because I had been involved in a fight on the playground. She quizzed me on the circumstances and then proffered the following advice.

"Eli," she had said, "you are a very smart boy and you don't need to resort to using your fists. You have a gift for language and a strong imagination. Use those skills properly and I guarantee you can forestall nearly any future antagonistic situations."

I wasn't sure why my brain had chosen this moment to bring that memory to the surface, as I figured I was well beyond the discussion phase with Miss Hess. But I wasn't gaining any ground in the fight and had come into this battle already winded, so I figured I had little to lose. I looked into the face of this raging, angry old woman and decided I needed to hit her where she lived.

"Archie Banks was a terrible magician," I said, my voice raspy but firm. "He was the worst. Just the worst. The man couldn't do a double lift to save his life."

It took a second for my words to register.

"You are wrong," she spit back at me. "He was a genius. A genius magician."

"On the contrary," I said, feeling very much like William F. Buckley going after a liberal opponent. "Archie Banks was undoubtedly a hack. He was a hack's hack. He sucked."

Okay, maybe I wasn't working with Buckley's lexicon, but I was making an impact.

"You lie, you lie, you lie," she screamed.

"He was such a failure, he even botched up his attempted suicide," I shot back, remembering Harry's description of Archie's unsuccessful effort to merely attempt suicide, with its disastrous results.

She froze, stopped thrashing around, and stared up at me, her mouth agape. I continued.

"What an idiot he was. He planned to be discovered before he could finish the job. And he couldn't even get that right."

She shook her head, her eyes filling with tears. "*Nein, nein, nein.* It was my fault. It was all my fault. I got busy, lost track of the time. And when I get home, it is too late."

She repeated the words "too late" over and over, and I could tell the fight had gone out of her. I reached for the gun, and she let me take it from her limp hand. She continued to whimper and began to curl into a fetal position as I pulled myself to my feet. Baxter was standing next to me, with several untossed cards still in his hand.

"Brutal stuff," he said quietly.

"Yes, she put up quite a fight."

"No," he said with a sad shake of his head. "Those things you said about Archie Banks. Mocking a magician's double lift? Brutal, old man, just brutal."

CHAPTER 20

The scene the police discovered on the roof was, at best, perplexing.

I stood next to Baxter, my face bloodied, my clothes rumpled and torn. He held Miss Hess's gun gingerly by two fingers, while in his other hand he gripped the rest of his trusty deck of cards. On the ground below us lay a little old lady, curled up in a ball and still whining, "too late, too late, too late" along with indecipherable Germanic mutterings. Scattered randomly on the fake grass around her were numerous playing cards.

Baxter took it upon himself to bring the police up to date while I continued to catch my breath. When Megan saw me, she gasped, and ran to get some first aid implements while Harry questioned me on the details of the preceding few minutes.

"I read this phrase in Jake's lecture notes tonight that really seems to apply to this situation," I said after I had recounted the details of my fight with the surprisingly scrappy Miss Hess.

"Something Jake North wrote is germane?" Harry said with surprise. "Do tell."

"He clearly had a ghostwriter helping him," I explained. "Anyway, the phrase was something like, 'One wrong piece of information can color an entire trick in the minds of the audience.'"

Harry nodded in agreement at the concept. "Yes, we made some wrong assumptions on this one, that's for sure."

"Like the idea that Archie Banks had no heirs," I suggested. "When he clearly had a devoted girlfriend. I'm not even sure if devoted is a strong enough word. And speaking of strong, Miss Hess fooled me on that one."

"She fooled all of us," Harry said, looking over at the old woman. She was now handcuffed, and the police were about to take her back into the house and, presumably, off to jail for a good long time. McHugh, who had been Harry's second phone call after calling the police, was consulting with one of the young constables. He finished his chat and headed over to us.

"Well, she won't say a word about her situation," McHugh said quietly. "Very tight-lipped that one. I suspect the few words she said in front of Eli and Laurence Baxter are all we'll hear on the topic from her."

"But they certainly have enough evidence on her, just for the attack on Baxter alone, don't you think?" Harry asked.

McHugh nodded. "Most certainly. But it would be helpful, if not deeply instructive, to get the details out of her. They'll piece most of it together, little doubt about that, but it's always better to get it from the horse's mouth, as it were."

We all looked over at her. Her back was straight, her expression grim. A few hairs were out of place, but you otherwise wouldn't peg her as a recent Ultimate Fighting contender and near champion. She looked to be the perfect candidate for assistance from a Boy Scout at the nearest street corner, if you ignored the handcuffs.

One constable was holding the roof access door open while two others were escorting the old woman toward it. She turned and gave us one final, icy glare. I can't speak for the others, but she still had the ability to produce chills up and down my spine.

"Talk about holding a grudge," I said with a certain amount of reluctant admiration. "Over thirty years, just waiting for the right moment to get back at all of you."

"You have to admire her patience," Harry agreed.

"As Richard III so eloquently put, via our friend Mr. Shakespeare," McHugh added, "'What traitor hears me and says not "Amen"? England hath long been mad and scarred herself.'"

With that, the mad and barely scarred Miss Hess disappeared through the door and into the dark stairway.

* * *

"I'm afraid this hasn't been much of a vacation."

Megan shrugged. "I don't know, I think we'll be talking about this trip to London for years to come! And we don't need to bore our friends with photos—we'll have newspaper clippings and police reports."

We were seated in Laurence Baxter's dining room, enjoying what was likely to be one of our last breakfasts under his kind hospitality. I was once again partaking in a picture-perfect English breakfast, while Megan dined on scones and hot tea. We had the dining room to ourselves, either because we were the first ones up...or the last.

It may have been my imagination, but the entire household staff seemed lighter and happier now that they were no longer under Miss Hess' oppressively boney thumb. Even Gwendolyn, who had seemed so timid all week, was actually humming when she brought in my breakfast. When she put the plate in front of me, I once again flashed back to our first breakfast in London, at the *Fawlty Towers*-style hotel where we'd spent our first couple of nights. I looked down at the beautiful English breakfast in front of me and thought back with a smile at the nightmarish plate I had seen that first morning. And then another memory began to rise to the surface—something intrinsically connected to that breakfast, but I couldn't quite grab it.

"Am I the last? Or are you two the first?" Harry asked as he came into the dining room, pulling me out of my reverie. Before we could answer, his phone beeped, and he stopped in his tracks to retrieve it. It took a few moments to find which pocket he had left it in. Once located, he pressed the button on the front of the phone and squinted at it. He then started digging through his pockets again, this time for his glasses. After a few moment of fruitless search, he handed the phone to me.

"Eli, can you read this to me?"

I set down my fork and turned my attention to the phone while he crossed the room and grabbed a coffee cup, quickly filling it from the urn Gwendolyn had just replenished.

"It's from De Vries," I said as I scrolled through the messages on his phone.

"Is he already up and gone?"

"Apparently," I said, scrolling to the most recent text. Harry's blind futzing with the device had backed up the stream to several texts earlier, and I sorted through a lot of "Dr., what time is rehearsal?" and "Dr., I am on my way," and so on. I finally found the most recent communication from De Vries.

"It says 'At The Magic Circle, can you meet me? Need help with the illusion,' although it looks like spellchecker has changed the last word to 'delusion.'"

"Sometimes spellchecker is more correct than we give her credit for, " Harry quipped as he pulled out a chair and sat across from us.

"He goes on to say it will just take a few minutes," I added.

"Oh, I suppose that's fine. I had no firm plans this morning. What are you two up to today?"

"We haven't had much chance to do any of the standard, touristy things this week," Megan said. "I was hoping to get to the Tower of London."

"To see the Crown Jewels?" Harry asked.

"Well, that's what I'll tell them if they ask, but I really want to see where Richard III had his two nephews killed."

"I think the events of this week may be rubbing off on you," I said, surprised at her interest in such a gory tale but not opposed to it. "How soon do you want to leave?"

"I'd rather not rush," she said. "We have all day, and I'd love to spend a few more minutes in the greenhouse and take a final bath in the amazing tub in our bathroom."

Realizing I would be hanging around for at least two hours

with nothing to do, I offered to accompany Harry down to The Magic Circle, with the idea of Megan joining us there in time for lunch.

I handed the phone back and Harry pocketed it.

* * *

Fifteen minutes later, we found ourselves on the Overground Line, headed toward Highbury, where we switched to the Victoria Line to take us to Warren Station. The first leg of the trip was devoted to Harry's explanation of why Warren was the preferred stop and that only a fool would use the Euston Square station or—God forbid!—the larger Euston Station.

"There's too much monkeying around if you go to Euston Square, but no one believes me," he said, repeating nearly verbatim a speech he had made earlier in the week to Angus Bishop. "Warren is my stop. Out the door, cross the street, take a right, take a left, take a right, and you're there. No monkeying around."

I found little to disagree with about this route, although his tone suggested he was ready to argue the point at length if necessary. Recognizing the futility of it, I changed the subject.

"Any word from McHugh about our Miss Hess?" I asked, pointing out adjoining seats that had just opened up in the subway car. "She still clamming up?"

We moved quickly from our standing position near the door and scored the seats.

"She is indeed," he said as we settled in. "Not a peep out of her. But they've got a new, interesting theory about Borys and his teabags. Very clever stuff."

"What's the theory?"

"Well," Harry said, moving into storyteller mode, "you remember how Borys basically kept his precious teabags under lock and key? His stash no one else had access to?"

I nodded. "Because of that, the police theorized the poison must have been put in the tea kettle. And, at that time of night, Borys was the only one likely to need or use the kettle. When he was finished, the kettle would be washed and readied for the next day, destroying all evidence of the poison."

"Right. But after he died, when they were going through his things, they found several poisoned tea bags mixed in with the other tea in his stash."

"Exactly," I agreed. "Which took some of the heat off the household staff, because it was clear Borys had come into the house already possessing poisoned teabags."

"That's what Miss Hess wanted them to think," Harry said. "The new theory is it was actually Hess who dropped the poison in the tea kettle. And then she was the one who put the poisoned teabags into his secret stash. But she did it *after* he died."

"So she did put the poison in the water the night before?" I said.

"Which killed Borys," Harry replied. "Then, at some point, she went into his room and maneuvered the teabag switch. Might have been in the middle of the night, or it might have been during the hubbub when the body was discovered. Either way, it was magnificent because it confirmed—wrongly—that he possessed poisoned teabags when he came into the house. Which, subsequently, took suspicion off the household staff."

"And off of her, presumably."

"Presumably," he repeated. "It was brilliant. It's exactly Ascanio's Last Action Clean concept, but instead of using cards or coins, she used poisoned teabags."

Harry then did a quick imitation of possible police dialog.

"'Did someone in this house poison this man?' 'Why no, look, he had poisoned teabags with him when he arrived,'" Harry said with a laugh. "And the household staff—including Miss Hess—is completely clean at the end of the trick. Brilliant, just brilliant."

* * *

I couldn't confirm Harry's claim the Warren Street station was the best one to use when heading to The Magic Circle, but as we made our way along the route, it seemed pretty straightforward to me.

For my part, I was still thinking about Miss Hess and the events of the last few days.

"Remember the other night, after Jake's play, when you talked about how unsatisfying that mystery was?" I asked as we crossed Euston Road.

"I do indeed," he said. "And, for the record, it's several days later, and I still find it unsatisfying."

I was tempted to explain that a good part of his dissatisfaction may have been the result of one actor's unwillingness to learn lines and penchant for adding nonsensical clues to a mystery play while performing it. However, I decided not to go down that path.

"Well, I'm having trouble with some of the elements of the case against Miss Hess," I said as I hurried to keep up with Harry. He took a right once we had crossed the street, and I actually had to break into a trot to keep up with him.

"Such as?"

"Well, if you had asked me before, I would have said there was no way she could hold Angus Bishop's head under water for any length of time," I began. "But after going one round with her on the roof, I have reassessed my original appraisal. She easily could have held him under for thirty minutes or more without breaking a sweat."

"Yes, the old bird was a lot stronger than any of us guessed."

"And," I continued, "the explanation of how she poisoned Borys is completely plausible."

"Brilliant," Harry said again. "She walked away clean on that one. As I've always told you, Eli," he said, coming to a complete stop and turning to me. "When doing a trick, I would far rather start dirty and end clean. I don't care if I'm concealing a chicken in my coat for forty-five minutes, I absolutely prefer to end clean."

With his proclamation made, Harry turned and continued walking. I tried to think of a performing situation which would require stowing a chicken for forty-five minutes, couldn't come up with one, and then had to nearly run to catch up with him.

"The one event that doesn't ring true for me," I said when I finally got alongside him, "was the murder of Hector Hechizo.

Someone had to lure him to the hotel room in order to subdue him and inflict the thousand cuts which did him in. Everybody knew he was a ladies man, but I don't think Miss Hess has the drawing power she might have had back in the day."

"Well, while we're discussing elements which don't ring quite true," Harry said as we turned down Stephenson Way, which is more like a wide alley than an actual street. "There's something about the first murder—with the knife in the chair poor old Oskar sat in—which just doesn't gel for me. I was backstage for nearly an hour before the show started. And I didn't see Miss Hess back there once."

The Magic Circle building was visible at the end of the block. Harry was walking on the narrow sidewalk, so I strode alongside him in the street, watching my step to ensure I didn't trip on any of the uneven cobblestones.

"According to Meagan, who showed up at the last minute, Miss Hess was in the coat check until right before the show. Maybe she got it all set up earlier in the day," I suggested.

"Perhaps," Harry said with a shrug. "But I don't know. The way McHugh has described it to me, that chair was like a mousetrap. It had to be set. And experience has taught me once you set a mouse-trap, you don't move it for fear of taking off your finger. So I'm not quite sure how she pulled that trick off."

The front door was ajar, and we walked in, expecting to see the traditional bustle of members in the Club Room just off the front door. However, the first floor was strangely vacant and quiet.

"They all must be up in the theater," Harry said. I began to move toward the spiral staircase, but he shook his head. "We'll take the lift; it's easier on my knees."

I followed him into the lift and continued to think about the events from the last few days, which weren't gelling for either one of us. I also kept thinking back to my English breakfast—the night-mare one, not the lovely one served at Baxter's house—although I couldn't figure out why it kept popping up in my brain.

Moments later we were deposited in a back service corridor just outside the theater on the third floor. We made our way past a couple empty dressing rooms and then pushed open a door which took us into the auditorium. Harry, who really knew his way around the building, moved confidently through the door and then came to a dead stop.

"Doctor!" he yelped, and at that moment, in a flash, I understood what had been odd about the text from Davis De Vries I had read to Harry at breakfast. I realized the two old friends began every communication with the letters "DR," followed by their message. This was true of all of the texts, with the exception of the one that had lured us to The Magic Circle.

There was no time to pass this realization along to Harry, as the cause for his sudden outburst was before us on the stage. Davis De Vries was slumped next to his illusion, the Catherine Wheel. He was either unconscious or dead; from this distance it wasn't apparent. But what was clear was he had been tightly shackled to the machine, lengths of chain encircled him and bound him firmly to the large metal illusion.

I heard a sound and turned to my right.

And for the second time in as many days, I found myself facing someone aiming a gun at me.

CHAPTER 21

"Y ou should see the looks on your faces, luv," she said with a grin. "Classic, just classic."

It was Angelika, standing in the main aisle near the front row of seats, looking over at us as Harry and I stood frozen in the doorway. She wasn't alone. The kid from Davenport's magic shop, Liam, was hovering next to her, looking pained and uncomfortable. It may have been due to the situation, or it might just have been traditional teenage angst.

I had only seen the two of them side by side once before, when I was rushing backstage after the onstage stabbing of Oskar Korhonen. So I think I can be excused for not having seen the family resemblance at the time, but it was clearly evident as they stood before me. And it may have been my imagination or the adrenaline (or both), but I thought I also saw a resemblance to Miss Hess.

And suddenly the recurrence of the nightmare English breakfast image made sense—I wasn't remembering the breakfast, I was remembering the family I had seen while eating that monstrosity. The family at one of the other tables—the ones I thought might be Russian—who were squirreling away food for a missing family member. I was eating that horrible English breakfast while they conversed.

"*Etta dyedooshkye,*" the old Russian grandmother had said to her offspring.

"It's for PopPop," had been her daughter's translation to her child.

They were doing it for their father and their grandfather!

I looked over at Angelika and Liam and realized I must have a sort of idiotic and not particularly helpful superpower—the rare ability to put together all the clues in a life-threatening situation, but always about ten seconds too late. It had happened before and clearly had just happened again.

"Looks like we're here just in time for an Archie Banks' family reunion," I said with far more bravado than I actually felt. "It's a shame Dad's still dead and Mom's on her way to a long spell in prison."

"I'm sorry?" Harry said, looking from his friend chained to the illusion to the woman holding the gun on us. "What family reunion?"

"Harry, unless I'm very much mistaken, the woman pointing the gun at us is the daughter of Archie Banks and Miss Hess. And the kid is her son. Archie's grandson."

"Just so," Angelika said.

"*Etta dyedooshkye,*" I said to no one in particular.

"So we were wrong about Archie having no heirs," Harry said quietly.

"By a generation or two," I agreed. "And I think the addition of these two players neatly explains the issues we were having with this so-called mystery. It was Angelika who lured Hector to his death at that nearby hotel. He certainly would have been open to following her there."

"Or anywhere, for that matter, knowing Hector," Harry added.

"My mistake was forgetting she mentioned being trained as a nurse. That would have given her the skills she needed to drug and intubate him."

"And I had thought my education was a bloody waste of time," she said with a wry smile. "How wrong I was."

"And I'm guessing young Liam here was the one in charge of

212

moving the chair on stage for that first night's show," I continued. "My guess is he was also responsible for setting the trap for whoever was unlucky enough to take a seat on the chair."

He scowled up at us. "Just did what I was told," he said with an insolent growl. "Didn't want to be part of this rubbish plan from the start."

With her free hand, Angelika gave him a quick rap across the back of the head. "Enough of your whining, ya spotty git. Take the cuffs and lock them to the wheel."

She pointed to a small pile of handcuffs on the front of the stage. Liam meandered over and picked them up, then headed toward us, gesturing we should move over to the Catherine Wheel.

"I only saw you interact with Miss Hess a couple of times," I said to Angelika, who kept the gun aimed at us as we moved across the stage. "You were both so mean and disagreeable to each other. I should have recognized immediately you could only be related."

"Family. Ya gotta love 'em," Angelika said with a sardonic smile.

And then Liam got to work.

* * *

I didn't do any escape illusions in my act—besides an occasionally funny but no longer PC routine with a Chinese finger trap—but I'd been around enough of them to distinguish the difference between real handcuffs and the gaffed variety. Sadly, the cuffs Liam was using on us were decidedly genuine.

Davis De Vries was slumped on the floor on one side of the wheel, but I could now see he was still breathing, which was currently the only good news we had. Liam made Harry sit on the opposite side of the illusion and locked him in tightly, with his arms positioned between two of the large metal spokes.

He got more dramatic with my binding, cuffing me with my arms outstretched, like I was in midst of performing the illusion. Unfortunately, he was using very solid (and very real) handcuffs, as opposed to the leather break-away straps which were part of the trick. To complete the effect, he also cuffed my ankles to the apparatus.

"As interesting as all this might be," I said to Angelika, who had kept her pistol trained on us the whole time, "I'm not really sure how tethering us to the Catherine Wheel completes the revenge plot your crazy old mother hatched. I don't remember anything in your dad's wacked-out suicide note about 'you tied me up and gave me annoying welts on my wrists.'"

"I don't think that's where she's headed on this one, Eli," Harry said quietly.

"Right you are, dearie," Angelika said with surprising warmth. "We'll be sticking to both the spirit and the letter of the old man's note on this, our final performance."

I wracked my brain, trying to remember what the final statement in Archie Banks' suicide note had been, but I was coming up empty.

"Let me give you a hint," she said, sensing the blank I was drawing. "What do you think of when I say The Magic Castle? And Halloween?"

I knew there was a connection, but it wasn't coming to me. Then I heard a slight gasp from Harry.

"The Halloween fire at the Magic Castle in Los Angeles," he said slowly. "It was a few years back. No one was hurt, but it did plenty of damage."

"It did indeed," she said. "But it will be a mere footnote compared to The Magic Circle fire we're creating today. This will be one for the history books."

The phrasing from Archie Banks' suicide note came back to me. "'While my career goes up in flames, you ride high on success,'" I recited, "'fueled by the failure you heaped upon me.'"

"That's my old dad, always had a way with words. And," she added, seeing a thought cross my face as I glanced up at the ceiling, "don't be thinking the sprinkler system you just took a gander at is going to do you a bit of good. My smart boy here has hacked the security system and shut them off, along with all the fire alerts."

Liam was just finishing attaching the final handcuff to my leg. "It was dead easy," he said, both proud and annoyed. "A toddler could have pulled it off." He stood up and stepped back, assessing his work. "There, these three gents aren't going anywhere anytime soon."

"The same cannot be said for us," Angelika said, waving her son off the stage with the pistol. "We have some burning issues to attend to downstairs in the library. Don't worry, though. You will see—and feel—the results of our handiwork soon enough."

They both headed up the aisle together, and then Angelika turned back.

"I meant to tell you, by the way," she said, "I really enjoyed that card trick of yours. The Ambitious Dog. Nice stuff, a solid fooler."

"What, were you another happy attendee of Jake North's bogus magic lecture?" I said, for just a moment feeling more annoyed about that whole kerfuffle than my current critical situation.

"No, the lecture notes," she said.

"Well, I hate to burst your balloon about Jake North," I said, using the only weapon at my disposal, "but he didn't write those notes. He couldn't have."

"I know that, luv," she said, opening her purse and sliding the pistol into it. "That's because I wrote those bloody lecture notes. He paid me. By the way, that bloke is a complete wanker."

"How nice," I said, my voice dripping in sarcasm, "that in our final moments together, we were able to find some common ground."

"Yes, I believe there's hope for humanity yet," she said.

And then she and her son disappeared up the aisle and out of the theater.

* * *

We were silent for several long moments, while the gravity of our situation settled over us.

215

"Well, here's another fine mess," I said. From my shackled position, I could look down out of the corner of my eye and barely see Harry, bound to one side of the machine. However, I was able to hear him chuckle at my attempt at humor.

"Well, I died on this stage on many occasions years ago," he said. "This will just be one more time."

"And what was it that did you in the last time?"

He chuckled again. "It was an ill-advised attempt at a sub-trunk transposition," he said, and I could hear the smile in his voice. "With an assistant who was less than agile, shall we say."

"Not Aunt Alice?"

"Oh, no, this was before I met your Aunt," he said. "You've seen The Pendragons' version of the substitution trunk, right? Metamorphosis?"

"Seen it? I've studied it. Obsessively. I've gone through it frame by frame on YouTube, like it was the Zapruder film," I said. The trick was one of the closest things to a miracle I had ever seen, in which magician and assistant switch places—from inside a trunk to out—in the blink of an eye. Or actually less than that.

"Well, in our version, I believe there was enough time during the transposition to boil a three-minute egg," Harry said. "That girl moved like molasses, only slower."

"Where is she today?"

"Probably still trying to get out of that damned trunk," Harry said.

I looked around the empty theater, thinking about the fire Angelika and Liam were setting elsewhere in the building.

"A lot of flammable stuff downstairs, is there?" I asked.

"Oh my, yes," Harry said. "The library is down there. Hundreds of books, maybe thousands. Not to mention all the ephemera—posters, handbills, that sort of thing. A real tinderbox, really."

"Hmmm," I said, not really sure how to respond to this news. "Well, if nothing else, this settles a discussion Megan and I had earlier this week."

"About?"

It was sort of bizarre, really—Harry and I were just chatting about this and that, as if nothing dire was happening.

"When we were out at Highgate Cemetery," I said. "We got to talking about whether we each wanted to be buried or cremated."

"I'll say this for you, Eli," he said. "You sure know how to sweet talk a girl."

"Anyway, I was making the case for cremation. Looks like I'll be getting my wish."

"Oh, I don't know," Harry said. I could hear him shifting his position, probably trying to get more comfortable. "Since we're on the third floor, and they're likely starting the fire in the basement, we can take some relief in the fact we'll probably die of smoke inhalation and not actually be burned alive." When this got no reaction from me, he offered a quick addendum. "Or no relief at all, I suppose."

A few more long moments of silence. I sniffed the air, sure I was beginning to smell smoke, although it easily could have been my imagination.

"Lucky thing for De Vries," Harry said out of the blue.

"How do you figure?"

"He's already out. By the time he wakes up, we'll all be dead."

I wasn't fully tracking on that logic, but I turned my head in the other direction to see if De Vries might be coming around. From my limited angle, he looked just as unconscious as he had when we walked in.

"Too bad for the old guy," I said. "He never got to see the debut of the Catherine Wheel."

"The Davis De Vries' Catherine Wheel," Harry corrected.

"Yes, of course," I said. And then a thought occurred to me. This might be, I began to think, one of those rare moments where I figured out the solution *before* the disaster, as opposed to in the midst of it. Although, to be fair, we were sort of in the thick of it already.

"Harry, remember that speech you used to give to young magicians about how there are all kinds of rooms in the house of magic?"

"I do indeed. I borrowed the concept from Eugene Burger."

"And you'd say something like, 'It's okay to spend most of your time in your own room, but you should also get out from time to time, in order to have some idea of what's going on in the rest of the house.'"

"I think I was more elegant in my phraseology, but that's the gist of it."

"Even as a kid, I remember how it always drove you crazy when magicians would only focus on one area of magic, like cards or coins, and be completely ignorant about everything else."

"Well, when I was starting out," he said, "a magician was a generalist. It was required. You had to have a close-up show, a walk-around show, a cabaret show, a kid's show, a big-box illusion show. Otherwise you'd starve."

"That's not the case today, is it?"

"Kids today, they have no idea," he grumbled, starting to warm to the topic, and then he stopped. "Is this really the time to get into that old argument, Eli? Or are you just trying to take my mind off our imminent fate?"

"A little of both," I admitted. "It just occurred to me, in the short conversations I had with Angelika and Liam, they both seemed quite well-versed in their own area of magic. But they also seemed woefully unaware of anything outside their small sphere."

"Well, if they happen to wander back in, be sure to hit them with that," Harry said. "They will likely buckle under your biting observation and free us with their deepest apologies."

"The point is, when they shackled us to the Catherine Wheel—"

"The Davis De Vries' Catherine Wheel."

"Will you let me finish?" I snapped.

"Sorry, I'm getting a bit punchy. You were saying?"

"When they shackled us to this illusion, they thought they were binding us to a huge, solidly built metal device. An impenetrable fortress. When in reality..." I let my words hang in the air, but Harry finished my thought for me.

"But in reality, it was designed to be set up or taken down in twenty minutes. And packed away in two cases."

"And, as De Vries was so fond of reminding everyone," I continued. "It goes together and comes apart without any tools."

"Without any tools," Harry repeated slowly.

I turned, as far as the cuffs would let me, and started to examine the spokes of the large wheel. I could hear Harry doing the same thing at the base of the illusion.

"Hard to be sure," I said, "but it looks like the spokes might break down into maybe three pieces each. I can see the seams between the joints."

The method Liam had used to bind me to the machine provided me with very little movement of my hands. However, the clanging and scraping I heard coming from Harry's area suggested not only did he have more freedom of movement, but he had also started to make some progress.

"What do you think?" I asked, unable to see what, if any, advancement he was making.

"Well," he said, the strain of reaching around the spokes apparent in his voice, "I don't want to make any promises I can't keep. But, we may get out of this contraption faster than my tortoise-like assistant was able to maneuver out of the trunk, lo those many years ago."

There was more scraping of metal on metal, more grunting, and then a sound that made me smile with relief. It was Harry, and all he said was one word.

"Bingo!"

CHAPTER 22

Turns out, when you're in London, you don't dial 911 for emergency services. You dial 999. This was something I learned the hard way in the first few seconds after we released ourselves from the Catherine Wheel.

Thankfully, Harry was aware of this key difference and set me straight when the first attempts on my cell phone produced only an annoying buzzing sound on the other end.

The blaze, such as it was, was handled quickly and professionally by the London firefighters. Much to the relief of Laurence Baxter, they were able to squash the fire in The Magic Circle library, while causing very minimal water damage to the rest of the building.

"They tell me we'll be back up and running as early as tomorrow," Baxter announced to all of us later that day.

We were seated around his dining table for what was likely to be our last time as a group. Baxter sat at the head of his table, with Roy and Roxanne on his right and Megan and me on his left. McHugh sat next to me, with Harry seated at the foot of the table. Davis De Vries, who had spent the afternoon in the Emergency Room, was seated on Harry's right. He was slowly sipping soup and seemed to have nearly completely recovered from that morning's conk on the head.

"It took virtually no time to find Angelika and her son," McHugh said, bringing us up to speed on the investigation. "And, unlike their closed-lipped mother, neither one of them has been the least bit reticent about offering up the salient details of the case."

Gwendolyn entered silently, supervising a new, young maid in the proper manner of removing empty soup bowls from seated guests. In the absence of the spooky housekeeper, she had been promoted and was clearly enjoying her new role.

"Second Girl," she whispered harshly. "Serve from the left, remove from the right. How many times must I repeat the simplest commands?" She continued to glare at the young lady as they headed back into the kitchen, and I realized that while Miss Hess was no longer haunting the house, her spirit lived on.

"It was quite the scheme," Roy said, reaching for a bread roll, which Roxanne slapped out of his hand.

"Carbs," was all she said as she did it.

Roy, undeterred, quickly faked with his left and grabbed a roll with his right. "International calories don't count," he said as he split the roll and began to lather it with butter.

Roxanne sighed and rolled her eyes. "Death wish," she said. "Nothing but a death wish."

"Hey, if Miss Hess couldn't take me down, what chance does cholesterol have?" Roy said, taking a bite of the roll. He looked up suddenly, a perplexed expression on his face. "You know, I never did hear what her plan was for me. Which line in the suicide note was I supposed to bring to life? Or, actually, death." He looked down the table at McHugh, who turned to Harry for help. Harry shook his head, so McHugh plowed ahead.

"The thing is, Mr. Templeton," McHugh began, "in talking to Angelika Sutherland and her son, it quickly became apparent you were not, per se, a crucial figure in the overall conspiracy."

"What do you mean?" he said, still chewing.

"I mean, to the best of our knowledge, there were no concrete tactics pertaining to your disposal."

"I know it's English, but you're going to need to translate for me," Roy said. "I only understood 'there' and 'your.'"

McHugh turned back to Harry.

"He means you weren't on her list, Roy," Harry said gently. "They said, according to Angelika, that Miss Hess had no memory of you ever having any interaction with Archie Banks. She had no plans to kill you."

This statement silenced the usually talkative Roy for a long moment.

"What the hell," he said finally. "So what is it? I'm not good enough to be on her high and mighty kill list? I was in the thick of it with the rest of you clowns, I shunned that bastard Banks, I shunned him good. Let me tell you."

Roxanne patted his hand, but he yanked it away.

"I was a Magi like the rest of you, or a Magus, or whatever the hell the right word is," he snapped, holding up his left hand and pointing at where his ring should be. Roxanne indicated his other hand, which he quickly held up, now pointing at the actual ring. "I've got the ring. I'm in the club. I'm good enough to be killed, that's all I'm saying. Jeez."

He took another bite of his roll, still shaking his head and mumbling. Roxanne patted his hand warmly.

"It's okay, honey. I want to kill you most days, and that's gotta be good for something."

This seemed to mollify him, if only a little. "Thanks, sweetie," he said. "I can always count on you."

"If I can divert our attention from this mini-drama for just a moment," Harry said, clearing his throat as he stood up, "I'd like to propose a toast. Or two. Or more."

He raised his glass and everyone at the table followed suit. He surveyed the group for several seconds before beginning his toast.

"First, to absent friends. They tell me Angus Bishop is showing good signs and the doctors feel he may come out of the coma in the next day or so. And, to add better news to good news, he will likely suffer no permanent damage." Harry held up his glass a little higher. "To Angus."

"To Angus," we all repeated.

"And to our absent friends who were, sadly, not so fortunate.

Oskar Korhonen, Borys, and Hector Hechizo. What can one say but we were lucky to tread this path with them. They will not be forgotten by those of us still on this journey called life, as we will carry them in our hearts. As I believe one of us said at our first Magi meeting, paraphrasing Shakespeare, 'We are bound unto our souls with hoops of steel.'"

Davis De Vries said, "Hear, hear," to this and we all repeated it, raising our glasses again.

"And to our host," Harry continued, "who has provided food and lodging this past week, which are, simply, without equal. To the epitome of class and good taste, I give you Laurence Baxter! No, wait. *Doctor* Laurence Baxter!"

We all raised our glasses and said as one, "*Doctor* Laurence Baxter!" He nodded humbly and smiled.

"And, if I may be indulged," Harry said, his voice dropping, "one final, personal toast." He turned to me and held up his glass. "To my fine nephew, Eli Marks, whose quick thinking saved not only my life and the life of Davis De Vries but very likely The Magic Circle itself. To Eli!"

"To Eli!" the rest of the group responded, each holding their glasses high. I wasn't sure if I was supposed to make a short speech, but it didn't matter, as Harry was moving forward.

"And, Eli, if I could ask of you one more favor," he said, still standing and looking over at me, a wide smile across his face.

"I'm yours," I replied, not really tracking with the fact he hadn't asked me for any earlier favors.

"It would involve extending your stay in London by a day or so."

I glanced at Megan, who smiled at the idea.

"No problem. What can I do for you?" I said.

"It's actually not for me," he said. "It's for a friend."

"A friend of yours is a friend of mine," I said as magnanimously as I could, but I was beginning to tire of the exchange. "Name it."

Harry turned from me to glance at De Vries. The two men exchanged a look and then both pivoted back to me. It took longer than it should have to sink in. And then finally the other shoe dropped.

So that's how, two days later, I once again found myself strapped to Davis De Vries' Catherine Wheel.

Only this time, it was in front of a paying audience.

* * *

I didn't throw up.

Although, that was never a foregone conclusion and it remained a viable option throughout. But in the end, I kept my wits—and my lunch—about me.

Rehearsals went well, and I quickly discovered just how ingenious De Vries' device actually was.

"The principle behind it is sublime," Harry said as we got ready for the first run through. "I mean, except for sporadic projectile vomiting, it really is brilliant."

"Now that I see how it works," I said, walking around the large obelisk and giving one of the spokes a quick, testing tug, "I'm surprised at how simple it is."

"It takes a great mind to come up with something this simple," Harry said as I stepped back to admire the whole contraption. "Coming up with complex solutions is easy. Making it simple is the hardest thing there is."

"Just like in the mysteries you love?" I suggested.

"Exactly," he agreed.

"Well, let's take this buggy for a spin and see how she does at performance speed."

The rehearsal went well, and the show went even better.

Because the stage at The Magic Circle lacked a trapdoor, we opted to end the trick with one of the assistants being wrapped in the large silk and then unfurling it to reveal that the magician—no longer on the spinning and flaming Catherine Wheel—had now transformed into the assistant. It was a graceful conclusion to the illusion and one the audience greeted with a long and sincere standing ovation.

Instead of taking my bow, I gestured to the side of the stage, where Davis De Vries had been standing, watching the trick from the wings. He waved my gesture away, but Harry gave him a gentle shove, and soon De Vries was center stage, accepting the applause he so richly deserved.

He turned to me and smiled as the audience continued to applaud wildly. I had never seen him so happy.

* * *

Laurence Baxter had ordered champagne—of course he had, he was Laurence Baxter—and we all stood backstage for a short celebration after the show. Davis De Vries, still a bit giddy from the success of the trick, clapped me on the back, and I had to react quickly to keep from sloshing all the champagne out of my glass.

"Thank you again, Eli," he said. "It was everything I imagined and more."

"And, as a special bonus," Roy Templeton added, "no puking."

"While we're all gathered here," Baxter interjected, deftly changing the subject, "we are all here, aren't we?" He did a quick head count—Harry, De Vries, the Templetons, Megan, and myself. Assured he had a quorum, he continued, digging into his suit coat pocket as he spoke.

"It has been many, many years since we presented one of these, but I believe in this instance it is well earned." He removed a small black ring box from his pocket and turned to me. "Eli, I speak for all of us when I say it would be our very great pleasure if you would consent to become one of the Magnificent Magi." He popped open the box, revealing the familiar ring within— although, unlike the ones worn by all the other members, this one was brand new. The red ruby in the center actually sparkled under the stage lights.

I was speechless. Roy Templeton grabbed the box out of Baxter's hand.

"Here, let me, before you prattle on and take all the drama out of it. You Brits have no sense of ceremony," he said, pulling the ring out of the box and gesturing for me to put out my hand. I did as he requested, and he slid the ring into place.

"Eli," he intoned, "I award you this ring for meritorious conduct, extraordinary valor, and conspicuous bravery against the wicked Miss Hess. You are now a member of the Magnificent Magi."

"Thanks," I said, "but isn't that almost word for word what Oz said to the Cowardly Lion at the end of *The Wizard of Oz*?"

Roy feigned complete innocence. "Never seen it. They must have gotten it from me," he said with a wink.

"Well, as long as gifts are being presented, this seems as good a time as any to present this to Harry," De Vries said, picking up a large, flat box which had been leaning against a wall.

"A gift? For me? What in the world for?" Harry said, looking truly puzzled at the box De Vries handed to him.

"For your invaluable advice and counsel on the creation of the Catherine Wheel," De Vries said.

"You mean the Davis De Vries' Catherine Wheel, don't you?" Roxanne asked and Roy gave her a quick, congratulatory high-five.

"Nice one, babe," Roy said.

"Actually, if it weren't for Harry, I would have gone with The Vitruvian Man as the name for it. Or the Ixion, God help me."

Roy grimaced. "Whatever's in the box, it's not enough. You oughta write Harry a check as well."

"So, what *is* in the box, anyway?" Megan asked impatiently as she helped Harry open the unwieldy carton. Once they were able to get one side of the box open, Harry slid out a large, purple velour bag. It was cinched shut with a gold braid. While Megan held the bag, Harry worked on untying the braid. Finally, he pulled out the items within.

"Oh my," he said in awe. "Are these what I think they are?"

"They are indeed," De Vries said. "They are the set of Linking Rings which once belonged to Ching Ling Foo."

"They are magnificent," Harry said, examining each of the

metal hoops. "How in the world did you even know they were of interest to me?"

"A little bird told me," De Vries said, stealing a glance in my direction. I gave him the slightest of nods in response.

"They are spectacular," Harry continued, letting Laurence Baxter take a look and then giving Roy Templeton a chance. "A genuine piece of magic history. I will treasure them, De Vries, treasure them."

"It is small repayment indeed for your help on the planning and execution of the Catherine Wheel," De Vries said.

"Hold on, buddy," Roy said as he examined one of the rings more closely. "You may want to demand your money back."

"Why, what's the problem?" De Vries said, sounding a little panicked.

"One of these is defective," Roy said, holding it up. "See. The sucker's got a gap in it."

The response from the rest of the group was loud and profane, but I paid it no notice. I was too busy admiring my new ring and the special membership it represented.

And looking at the Magi ring reminded me of another ring I'd been carrying around all week.

CHAPTER 23

W ith all the flight rescheduling we had done over the previous ten days, it took a bit of juggling, but we finally arranged it so Harry, Megan, and I all took off from London and landed in Minneapolis at about the same time. Not the exact same time but close. The reason for the discrepancy was that Harry was flying out of Gatwick airport, while Megan and I were departing from Heathrow. Such was the downside of non-refundable tickets and multiple rebookings.

So we all said our goodbyes in the drive in front of Laurence Baxter's mansion, with Megan and me getting a cab and Baxter himself driving Harry to Gatwick. Hugs all around with Roy and Roxanne, while Davis De Vries stuck with the more traditional handshake and a warm pat on the back. Although we'd been unable to see him, word from the hospital was Angus Bishop was upright and taking liquids, which Roy suggested would be the perfect title for Angus' memoir "if the old sot ever got sober enough to write one."

We successfully avoided the dreaded Minnesota Long Good-bye, which generally added thirty minutes to any departure, by saying we were afraid we'd be late for our flight. Five minutes later, Hampstead Heath was behind us.

As we settled into the backseat, with our luggage piled

unsteadily on the floor in front of us—an odd design flaw in London cabs, as they appear to lack useable trunk space—I got a sudden feeling of sadness. Megan picked up on it immediately, as I must have given out a particularly woeful sigh.

"What's wrong?"

"Nothing," I said. And then I came to a decision—I had meant to do this all week, and now was as good a time as any. "I've been meaning to do something since we got here, but other things kept getting in the way."

"Like murders and dead bodies and fires and things?"

"Exactly. But I want to try out this new trick before we leave London. Can I borrow your ring?"

Intrigued, she pulled off her grandmother's ring she always wore and placed it in my hand. I took off my new Magi ring and set it alongside her ring in my hand. I closed my fist, made some magical motions over it with my right hand, dropped the rings from my left to my right hand, and then held them up for her inspection.

Both rings were now joined together, one looping seamlessly through the other. I let them dangle before her eyes for a few moments, as she clapped her hands together in surprise.

"Oh, Eli, that's wonderful."

"Wait," I said, taking the conjoined rings and placing them back in the palm of my left hand. "There's more."

A few more magical-looking hand motions, a toss from the left hand to the right, and I once again held up the rings. But now, instead of just her ring and my ring, there was a third ring in-between. It connected the two rings.

Megan looked at it, her eyes widening.

"What kind of ring is that?"

"Well, I don't know what they call it over here, but back in the States we call it an engagement ring."

"My answer is yes," she said quickly as she broke into a wide grin.

"I haven't asked the question yet."

"You forget, I'm psychic."

I'm not sure who made the first move, but seconds later we were kissing. Out of the corner of my eye, I could see we had attracted the attention of the cab driver, who studied us via the rearview mirror.

"I suppose we should set a date. And things," I suggested.

"I've always wanted to honeymoon in London," she said, still beaming.

I looked out the taxi window as we zipped along.

"Funny. We're already in London."

"Well, let's just stay," she said. "Who says we can't have the honeymoon first?"

I shrugged. "I don't know. Tradition?" I suggested.

"Ah, we'll get around to the wedding eventually," she said. "I traditionally don't let traditions get in my way."

"I think that's one of the things I love about you."

"So we're staying?"

I did a mental check of my calendar for the next week. No work obligations occurred to me, which really should have indicated bad news for a freelance magician, but I wasn't exactly in that mode at the moment.

"Works for me," I said.

"Me too," she said, and then her face brightened. "And we can go back and stay at that great little hotel I loved!"

Before I could protest, she passed the address onto the driver.

And my fate was sealed.

ALSO BY JOHN GASPARD

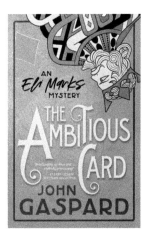

THE AMBITIOUS CARD

An Eli Marks Mystery (#1)

The life of a magician isn't all kiddie shows and card tricks. Sometimes it's murder. Especially when magician Eli Marks very publicly debunks a famed psychic, and said psychic ends up dead. The evidence, including a bloody King of Diamonds playing card (one from Eli's own Ambitious Card routine), directs the police right to Eli.

As more psychics are slain, and more King cards rise to the top, Eli can't escape suspicion. Things get really complicated when romance blooms with a beautiful psychic, and Eli discovers she's the next target for murder, and he's scheduled to die with her. Now Eli must use every trick he knows to keep them both alive and reveal the true killer.

THE BULLET CATCH

An Eli Marks Mystery (#2)

Newly-single magician Eli Marks reluctantly attends his high school reunion against his better judgment, only to become entangled in two deadly encounters with his former classmates. The first is the fatal mugging of an old crush's husband, followed by the suspicious deaths of the victim's business associates.

At the same time, Eli also comes to the aid of a classmate-turned-movie-star who fears that attempting The Bullet Catch in an upcoming movie may be his last performance. As the bodies begin to pile up, Eli comes to the realization that juggling these murderous situations – while saving his own neck – may be the greatest trick he's ever performed.

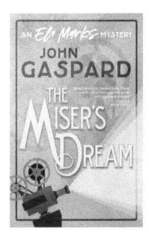

THE MISER'S DREAM

An Eli Marks Mystery (#3)

A casual glance out his apartment window turns magician Eli Marks' life upside down. After spotting a dead body in the projection booth of the movie theater next door, Eli is pulled into the hunt for the killer. As he attempts to puzzle out a solution to this classic locked room mystery, he must deal with a crisis of a more personal nature: the appearance of a rival magician who threatens not only Eli's faith in himself as a performer, but his relationship with his girlfriend.

But the killer won't wait and starts taking homicidal steps to bring Eli's investigation to a quick and decisive end. Things get even worse when his magician rival offers his own plausible solution to the mystery. With all the oddball suspects gathered together, Eli must unveil the secrets to this movie-geek whodunit or find himself at the wrong end of the trick.

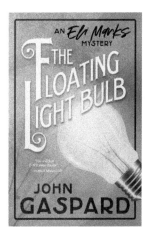

THE FLOATING LIGHT BULB

An Eli Marks Mystery (#5)

When a magician is murdered in the midst of his act at the Mall of America, Eli Marks is asked to step in and take over the daily shows-- while also keeping his eyes and ears open for clues about this bizarre homicide.

As Eli combs the maze-like corridors beneath the Mall of America's massive amusement park looking for leads, he also struggles to learn and perform an entirely new magic act. Meanwhile, the long-time watering hole for Uncle Harry and his Mystics pals is closing. So in addition to the murder investigation and the new act, Eli must help the grumpy (and picky) seniors find a suitable new hang out.

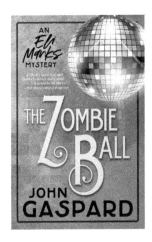

THE ZOMBIE BALL

An Eli Marks Mystery (#6)

Eli's asked to perform his magic act at a swanky charity gala, *The Zombie Ball* – a former zombie pub crawl which has grown into an annual high-class social event. What begins as a typical stage show for Eli turns deadly when two of the evening's sponsors are found murdered under truly unusual circumstances.

Compounding this drama is the presence of Eli's ex-wife and her new husband, Homicide Detective Fred Hutton. Under pressure to solve the crime before the 800 guests depart, Eli and his detective nemesis go head-to-head to uncover the bizarre clues that will unravel this macabre mystery.

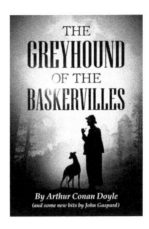

THE GREYHOUND OF THE BASKERVILLES

This is new edition of Arthur Conan Doyle's classic mystery, "The Hound of the Baskervilles." It's the same story. Mostly.

That is, it contains the same characters, the same action, and much of the same dialogue. What's different?

Well, it's a little shorter, a little leaner, a little less verbose in some sections. But the chief difference is that it's now narrated by a dog. A greyhound, in fact, named Septimus.

In this new edition, he tells his story of how he became "The Greyhound of the Baskervilles." Same story, new tail.

THE RIPPEROLOGISTS

The Ripperologists is a contemporary thriller about two competing experts who are forced to work together to beat the clock when a copycat serial killer begins recreating Jack the Ripper's 1888 murder spree.

Set against the backdrop of the fascinating subculture of Ripperologists, the story takes equal stabs at the disparate worlds of publishing, Ripper studies, fan conventions, and Internet chatrooms, as our two unlikely heroes employ their (often contrary) knowledge of a 120-year-old phantom to hunt down a modern killer.

ABOUT THE AUTHOR

In real life, John's not a magician, but he has directed a bunch of low-budget features that cost very little and made even less – and that's no small trick. He's also written multiple books on the subject of low-budget filmmaking. Ironically, they've made more than the films.

He's also written for TV and the stage.

John lives in Minnesota and shares his home with his lovely wife, one or more greyhounds, a few cats and a handful of pet allergies.

Find out more at: https://www.elimarksmysteries.com

 facebook.com/JohnGaspardAuthorPage

 twitter.com/johngaspard